INTO THE BADLANDS

a novel

Brian J. Jarrett

Elegy Publishing, LLC
St. Louis, MO

Cover photo by Evgeni Dinev, FreeDigitalPhotos.net

Editing and proofreading by Sandi Powell.

2011.ITB.1.24 (Third Edition)

ISBN: 1468123424

ISBN-13: 978-1468123425

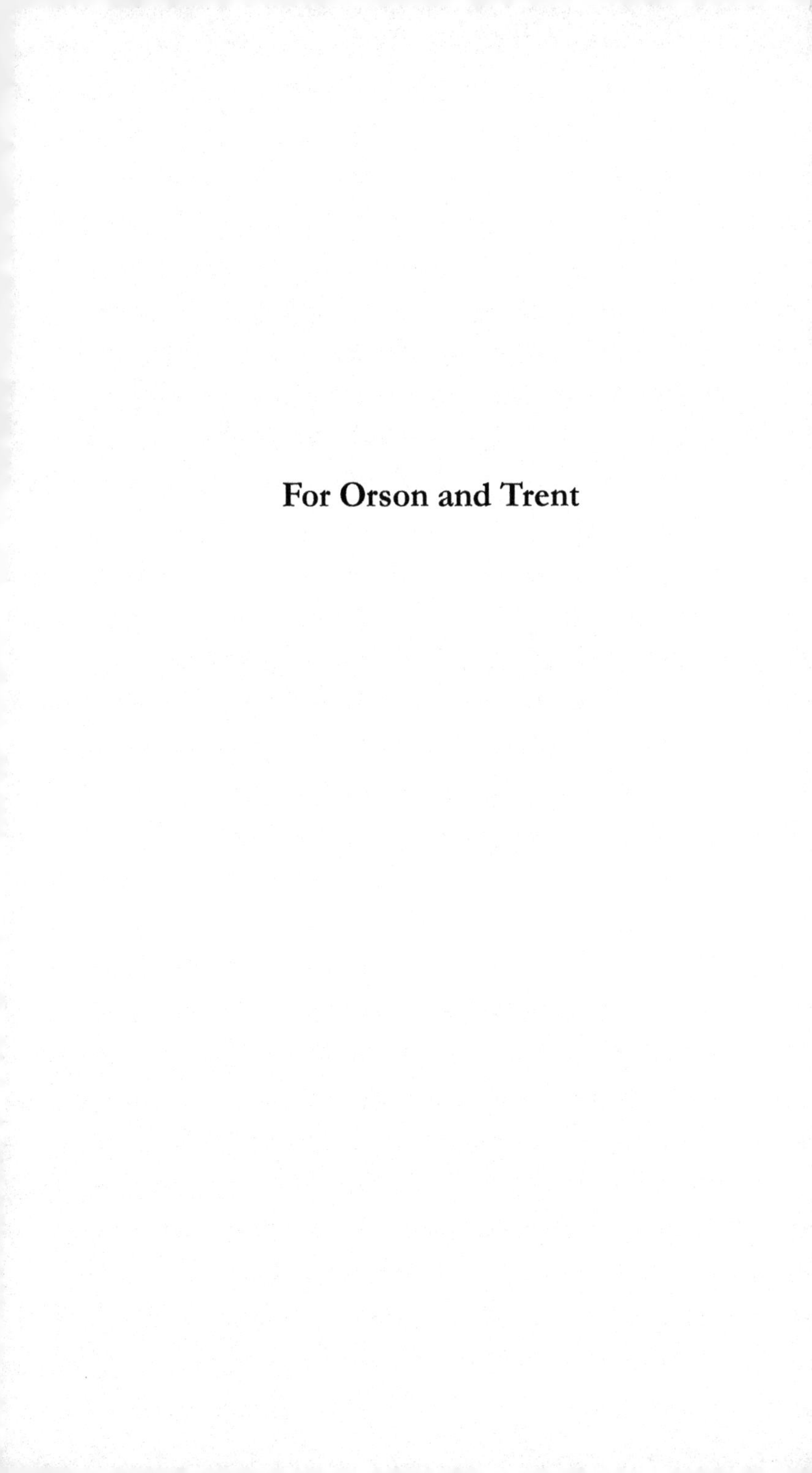

For Orson and Trent

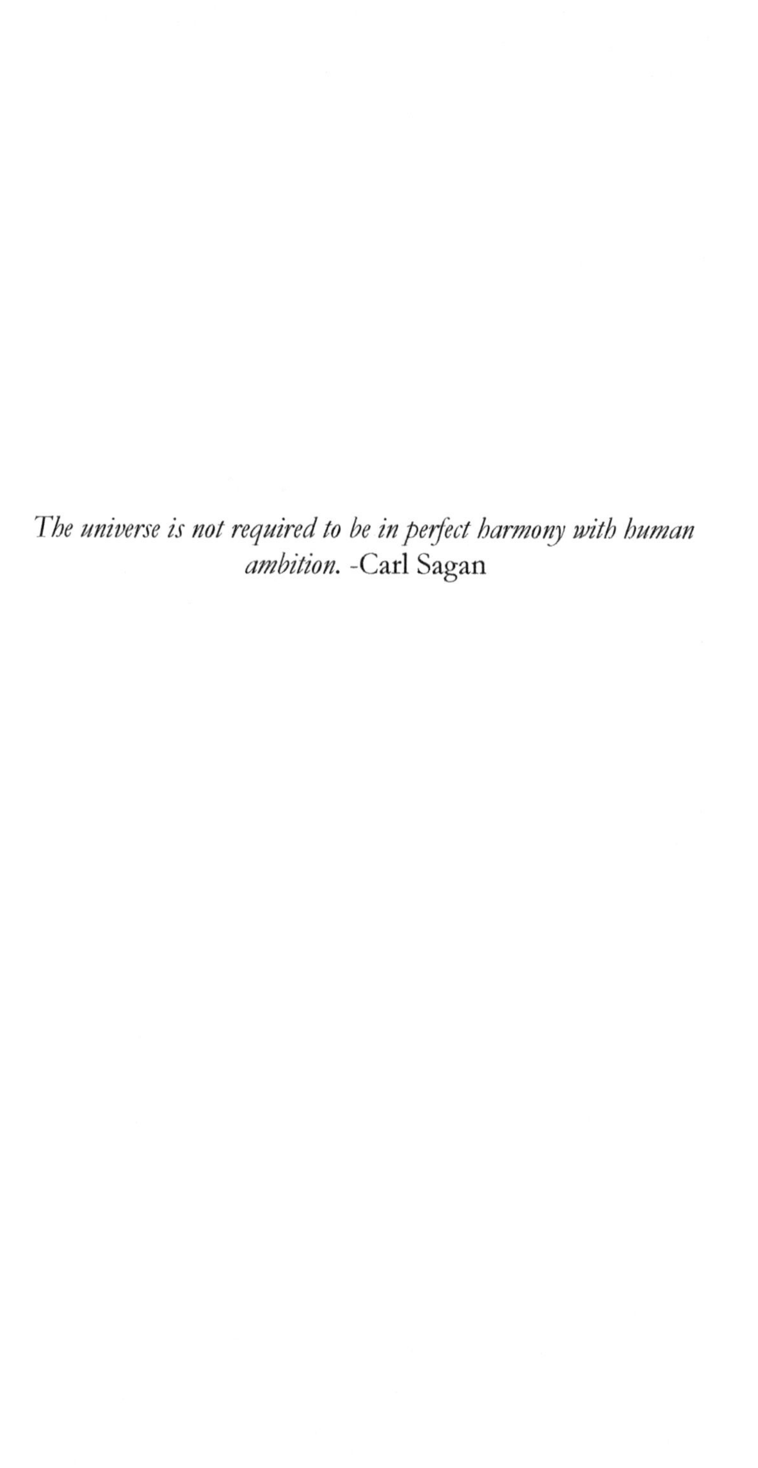

The universe is not required to be in perfect harmony with human ambition. -Carl Sagan

Contents

Acknowledgments

The author would like to thank the following people for their invaluable time and assistance with this project; it wouldn't be what it is without them.

Pete, Allyson, Brooke, Jerome, Scott, Sandi, Jerene, Tim, Bevin, Adam, Melonie

Chapter One

Zach Brady sifted through the paltry remains of what had once been a sporting goods store, diligently searching for anything that might still be of use. Rotting, empty boxes spilled from cabinets and shelves like the organs of a gutted animal. Despite the cold he could still smell the stink of mold and rot in the air, even through the mask covering his mouth and nose.

His father and his younger brother were two aisles down from him, both engaged in searches of a similar nature. Zach felt that searching this store was pointless, but his father said it was necessary if they wanted to survive the winter. He always listened to his father.

He spotted a cabinet two aisles over. The doors were closed; that could be a good sign. Sometimes it meant there was actually something useful hidden inside. His dad had taught him the difference between what was useful and what wasn't. It turned out toys weren't all that useful. Zach didn't really agree, but he was only ten years old and Dad made the rules. His father did allow him a single toy, though; he chose a '57 Chevy Hot Wheels car. It was even small enough to fit in his front pocket.

Zach walked to the cabinet, stepping lightly around the fallen debris littering the floor, being careful with each step to test his weight on the decaying floor. The snow made it difficult to see what was actually beneath his feet. It had been a long time since this place had seen a roof overhead. He'd fallen through a rotten floor once before and he didn't want to do it again.

When he reached the cabinet and opened the doors he found only some ragged sheets of decomposing paper, some pens, and some paperclips. That was as good as empty. He couldn't help but be disappointed. Their supplies were dwindling and they needed a find soon. He thought his dad was scared but was trying not to show it. It made Zach feel better when his father was brave. It made him feel he could be brave too.

Suddenly he noticed how quiet things had become. He couldn't hear his father and brother anymore. Wind whistled through the broken windows. A crow cawed once in the distance. Then he heard a sound come from the end of the aisle behind him, a sound like someone walking. His stomach clenched and despite the cold air against his cheeks, his face flushed hot.

He rose and turned slowly. At the end of the aisle, no more than sixty feet in front of him, stood a gaunt, dark figure. Dead leaves and small twigs infested its long, matted hair. Its breath escaped in small plumes, visible in the cold, dusk air. The figure stood slightly hunched, watching him. Its head turned to the side, its mouth twitching and jerking. It was dressed in dirty, disintegrating rags that barely covered its body.

It stood, simply breathing and watching. Zach froze while the thing just continued to stare. He knew that calling out to his father could provoke it, but so could running away from it. If this carrier was paralyzed badly enough he could maybe outrun it, but he also knew there was no guarantee of that. Sometimes carriers were so delirious they just walked away, not often, but sometimes. He hoped this one would just walk away.

Zach's eyes shifted left and right; he could find no obvious exit. Shelves, boxes, and other garbage boxed him in.

Suddenly, the figure stopped moving and stood very still.

Zach reached slowly for his gun and unsnapped the holster. In the eerie silence of the store it made a deafening clicking sound.

It leapt.

Zach backpedaled, surprised by the thing's speed. It had appeared to be starving, even near death, but the prowess and agility it displayed was terrifying. Zach tripped over some trash on the floor, landing on his backside. Boxes fell around his head, blocking his view.

He reached down to his holster to retrieve the gun. It was gone! He desperately searched for the gun under the trash and snow covering the floor, but he couldn't find it. Panic coursed through him like an electric shock. The thing continued to run, jumping over trash and boxes, closing the gap between them with alarming speed. Zach stood up and tried to run. In his haste he tripped and fell on a rotten tree branch that had fallen through the decaying roof.

Now on his hands and knees he quickly looked up, surveying his escape route. He still didn't see one; all the shelves now looked like a labyrinth. The gun was still missing and he couldn't think. He was frozen in place, utterly terrified. He realized with sickening certainty that he was going to die in the trash; torn limb from limb by the monster behind him. In a last-ditch effort he opened his mouth to call out for his father's help.

Before he could make a sound he saw a tall figure dressed in camouflage, wearing goggles and a surgical mask over a long beard running toward him. The man gripped a baseball bat in his hands.

Daddy.

His father jumped over him, swinging the bat with

incredible force. Zach watched as the bat connected just above the thing's nose. Its head snapped backward from the impact as its bare, frostbitten feet flew out from under it. It landed on its back, motionless, dead before it hit the floor. Standing over the miserable figure, his father delivered one final blow to the thing's head, splitting it into pieces.

Ed Brady turned to his oldest son, a few small dots of the carrier's blood clinging to his goggles.

"Oh, Zach," he said through the mask, shaking his head, his voice wavering.

Zach began to cry.

Ed held his son for only a moment, attempting to quell the tears. A moment was all the time they might have before more of the infected showed up. This attack had been too close. Zach knew better than to wander off, but the boy was so young; it was an understandable mistake. Dangerous, but understandable.

Ed's youngest son Jeremy emerged from the shadows. He was a thoughtful and precocious eight year old, streetwise beyond his years. Jeremy instinctively scanned the aisles for movement before fixing his gaze upon his father and brother.

Ed looked down at Zach and Jeremy. "We have to go, guys. Where there's one there's bound to be more, you know."

The boys nodded in agreement.

"There's nothin' here anyway," Jeremy said.

Ed didn't reply.

The trio quickly searched the trash, eventually locating Zach's missing gun. Quickly but carefully they made their way out of the store. The arctic wind bit into them as they passed through the broken front doors of the decrepit building and into the winter night.

After scanning the parking lot for carriers Ed picked up some snow with a gloved hand, rubbed it on his goggles and wiped them clean. Next, he wiped his wax-laden surgical mask in the same fashion. Finally, he cleaned his gloves in the snow.

Carrier blood.

He knew what that could mean.

He inspected both of his children; they were apparently clean…this time. He wondered just how exposed he'd been back there. His concern was for the kids; if he was alone and had been exposed he could live and die by that. With the kids involved, however, it would mean leaving them without their protector. It would be their death sentence. He had to make sure his children would live to see a different world than the one in which they now suffered so greatly.

He turned to his oldest son. "Zach, go get the sled and bring it over here."

Zach complied without hesitation. In their world, survival depended on following the rules.

Ed hitched the sled to his own waist using a frayed, nylon rope they'd picked up at a Home Depot right after they left the border town. The sled, procured from a Toys "R" Us when the snow began to fall, contained anything they couldn't fit into their backpacks: extra food, blankets, plastic sheeting, rope, and more.

They ran through their pre-travel checklist: boots tied, backpacks zipped, masks and goggles on, what guns they had holstered and ready. Their map was their ever-present guide, tucked away in Ed's front pocket. Their baseball bat and machete were close at hand as well. Those weapons usually saw more action than the guns anyway.

A scream sounded in the distance, deep in the surrounding wood. It was the sound of pain and insanity. Ed shuddered. He supposed he'd never get used to that sound.

"Let's go."

As the snow continued to fall from the dark sky above them, Ed and his sons trudged on through the accumulating drifts. The sled he pulled moved smoothly across the powdery surface, producing a soft, consistent scraping sound. It was almost soothing in the heavy silence of the snowy night.

Wool socks covered their feet. They never ignored their feet; frostbite led to gangrene, and gangrene led to death. Once feet froze, death wasn't far behind. It was a hard lesson of winter after the outbreak. Ski masks covered their faces now, their eyes protected by goggles, their bodies covered by multiple layers of scavenged winter-wear. They looked like homeless mountaineers engaged in a futile search for some mythical peak.

The snow fell heavily for several hours before finally letting up. Eventually, it stopped altogether, the clouds moving out not long after that. The nearly full moon shone brightly down from above them with cold indifference, effectively illuminating the area around them and allowing them to see surprisingly well. The strip mall they'd left was long behind them, but the memory of Zach's encounter with the carrier was still fresh in all their minds.

According to the map, they were traveling along what had once been Interstate Highway 64, heading due west. In this part of the country, highway exits had initially served to offer travelers a respite from the rigors of the open road. They also unintentionally served to break up the long stretches of tree-lined roadway.

Despite the brightness of the moon, the surrounding forest remained the deepest of all blacks. Having left the strip mall far behind, Ed and his sons now walked a barren stretch of road bordered by a Stygian nightmare. The snow had accumulated significantly, making travel even more difficult. Summer travel was easier, but the favorable conditions also meant it was easier for the carriers as well.

By the light of the moon, they could see scores of corpses littering the highway. Most belonged to the infected and were at least partly devoured by wild animals, or possibly by other carriers. The bones and the cartilage, however, remained largely intact. Ed noticed some of the bodies were fresher than others, suggesting they'd died more recently.

That meant people were still being infected.

The infected were dying, but not quickly enough. Survivors killed many carriers shortly after the infection broke out, and the army's first strike killed even more. In the end, however, there were so many infected they couldn't possibly all be contained or killed.

That had been civilization's downfall.

Some time after the outbreak the remaining infected began to develop rudimentary survival techniques. They would often hunt city and suburban streets in packs, eating whatever people and animals they could catch. The infected ate anything already dead as well, including infected bodies. While the living carriers wouldn't hesitate to eat an already infected dead body, they tended not to attack other living infected humans. This peculiar behavior led to speculation by survivors that the virus had been a form of germ warfare, the behavior engineered.

With the cloud cover gone it was inevitable the temperatures would drop. Ed and the boys needed a camp and a fire. There were plenty of cars forever stranded on the highway; normally they just found one with windows intact and holed up in it. As cold as it was on this night, however, they desperately needed heat, so they staked out two cars parked nearly side by side to build their fire between.

After identifying their campsite, the three of them walked together to the edge of the forest to gather deadwood for the fire. They rarely separated; this task was no exception to that rule. After the incident back at the sporting goods store, Ed felt this was even more imperative. He still blamed himself for allowing Zach to go off alone for so long. They were lucky, indeed.

They made short work of the firewood retrieval, each carrying as much as they could back to their campsite. Five trips provided them enough wood to keep the fire going the entire night.

Back at their impromptu camp, Ed looked inside the two cars; they were both filled with the forgotten corpses of another time. Most of the infected had difficulty opening car doors; otherwise, they'd have eaten their fill of the car-bodies long ago. He had the boys close their eyes while he removed the corpses from the cars, dragging them a sufficient distance from the camp. It was gruesome work, and one more nightmarish image he didn't want his children to have to endure. He could only imagine the circumstances that led these poor folks to die in their cars. He tried not to dwell on it; he couldn't mourn for the lost world forever.

Once Ed got the fire going they all removed their gloves and held their hands toward the flames, rubbing their fingers together. The smell of smoke was strong and comforting. The cars they'd camped between served to block some of the biting wind, reflecting some of the fire's heat back toward them. It wasn't necessarily cozy, but it would suffice for the night.

Ed and the boys were in their third winter since the outbreak. Two of those winters were spent on the road. They had been in the border town for the first winter immediately after the outbreak, at least until the food ran out and things in the town broke down completely.

That had also been before Sarah died.

Ed promptly shook that thought from his head.

They sat on a folded blanket, placed on top of a sheet of plastic to keep the snow melt from soaking their clothing. Another simple truth in these cruel winters: get wet and death wasn't far behind. They covered themselves with an unzipped sleeping bag, huddling closely together between the cars, Ed's back supported by a rotten, flattened tire. Jeremy's head rested on Ed's shoulder while Zach sat, leaning against his father's chest.

They sat this way for a very long time, not speaking. They'd had close calls before, but they were all still shaken by what had happened at the sporting goods store only hours before. They were lucky, Ed knew that, and he wondered how long they could carry on until their luck ran out. He wondered if the question wasn't *if* the virus or the carriers would catch up to them, but *when.* He asked himself that question frequently, more often than made him comfortable.

After some time, Jeremy spoke. "Daddy, do you think Mommy is watching us right now?" It was a question he'd asked before.

Ed didn't have an answer. He wanted to always tell the boys the truth; they deserved that much. Sometimes, particularly when the truth was harsh, it was a difficult thing to do. "I don't know, buddy. I hope so."

"Do you think she knows we're okay?"

"If she's watching us then yeah, I think she does."

Jeremy paused for a moment, thinking. "Good."

"I miss her," Zach added.

"I do too. We all do," Ed said.

"I think she'd be proud of us," Zach said. "Really proud."

Ed smiled. "Yeah, she would, wouldn't she? She really would." That time telling the truth was easy.

The fire crackled as it ruthlessly consumed the deadwood they'd gathered. Smoke blew haphazardly into the air as small embers traveled on updrafts, burning out after a few feet. Occasionally the burning wood cracked so loudly they looked to the woods for intruders. Thankfully there were none.

More silence followed. Ed and the boys watched the hypnotic dance of the flames upon the wood. He pulled them closer. Despite the cold and the wind they were reasonably warm.

"Tell us again about the city by the river," Zach asked.

The city was what kept them all going. It was their religion now. It had also become a common bedtime story. They asked about it periodically and never tired of hearing the same thing repeatedly.

Ed cleared his throat. "I went there once, a few years before the infection broke. It was a nice city, built right on the river. Near the edge of the river was a giant steel arch, over six hundred feet tall."

"Did you climb it?" Jeremy asked.

"No, doofus, you can't climb the Arch," Zach said.

Ed continued. "No buddy, I didn't climb it. I didn't even go in it. But, when I last saw it, the setting sun lit it up like a giant orange candle."

Zach paused for a moment, thoughtful. "Do you think

anybody lives in the city anymore? Do you think what you heard was true?"

Ed thought about his answer, though they always asked the same question. "I don't know, maybe. I hope so. You know how the cities were overrun so fast. Everybody ran to the coasts to get away. There might not be anybody there, or it could be full of carriers."

"But the message you heard," Zach continued, "it said Saint Louis was a safe haven."

Ed nodded in the darkness. "But that was a while ago, and the message was spotty; the reception was bad and there was lots of static. It's hard to say for sure."

"Well, I think it's safe," Jeremy said, proclaiming this sentiment with his usual high degree of confidence.

Ed chuckled. "I hope so. Either way, we have each other."

Ed allowed the boys to drift off to sleep together. He planned to stay up for a few more hours before waking Zach for guard duty. He and the boys always slept in rotation; danger lurked everywhere and knew no bedtime. For now, he was content to sit with his two sons, to hold them close another day, and to fill their minds and their spirits with hope.

Ed had indeed happened upon a radio broadcast, that much was true, but it had only contained four words. *Saint Louis…(static)… safe haven.* While that *could* mean Saint Louis really was safe, it could also be just as likely that hidden under the static between those words the message might have really been Saint Louis is *not* a safe haven. That particular message might have been a dire warning to all those considering entry.

Or it all could be a lie; a fib orchestrated to lure the unwitting into a trap. The police, the armed forces, even the government eventually crumbled once the infection went into full pandemic. It came on too strong, too fast, and there was no plan in place to deal with a threat of that magnitude. It was truly unprecedented. It made the Spanish Flu look like a common cold season.

Now, without any law of the land in place, men had become more horrible than Ed had ever thought possible. Their evil was truly limitless. He'd seen some of the worst things imaginable since the outbreak; his children had seen more than their fair share as well.

The truth was there was no one left to save them. They were, in every sense of the phrase, completely on their own. Ed knew the reality was they couldn't keep moving forever. Eventually, their luck would run out. They'd be captured and killed by thieves or they'd be torn to bits by the hordes of rabid carriers that freely roamed the land now. Or, perhaps worse, Ed would be exposed to the virus, leaving his two children to fend for themselves in a world with no hope, no rules, and no allies.

He wondered if he could do what was necessary then. The three bullets he kept in the magazine in his front pocket were a constant reminder of the choice he might be forced to make.

Sarah's luck had run out. Try as he had, he hadn't been able to save his wife. His harsh lesson had been how powerless to change anything he really was. That knowledge haunted him each time he looked at his children. Was he just biding time, staving off the inevitable? He could only hope they couldn't see his increasing doubt.

Ed Brady sat on the surface of a deserted highway, surrounded by ghosts of the past, holding the fragile future in his arms.

The city by the river could mean salvation, or it could mean death.

Either way, it was their destiny.

Chapter Two

As she stood in the middle of the deserted highway, Trish Connor thought the worst thing about the end of the world might very well be the winters. They were particularly harsh, as if the nightmare she woke up to each day wasn't already harsh enough. At least when Tim had been alive it had been a little easier to bear; now she was in her second winter without him and it was the worst one yet.

Cold. So cold. Some nights she was sure she would freeze to death. She often thought that might be better. Each morning, however, she'd awaken to another day of relentless cold and raging hunger. She felt like the walking dead herself, an animated shell, empty on the inside.

Once, before everything went to hell, she'd been pretty. She thought maybe she still was, but it had been so long since she looked in a mirror she couldn't know. Worse, she feared she might not recognize herself anymore. She already could see how thin her body was, and she knew her face had to look like that of a corpse. She didn't have the courage to face all of that, at least not anymore.

If Tim had noticed any of this he hadn't let it show. Dead for more than a year now, his face was still bright and clear in her memory. He'd cared for her, protected her, and told her the sweet lies her heart so desperately needed to hear.

But now she could no longer fool herself into believing, not even for a moment, that everything would be okay.

She sometimes wondered why she continued to trudge on, eking out a pathetic existence in a world overrun with the stuff of nightmares. Sometimes she sat in the freezing cold, just before nightfall, and stared at the barrel of the pistol she carried. She had eight bullets; it would take only one to make it all go away. Click, boom, gone; all in less than a second.

But Tim wouldn't approve of that, not even from the Great Beyond. For her to give up now would be like spitting in his face. He had believed she was worth saving and that life was still worth living. He died in defense of that belief, and for that she both loved and hated him.

She was seventeen when she met Tim in high school. She was only nineteen when he died. In the two years they spent together she felt they'd shared a lifetime. They had been through so much together that they had become as close as two people could be. Their youth was irrelevant. Now she was twenty years old and completely alone in a living hell.

She would often sit in the cold, squeezing her fingers together, feeling the familiar thickness of Tim's class ring on her middle finger. He hadn't been able to give her a wedding ring, so he'd given her his class ring instead. Though too large to fit on her ring finger, it didn't matter. She made do. Nothing else in her possession could rival this ring's importance.

Now desperate and alone on a desolate highway, she found herself hungry and cold, covered in filthy, scavenged clothing. She stared at the seemingly endless stretch of snow-covered road in front of her for a very long time, trying to ignore the stinging bite of the relentless wind. Here on the open road the wind seemed to never stop.

She once avoided the road, but the empty farmland had soon overgrown its boundaries and she was now too weak to fight her way through the thicket. On the highway, grass grew only in the ever-widening cracks, not yet overtaking it. It would eventually claim the entire road, but for the time being it was passable.

Now the deep snow drifts made travel by any means other than the road impossible. Although the defunct highway still held thousands of abandoned cars she could easily maneuver around those. Many of the cars were still occupied by their owners; sad reminders of thousands of failed attempts to escape an inescapable fate. She rarely looked inside them anymore; they all held the same terrible thing.

Survivors had picked many of the bodies clean of their clothing and possessions; the birds had picked many more clean of their flesh. The rest just slowly decomposed in their cars, or on the highway itself. Trish had seen so many bodies she hardly noticed them anymore.

The truly dead were no longer her concern; the walking dead were what mattered now. Their bodies were alive, but their minds, their hearts, and their souls, those were long since dead and gone. They were no longer human; they were wild animals now. Vicious and relentless, the infected were absolutely mad with hunger and delirium.

Such was the way of the world now.

To her left an exit beckoned. Two hundred yards of pavement led to abandoned restaurants, truck stops, grocery stores, and then on to hundreds of deserted homes. Many had surely been picked over, raided, and plundered, but there weren't enough survivors to scavenge it all. There had to be scraps, something sustaining left behind three eternal years ago. It was risky because the infected could be anywhere, but it was better to die trying than passively freeze to death on a road to nowhere.

She was sure Tim would have agreed with that.

Nearly twenty minutes later Trish stood facing the door of a former Howard Johnson's, peering intently into the darkness within. A gentle snow drifted slowly down from an apathetic sky, dusting her shoulders and blanketing the ground around her in a thick, white powder.

Seeing no footsteps in the snow other than her own, Trish felt she could reasonably assume she was alone. It was impossible to tell if there were carriers inside. She decided she had little choice but to step into the darkened building and take her chances.

The glass in the unlocked door's window was mostly broken. She slowly opened it, being careful not to cut herself on any broken glass. She wondered why she still cared. Habit, most likely. The door scraped along the floor, pushing trash and other debris along the way as it opened. By all appearances, no one had been there for a very long time and she took that as another reassuring sign.

Once in she felt her way along the walls through the darkness, searching for a suitable place to curl up and wait out the seemingly endless night. She heard a scurrying from somewhere in the blinding dark and froze. Then she heard it again. *Rats*, she thought to herself. Compared to the carriers, rats were a mere nuisance now, a proverbial gnat buzzing around the ears. Still, she hated them.

She listened intently for the telltale signs of the infected; there was no breathing or growling, no shuffling of feet in the darkness. No dragging of paralyzed limbs, no maniacal screaming or delirious repetition of gibberish. No slurping of drool through rotten teeth. For now, she was alone.

She continued her way through the room, feeling against the wall until she eventually bumped into a table. She dropped to the floor beneath the table and scraped away enough debris to make something that loosely resembled a makeshift bed. She curled up in the fetal position, her back up against the wall, and prepared to wait out the night there.

She again listened for signs she wasn't alone; she heard

nothing but the rats and the howl of the wind as it drove in through broken windows. She hoped the rats weren't hungry; they'd been known to chew on sleeping people. She squeezed her fingers together inside the tattered mitten on her left hand and felt the shape of Tim's ring. She felt comforted and connected, as if linked by a tether through an invisible doorway to the Great Beyond.

As she drifted off to sleep, she asked two favors of a god she no longer believed in. First, she asked for vivid dreams of Tim; dreams where he held her and told her everything would be okay.

Then she asked that she never wake up again.

Sleep overtook her more quickly than she had expected. She never heard the three figures carefully open the building's broken door, nor did she hear their footsteps as they made their way toward their sleeping prey.

Chapter Three

"Check that closet over there. Maybe there are some coats or some blankets," Dave Porter said to his wife, Sandy, as they combed through an abandoned house two miles from the highway. Sandy nodded in acknowledgment as their friend Jim searched the kitchen for any food or equally useful items that may have been left behind.

"Nothing," Sandy replied.

"Dammit," Dave said. He turned to Jim. "Anything?"

"Nothing here either," Jim replied. "The cupboards are bare, not even a bone for a dog." He smiled, but dropped it when no one else returned it.

"We have to check the basement," Dave, his voice flat.

Jim and Sandy both looked at him, apprehension painted on their faces.

"Look," Dave continued, "I don't want to do it either, but it's our best chance."

"Not after what we found at the last place," Sandy said.

"I know, I know, but we have to," Dave continued.

"We didn't get enough at the last house. You both know that. Besides, whatever we find down there can't hurt us. You saw the windows in this place, not a single one broken. The door was still locked, for Christ's sake. Nobody's been in this place since the outbreak, not even the rats."

Sandy's lower lip trembled slightly. "I don't think I can handle seeing what we saw back in that last house. They were just so small…" She trailed off, biting her lip to keep from crying again.

Dave forced the hardness from his face. "Jim and I will go. You stay up here. If the coast is clear we'll call you down. We still have a couple more hours of daylight left, plenty of time to search the basement."

Consternation washed over her face. "I don't want to be up here by myself."

Dave sighed. He tried to be patient, but it was often difficult. "I know, but you said you didn't want to go down."

"I don't."

Jim turned to Sandy and put his hand on her shoulder. "It'll be all right, we'll be right back up in a flash."

Sandy nodded, but she seemed less than convinced.

Dave handed Sandy their only working gun before pulling his hatchet from his belt. She took the pistol, touching it like a slimy fish.

"Don't shoot unless I tell you to," he told her.

She nodded. "I won't."

Dave grabbed the flashlight they'd found during a prior house raid, and Jim held his ever-present hammer tightly in his hand as the two men walked toward the basement door. They reached the door and Dave turned the knob, slowly and carefully opening the door. It groaned and squeaked on its hinges as it gave way. They all listened intently for any audible signs of carriers seeking shelter within. Reassuring silence greeted them. Holding his hatchet tightly, Dave knocked three times on the door. That usually got the deadwalkers stirring. Despite the knocking they heard nothing from below.

Dave looked at Jim. "Let's go."

Jim nodded.

Dave placed one foot on the top step, testing his weight. The wood held. He couldn't be too careful; a broken ankle in this new world was a death sentence. He flipped on the flashlight. The batteries were low and the light was dim, but it would have to do. Taking a deep breath, he and Jim continued down the steps.

There were no windows in the basement. The light from above illuminated the steps, but couldn't pierce far into the darkness below. The flashlight was little help. Dave couldn't help but think they were headed into more of a cellar than a basement. He paused halfway down the steps, listening for movement in the darkness below. He heard nothing. He shone the flashlight back and forth quickly, scanning the basement for movement. There was none, so he deemed it safe enough to continue.

He continued to descend into the darkened basement until his feet finally touched the concrete floor. He heard the steps creak as Jim brought up the rear. Though unfinished, the basement had wooden frames erected where walls had been planned. By the dim light of the flashlight, these skeletal walls took on the sinister appearance of bars on a jail cell.

Dave made a right turn, choosing the direction at random. The light flashed across various objects; boxes, chairs, a workout bench, shelves, and more. It was all covered in dust, untouched for years. This was good. The basement smelled musty and dank, as if the air around them had absorbed the stagnant history of the past three years.

The pair entered into a small, unfinished room, framed in with the same partially finished walls. Jim stayed close behind in the darkness to avoid being separated. If there was one thing they had learned over the years it was that staying together was critical to their survival.

Three years ago, when the infection quickly became a global pandemic, many survivors fled to the coasts like rats from a sinking ship. Dave and Sandy had been married for only a month. Living near the eastern shoreline, they had little distance to travel to make it to the coast and settle into what they thought would be only a temporary shelter.

Weeks became months, months became years. The infected didn't die off as expected. Instead, they adapted, learned to hunt, and the virus, although devastating psychologically, wasn't itself fatal. Some of them almost still seemed to retain at least some humanity, despite their behavior and appearance.

Dave had openly disagreed with their border town's leadership. He was outspoken, even vehement. A folly of youth, in retrospect. That attitude and behavior had landed him few supporters within the town. Once they struck up a friendship with Jim, who was openly gay, things went bad very quickly. Before long they were framed for the theft of town supplies. Punishment for these trumped up charges had been severe: expulsion into the land outside the town's fences: into the Badlands. Though he couldn't prove it, Dave felt the town council had simply found a convenient way to get rid of their problems in one fell swoop.

Once outside the town's fences, the three outcasts found themselves wandering from one abandoned house to another, from grocery store to gas station, from truck stop to motel, all across an infected no man's land that had once been known as the Midwestern United States. If any form of government still existed, it was absent from this dismal wasteland, the concept long ago forgotten, abandoned, or just plain dead. Dave, his wife, and their friend survived for over a year with a combination of luck, teamwork, and determination.

Now two-thirds of that team stood in the basement of a long-abandoned house, searching for anything that could be used to buy them another day in Hell. Dave kept the flashlight trained on the path in front of him. He raised the beam and stopped.

In front of him, within the wooden skeleton of a room that would never be finished, an unknown tragedy had played out. Two corpses occupied the room, desiccated, frozen, and slowly rotting, captured in the final scene of a macabre and horrible play.

One, a woman, chained to the concrete wall, her head gone from the jaw up. The feeble beam cast by the flashlight showed dark stains on the wall behind her. A flick of the beam fully illuminated the other corpse, a man, sitting in a rocking chair. His head was gone; only a jagged stump and a partial jawbone remained.

It didn't take long for Dave to understand what had happened. In the seclusion of a forgotten basement a husband carried out a grim duty. She was infected; he wasn't. He'd ended her suffering before ending his own.

It occurred to Dave that not a single person living until now knew this had even happened, this final act of bravery at the end of the world.

And that made his heart break.

"Holy shit," Jim said quietly from behind Dave as he gazed upon the gruesome scene.

"Yeah," Dave replied. He could find no other words to add.

"Dave?" Sandy called from the top of the steps. "Is everything okay down there?"

"We're fine," Dave replied. "You?"

"I'm getting nervous up here by myself. What'd you find down there?"

After the horror they'd seen in the last house, he wasn't sure if Sandy would be able to handle this too. Those kids…

"You might not want to see this," Dave called up the steps.

A pause. "Oh no, not again."

"No, not that," Dave replied, "but still, it's not pleasant."

Sandy hadn't seemed able to adjust to life after the outbreak, much less life on the run from the infected. She had bad days and worse days. She was withdrawn most of the time, lost in her thoughts. She'd become almost childlike, relying on Dave to do almost everything for her. He loved her, no doubt, and his heart ached for her anguish. God knew he tried to understand. But there were days when understanding was difficult to come by. Sometimes he didn't want to have to think for her. Sometimes he just needed her to be strong on her own. The reality was that Sandy needed a protector and Dave had volunteered for that task, 'til death did they part. So he did his part, every day. It was his duty, after all.

With Sandy at bay, Dave turned his attention back to the room in front of him. He walked in, lighting the way with the flashlight. The shotgun used in this brutal yet merciful act lay on the floor beside the man's body, the barrel slightly rusty from the dank, basement air. Dave handed the light to Jim, picking up the shotgun. It looked functional, but the only true test would be actually firing it.

Judging from the scene in front of him, he assumed both barrels were empty. He broke the gun open and confirmed this. He took the flashlight back before handing the shotgun to Jim. A quick search of the room revealed a box with about a half-dozen shells. He placed the shells in his pocket before taking the flashlight back from Jim.

All of a sudden he felt the room squeezing him. The heavy air was suffocating. It was as if all the dread and despair that came with the outbreak was crammed into that little space.

He had to get out.

Suddenly Sandy called down again. "Dave, I don't want to be up here anymore. I want to come down."

He called back up to her. "Come on down, babe, just watch your step."

Sandy walked slowly down the steps, making sure to grasp the handrail tightly.

Dave walked back to the bottom of the steps, shining the light to illuminate her way. He took her hand as she stepped onto the concrete floor. "Just don't go in that room back there," he warned.

Sandy nodded.

The trio spent the next fifteen minutes with a single flashlight in the bitter cold, searching for supplies for their packs. They found some canned tuna, Spam, Vienna Sausages, some ramen noodles, and a book of matches. Apparently the homeowners had consumed most of the food before they met their terrible end. Jim discovered a hunting knife and a pair of boots too small for him. Sandy found a can of Sterno, partially burned, and Dave found a can opener. All but the boots went into their packs.

A loud bang abruptly sounded as something struck the floor above them. The trio froze, their muscles tightening. Dave extinguished the flashlight, and the three of them held their breath in the dark while they listened for any clue as to what had made the sound. They heard the floor creak, followed by what sounded like a paralyzed limb being dragged along.

Something was upstairs.

The three strained their eyes to see in the darkened room, but they could see very little besides the feeble light illuminating the steps from above. Something had definitely gotten into the house; there was little doubt it was a carrier.

Fuck! Dave thought. It'd been Sandy's job to lock the doors behind them; apparently she hadn't done it. That mistake might now cost them their lives.

Dave turned to his wife and his friend in the dark. "Let's see what this thing decides to do," he whispered. "If it leaves on its own then we grab the backpacks and get the fuck outta here."

"And if it doesn't?" Jim whispered.

"If it doesn't, then I'm going to catch it by surprise at the bottom of the steps." Dave turned to face both his wife and Jim, still whispering. "You guys stick together. Grab the backpacks and be ready. Sandy, give Jim the pistol."

"What about this shotgun?" Jim whispered back.

"I don't know…give it to Sandy."

Jim and Sandy swapped guns.

Dave continued. "I'm going to wait at the bottom of the stairs with the hatchet. If it comes down, I'll hack it to pieces." He leaned in, touching Sandy's shoulder. "Nobody shoots unless I say so. I don't want to take a bullet meant for whatever's up there. Besides, one bang from that gun and there'll be dozens of deadwalkers on us like stink on shit."

"Do you think there's more than one up there?" Sandy asked.

"I hope not," Dave replied.

Sandy reached up, placing her hand on top of her husband's hand. "Dave, I'm afraid."

"I am too, babe, but we have to face this head on; otherwise, we're all dead."

"Be careful, baby," she replied.

Dave could see she was ready to break down; she just wasn't equipped for this. He silently hoped she could hold it together and not get herself or the rest of them killed.

"I'll wait for your signal," Jim whispered.

Dave took some consolation in knowing that at least Jim wasn't trigger-happy.

They listened intently while the thing upstairs limped around above them. There was a crash as something was tossed carelessly to the floor, followed by more crashes and bangs. Whatever was up there was ransacking the place. Dave had no doubt it was a carrier looking for food. Carriers almost never figured out how to open metal cans, but glass they'd just break. And more often than not they'd eat the glass along with the food. It was a fitting last meal.

Finally the sounds stopped. As they waited, Dave counted the seconds off in his head. *Fifteen, thirty, forty-five, one minute*. He wondered for a moment if the thing might have just wandered back outside. Of course it could also be waiting for them, he considered. Doubtful, but not impossible. Some carriers were smarter than others.

Sandy's grip tightened around Dave's arm. "Is it gone?" she asked.

"Maybe. I think we need to-"

A footstep sounded on the top step, followed by another. The hair on the back of their necks stood on end. Dave felt butterflies fluttering in his stomach. As the group stood a mere twenty feet from the wooden stairs, dwindling sunlight shone down from above, illuminating the steps in a pallid glow. A shadow fell upon the steps, cast from a figure standing in the doorway above.

Another step; now they could see the thing's foot. It was clad in a dirty, mud-caked shoe, a shoe that hadn't been removed in three years. Tattered jeans barely covered the emaciated leg. Another step, this one a dead thud as the carrier's paralyzed leg followed obediently along.

"Remember the plan," Dave said quietly to the others. He broke from Sandy's grip and walked toward the bottom of the steps.

"Dave!" Sandy whispered, but he was gone. She saw his shadow flash in front of the stairs and then he disappeared into the darkness of the basement.

Another step, followed by the dull thud of the trailing limb. Dave wondered how the thing could even walk. He could only hope that this handicap would allow him the upper hand. Fighting the infected was incredibly dangerous; not only were they insane, but their insanity was catching. He'd have to get in and strike hard, then he could get his wife and friend out. He couldn't afford to fuck this up. If he did, they were all as good as dead. He couldn't even use the gun; it was too likely to attract more carriers. Having that gun and not being able to use it was like being stranded in the ocean on a life raft, surrounded by water and none of it fit to drink. Irony could be very cruel.

Another step, followed by the dead-leg thud. Dave removed the hatchet from his belt, wiping the sweat off of his hand before tightly gripping the handle. He was surprised his hands were sweating despite the cold. His muscles tensed as his senses leveled and focused. Fight or flight had chosen fight, and his body was readying for it. He swallowed hard, tasting the dank, cold air of the basement. With his eyes focused on the stairs, he waited for the right time.

Another step, followed by the thud. Then one more.

Now.

Dave lunged from the shadows, hatchet in hand.

Chapter Four

Trish awoke in terror as she was forcefully pulled from under the table in the dark building. She opened her eyes wide, searching the darkness for her attacker. She could see nothing. Her heart raced, kick-started by a boost of adrenaline. When she tried to scream a hand covered her mouth. She bit it hard and heard her attacker scream before a fist smashed into her face. The world spun as she went limp in their grasp. Flashing points of light flared in her eyes.

Though stunned, she didn't lose consciousness. Her mind raced for answers. Her assailants weren't carriers; carriers tore and ate flesh, attacking wildly and viciously. This was a kidnapping, and Trish knew there was only one reason to kidnap a young woman.

There were some fates worse than death.

The kidnappers dragged her limp body out of the building and into the open air. She could feel the coldness of snowflakes falling on her neck. The bite of the freezing night air and driving wind brought her to her senses. As she struggled against her captor's grip, she could make out three figures surrounding her in the dim light; two stood in front of her while one pinned her arms behind her back.

"Let go of me, asshole!" she screamed.

A man's voice came from one of the dark silhouettes in front of her. "Shut the fuck up, cunt!" He lunged forward, driving his fist viciously into her stomach. Trish doubled over in agony. The world spun around her as she dropped to her knees and vomited bile from her empty stomach onto the snow-covered asphalt.

Another heavy blow to the back of her head sent her drifting off into darkness.

When Trish awoke the first thing she noticed was the pounding headache; it felt as if her head would split open at any minute. She noticed a warmth in the air around her that she hadn't felt in weeks. Dazed and confused, she tried to move, but she quickly discovered her hands were bound. With a rush it all came back to her, and she quickly opened her eyes to look around.

She found herself in a small room, dimly lit with a single gas lantern. A small kerosene heater burned with glorious heat in the center of the room. Beside it a man dressed in dirty overalls sat on an empty drum. He was small and thin with stringy hair and pasty-white skin. He picked at his fingernails with a large knife.

The man on the drum noticed Trish open her eyes, stopping the work on his fingernails. He nodded toward a figure out of Trish's sight before flashing a blackened grin at her. Her stomach twisted in revulsion.

Another figure appeared from the darkness, pulled up a stool, and took a seat beside the first man. He was tall, black, and wore a dark red beret. They both stared at her without saying a word. She stared back, her wits returning and her fear rising. She knew no good could come from any of this. She found herself wishing a carrier had gotten to her instead.

"Who are you?" she croaked, her mouth dry and her throat parched.

"Shut the fuck up, bitch," the man on the drum said.

The large man with the beret chuckled.

Trish closed her eyes. To have come all this way, to have fought so hard, only to meet her end at the hands of these all too human monsters was unthinkable. Tim had always told her that the world wasn't fair; he was right again. She turned her thoughts to Tim, to the images of his face emblazoned upon her mind, and drifted off to blissful unconsciousness.

When Trish opened her eyes again she saw the same two men. Now they surrounded her, all less than three feet away. A third man was now in the room, again out of sight.

"Give her another dose," Trish heard the hidden man say.

"Not so much this time," the man in the beret said. "You just about killed her the last time."

The pale, black-toothed man replied. He was so thin he looked as though he might break under his own weight. "How the fuck am I supposed to know, Darnell? Ain't no instructions on the bottle, and I ain't no fuckin' doctor."

"Don't use the needle this time then. You always fuck that shit up. Give her the pills," Darnell replied.

"Which pills?"

The hidden man walked around from behind Trish and into the feeble light. She couldn't make out his features; she could only see his silhouette. He handed the scrawny man a bottle of pills. "The lorazepam, dummy. That's the only pills we got left. You keep this bitch quiet, or else she'll have the deadwalkers all over our shit."

Trish felt herself being lifted to a sitting position. Her vision spun as she became level. Fingers forced her mouth open, and she felt two pills being placed inside, followed by a cup of water to wash it down. Although part of her knew not to swallow the pills, that part was groggy, very tired, and had no energy to put up much of a fight. She was so thirsty that she almost swallowed unconsciously.

Then she was unceremoniously dropped back down to the table, too weak to support herself. She felt as if she were underwater, or behind a thick glass wall watching things unfold. Pain flared in her groin. She knew what must have been done to her; she'd been with no one since Tim.

She silently sobbed, tears spilling from her swollen eyes. She conjured up an image of Tim, strong and good, as she slipped back into an altered state.

Dreams of Tim and dreams of carriers clouded her mind. At times Tim would disappear and the carriers would attack her instead of him, but she could never die. She dreamed of her parents once. In this dream she was eight years old, sitting in her backyard by a pool, despite the fact that her parents had never owned one. In the dream her parents were young and in love, the way they'd been before the divorce. Her mother was beautiful, kind, and happy; unaware of the bitter woman she would become. Her father was still alive; his eyes sparkling in the bright sunlight, without an inkling of the drunken car crash that would take his life two weeks before Trish's sixteenth birthday.

Once she awakened to the pressure of another body on top of her. The pain was so intense. Not just in her groin, but all over her body. Thankfully she dropped off again into a deep sleep. She remembered being awakened to drink periodically, but she was offered no food. That hardly mattered; she wasn't even hungry anymore.

The pills were provided regularly, along with consistent injections. She had no idea what they were shooting into her. She spent most of her time unconscious. When she was awake she tried not to think about what was happening. She preferred the unconsciousness; with it she could fade away and pretend she was anyone or anywhere else.

Time passed in strange random bursts, running together and melting into a confusing, soupy mess. Trish wasn't sure if time was passing in hours, days, or weeks. She knew she was getting weaker, but death never came, no matter how much she wished for it. The agony seemed as if it would never end.

Sometimes the lantern was lit, often it was not. When it was lit she could mostly see her captors and her surroundings. She remembered eating some crackers once, and drinking water periodically, and she was once washed between her legs. She remembered all three men on top of her at one time or another, like monsters devouring crippled prey.

Eventually, after an indeterminate amount of time, she began to feel more lucid. She was sleeping less and noticing more. She could only assume they tapered down the dosage of whatever drugs they were feeding her, or maybe her captors were just running out of the stuff. The return of her lucidity also brought with it the despair of her plight. She wanted to die. Her body ached; her pelvis and legs were bruised until they were almost black. Her throat burned from thirst. Hunger still showed no signs of returning. She'd hung on long enough; she'd done her best. Tim would forgive her if she let go. She deserved relief.

At some point she awakened to find herself lying on her side, still on top of the wooden table she'd been on since arriving in her prison. She was cold, despite having been covered at some point with a thin blanket. Often she was left with just one of the kidnappers, usually the skinny one with the missing teeth. She discovered that was the case now. She remembered they called him Trey on a few occasions.

Trey was picking his fingernails with the knife again as part of what appeared to be his favorite pastime. She decided to speak to him, to reason with him, to appeal to his humanity, if he possessed any. It was worth a shot. She lifted an arm and attempted to wave it in the air; it felt as if it was made of lead. Still, the slight movement was enough to catch his attention. He looked up from his fingernails and stared at her.

Trish opened her mouth, but nothing came out. Her lips were dry and her head pounded. She was seriously dehydrated. She swallowed hard and tried again.

"Come..." she croaked.

Trey continued to stare at her, unmoved. His filthy face wore an utterly vacuous expression.

"Come...here," she tried again. The attempt at speech brought on a mild coughing fit, her head pounded with every cough. Eventually it subsided.

"Fuck off, bitch," Trey replied.

"Come...here," she tried again. A tear streamed from her left eye.

He stood up and walked closer, stopping a few feet away. "Shut the fuck up."

He was stupid and cruel, Trish knew, but she had to try. She swallowed again. She needed out, she needed peace, she needed eternity.

"Kill me," she begged. "Please."

Trey looked puzzled at first, but then his expression changed. He pulled a knife from a sheath attached to his belt and lunged forward, placing the blade against her throat. Trish tilted her head backward, exposing the area.

"Do it," she pleaded, closing her eyes. She waited; she was ready. It couldn't hurt more than she already hurt.

Trey chuckled. "Bitch, you're gonna die one day, but I ain't gonna be the one to kill ya. Not yet, at least." He turned away and walked back to his chair, resuming his fingernail work by the feeble light. "Kill me," he mocked, chuckling to himself as if remembering a funny joke heard earlier in the day.

Trish's spirits, previously bolstered by the thought of relief, now dropped. This man was a monster; they all were, all three of them. At the end of the world humans behaved as they always had. They killed and took what they wanted. Overwhelmed with grief and hopelessness she sobbed quietly, the tears again running down her cheeks and dripping down upon the rough, wooden surface of the table beneath her.

It wasn't long until sleep found her again.

Trish awoke. Her throat burned and her head ached. Her body reeled from pain. More pills, more sleep. Swimming time and blackouts. The molestations continued, though less often. Were they bored? She couldn't tell. How long could it continue to go on? She didn't know. How much time had passed was a mystery; hours and days were just a blur now.

Her captors came and went from the room. They kept the kerosene heater burning and a guard, usually Trey, posted in the chair. The room was always dim, lit most of the time by the small lantern. Trey worked on his fingernails by the light of the lantern and would continue the work by candlelight when chastised for using too much lantern fuel.

Ultimately, complete lucidity returned; painful, clear, brutal, and honest lucidity. Her throat still burned and her stomach cramped. She was awake, but kept her eyes closed, feigning sleep and wishing for death. It could come in any form and from any source at this point; she would welcome it without prejudice. She began to see her torturers as saviors, the only people in the world who could deliver the sweet kiss of death and release her from the hell in which she now barely survived.

Her attackers must have stopped the drugs altogether. If this was true then there was only one reason for that: they were finished with her. This realization initially caused Trish some fear, but it also carried with it joy and hope. It meant that soon she could be released. Even if there was no shared afterlife she could at least join Tim in the same dark abyss. Together forever, blanketed by the same eternal darkness. No more pain, ever. With her wits again about her she felt for the familiar comfort of Tim's ring on her finger.

It was gone.

She opened her eyes and looked down at her left hand just to make sure the ring was really gone. It was. Those bastards had stolen it right from her hand. At that moment something inside her changed; what had once been overwhelming sadness and despair was now seething anger. She was immediately filled with rage, indignation, and hatred. She felt it overtake her body, starting in her aching stomach and radiating outward toward her limbs. She was weak, but she wasn't dead, at least not yet.

Those motherfuckers, she thought.

Then, instead of making plans to die, she started making plans to kill.

She looked around the room; only Trey sat in the familiar guard chair. As usual he was engrossed in his fingernails. She began to formulate her plan. She continued scanning the room with her eyes, being careful not to move her head, making out whatever she could in the shadows. There were at least some supplies in the room; this looked like a home base for these creeps. She was careful not to move her head to avoid drawing attention to herself.

There were clothes in the room, some pants and some heavy coats. She saw a large container of what appeared to be water with several canteens sitting on a shelf above it. There were boots and perhaps three dozen cans of various foodstuffs, the labels unreadable in the dark room. There were no guns, at least none she could see. This was where they stored their gear, the things they needed to go out kidnapping and raping innocent women.

She turned her sights back on Trey; small, scrawny, and weak. He was a toadie, a lackey. She'd seen enough to understand that he was the low man on their totem pole. She remembered him on top of her between her blackouts, but only once or twice. He had always been made to go last, after the other two had gotten their fill. The idea mortified her, but she quelled that feeling; she had plans to make. While the other two might have had enough of her, Trey hopefully had not. That could be her opportunity.

She also felt confident that Trey wouldn't kill her, not without the others' permission. It was doubtful he would defy them. He might beat her, but she could handle that. She'd been through worse than that already.

She closed her eyes and finalized her plan. If she was going out then she was going out fighting. She took a moment to think of Tim, to use him as inspiration, before she opened her eyes again.

She turned her head toward Trey and spoke. "Trey." The words came out as a raspy whisper. "Trey," she repeated, louder this time.

Trey looked up from his work. He stood up slowly, his fingernail-picking knife gripped in his hand. Trish had never addressed him by name before; this seemed to get his attention though he didn't reply. Instead he just stared, that empty and stupid look spread across his scrawny face.

"Trey, come here," she said, hoarse from thirst. Her head pounded from the dehydration.

"Fuck all that," he replied.

"No, please. I need something."

"I ain't giving you shit."

"I'll give you something in return."

This piqued his interest. "You'll give me what?"

"Come closer."

He inched closer, craning his neck to hear.

"I need water. I'm thirsty. I'll return a favor with a favor."

He paused, thinking. "What kind of favor?"

"You know what kind of favor."

"Bullshit. You won't do it."

"I will, but for water. I need water first."

Trey paused again, thinking. She could only imagine what effort the act of thinking must be for him. He glanced at the door then back at Trish then back at the door again. He sheathed the knife. She hoped this was a good sign. If the other two were there he wouldn't make a move, but if they weren't he just might take the bait.

"Until I finish, right?" He whispered this question as if he didn't want anyone else to hear.

"Until you finish. But water first."

Trey took another look at the door; this worried her. Maybe the other two were out there after all. It didn't matter; she was already committed to the plan.

Trey walked to a large, white container and removed the lid before dipping a canteen into the water. Once the canteen was partially filled, he moved over to where Trish lay. She lifted herself into a sitting position, struggling against her own weight. The world swam around her; she wasn't sure how long it had been since she'd been vertical. Her hands were bound in front of her by a strip of cloth that had been wrapped several times around her wrists before being tied.

Trey handed Trish the canteen; she took it in her bound hands. She touched the canteen to her lips and drank; the water tasted like heaven. She gulped as much as she could, pausing before taking another long drink. In a few seconds the canteen was empty.

"More," she asked.

Trey shook his head. "Fuck no. A deal's a deal. And you better not fuckin' weasel out on me, or I'll kill you."

No, you won't, she thought to herself. *Not without their permission.*

"Help me off this table and to my knees then," she said.

He stood, not moving, simply staring at her.

"How else am I supposed to get down there?" she asked.

Apparently convinced by this simple logic, he balanced her as she slid off the table. Her legs were weak, but she found could stand on them. The thin blanket fell off her impossibly thin frame and she recoiled at the sight of herself. Back in school she'd seen images of Nazi concentration camp victims who had a similar appearance.

"Help me to my knees," she asked. Trey obliged. "Now unzip your pants and unbuckle your belt."

"You try anything funny and you're fuckin' dead," he warned, removing the knife from the sheath again.

Trish said nothing.

As Trey unbuttoned his pants and unzipped his fly, Trish pulled his pants down to his knees, exposing his erect penis. He smelled of sweat and urine. As she took his penis in her hand she heard him gasp; she glanced to the side and saw that his grip on the knife had relaxed. As she began to work his penis she felt his body relax.

It was time.

She took his penis in her mouth and his testicles in her bound hands. Then, in one orchestrated motion, she bit down as hard as she possibly could, squeezing his testicles even harder. He screamed and instinctively hit her in the head with his free hand. She held on despite the blow, tasting the metallic flavor of his blood as she bit down harder. She bit with all her might, grinding her teeth back and forth on his member. He screamed again, striking her repeatedly in the head and temple.

In an attempt to stop the beating, she reached up, grasping his hand in both of her bound hands. She wasn't strong enough to keep her grip, however, and he wrestled it away. Despite this he didn't stab or cut her with the knife in his other hand. Her gamble had paid off; he was too afraid of his crew to kill her, even as she tried to bite his dick off.

As he pulled his hand away he struck the top of her head with the handle of the knife, leaving a large gash behind. The pain was intense; it hurt so badly that she almost let go. Instead of letting go she pushed him backward. He fell, unable to keep his balance with his pants around his knees. He continued to fall backward, arms flailing. Trish released his bleeding penis, twisting his testicles one last time before he flew out of her grip. He struck his head on a shelf behind him before landing hard on his back. His head hit the concrete floor with a sickening thud.

As he struck the ground, the knife flew out of his hand, sliding a few feet away. He screamed again as he curled into the fetal position, holding his injured genitals. Blood from the laceration on Trish's head flowed into her left eye, obstructing her vision. She quickly wiped it away.

She lunged toward the knife, scrambling across the dirty warehouse floor. *Oh please, oh please, oh please, oh please* she repeated in her head as she reached out and grasped the knife in her hands. Adrenaline now powered her weakened muscles. In the background she heard Trey still screaming in pain as he lay on the floor. Picking up the knife, she crawled back toward the screaming man on the floor. The door didn't open and no one rushed in. They were still alone.

As she reached Trey she raised the knife above her head, preparing to drive it into his chest. Just before she could deliver the stab, his fist connected with the side of her head. He was weak from pain and the blow held little force, but it caught cleanly enough to knock her off-balance and to the floor. She retained her grip on the knife, despite the fall.

Trey rolled to his stomach, attempting to get up, his pants still around his ankles. Blood dripped to the floor from his lacerated penis. Trish recovered and jumped on his back, forcing him back to the ground. She lifted the knife up high into the air before driving the blade into his back as hard as she could. Trey screamed again, louder than ever. Once buried, she twisted the blade back and forth. Blood began to pour from the wound, soaking his clothing and pooling on the floor. Trey screamed like a wounded animal.

Trish pulled the knife out and immediately drove it into his back again. Again and again and again and again she plunged the knife into him. She cried as she stabbed. She lost count of how many times she stabbed him before he finally stopped screaming. He made sticky drowning sounds as the blood poured into his punctured lungs, pooling on the floor around his body.

Eventually she stopped stabbing. The crying stopped as well. She looked down at her captor before pulling the knife out of his back. The blade made a sloppy, sucking sound as she removed it from his soggy body.

Then she stabbed him one more time for good measure.

She'd done it. The bastard was dead. Now it was time to get out of there.

Bracing the knife handle between her feet, she sawed through the bindings around her wrists. As the bindings fell away, she picked herself up to a standing position. She fell immediately back down again, dizziness overtaking her. Ignoring the instability, she got back up again. Pain roared through her head from the impact of the knife blade, but she stood without falling.

Now free, she grabbed some pants, socks, and boots. She put them on her naked body moving as quickly as possible. It was difficult just bending over. She was unable to find a backpack or bag, but she found a pillowcase that had apparently served as a bag before. She filled it with as many canned goods as she thought she could carry. She then filled two canteens from the shelf with water, slinging the straps over her shoulders before pulling on a coat from a hanger attached to the wall.

She discovered that along with Tim's ring her captors had also taken her gun. Unable to find a replacement pistol, she rushed to Trey's body to search for a weapon of any kind. Apparently he couldn't be trusted by the others to carry a weapon, as she couldn't find anything on his body. As she worked she checked the door periodically. It remained closed. She hurried as quickly as she could, but she felt as if she were moving in slow motion. She was so weak and malnourished that everything was an incredible effort.

Giving up on Trey, she ran back to the pillowcase and attempted to lift it. It was too heavy. She pulled out some cans until she could pick up the bag. Satisfied with the weight, she slung the pillowcase over her bony shoulder.

She looked down at the sloppy corpse on the floor, spitting a mixture of saliva and blood on it. "Fuck you, Trey," she said, picking up the knife. She turned toward the door to leave.

Then, from the other side of the door, she heard the sound of another door opening, followed by footsteps.

Chapter Five

As the hatchet struck the carrier's good leg, Dave turned his head to avoid contact with any blood spatter. The blade connected solidly above the thing's exposed ankle, separating the skin and stopping when it hit bone. The carrier shrieked with terrible ferocity as the hatchet sliced the skin and muscle. With both legs now unable to support its weight it tumbled headfirst to the bottom of the steps, striking the concrete floor squarely with its shoulder. Dave heard a loud crunch as the thing's collarbone snapped upon impact.

Despite the broken bones, it tried to get up. Immediately Jim appeared and delivered two hammer blows to the base of the carrier's neck. A short scream slipped out of Sandy's mouth before she had the good sense to muffle it. After the hammer blows the thing stopped trying to get up again. It now just moaned loudly, the sound of a mortally wounded animal. As if filled with fluid, its lungs made wet, slurping sounds when it breathed. The tragic figure squirmed on the floor, writhing in pain, bleeding and moaning.

They all knew that noise could draw other carriers, provided they weren't already there. Even if it wasn't human anymore the thing was still suffering. Dave lifted the hatchet and drove it forcefully into the back of the carrier's neck, burying it deeply into the thing's spinal column. It went limp and silent. He pulled the hatchet out, shaking the infected blood off to the side.

"Sandy! You okay?" Dave called.

A pause. No response.

"Sandy!"

"Yes, I'm okay!" she replied, shaken. She sounded as if she'd been crying.

Dave flipped on the flashlight and quickly found Sandy in the darkness.

He turned to Jim. "We gotta get moving right now."

He turned back to Sandy. "Grab the backpack and let's go."

Sandy picked up the backpack, slinging it over her shoulder as she and Jim filed in behind Dave. On his way up the steps he stepped over the carrier. As he did, he envisioned for one sickening moment the thing reaching up and grabbing him by the leg. It didn't happen, but it was a difficult feeling to shake. It wasn't until he cleared the body that he noticed how badly it smelled. If death wasn't horrible enough on its own the virus made it even worse.

The three of them climbed the steps: Dave first, followed by Sandy and Jim. Dave paused at the top of the steps and looked around the main floor of the house. It looked empty. Daylight was fading, but there was still enough light to see clearly. He could see the pots and pans and other items the carrier had knocked to the floor during its rampage upstairs.

"It's clear," he called back to the others. "Let's go."

Dave walked to the front door only to find it was standing wide open. Sandy had forgotten to lock it. He closed his eyes, frustrated, exhaling to drain the tension. *The best laid plans of mice and men often go awry*, he thought. He'd told her a dozen times not to leave the doors unlocked; this time it almost got them killed. They were lucky, indeed. Moving toward the door, he turned back to Sandy and Jim to get them moving.

Suddenly Sandy screamed, running to the kitchen. Dave turned toward the door just in time to see a large carrier, this one at least six feet tall, running toward him. He barely had time to react before the thing was through the open door and upon him. The bloody hatchet flew from his hand, landing on the floor a few yards away. Dave landed squarely on his back with the carrier on top, his head striking the wooden floor. Sandy screamed from the kitchen as she huddled in the corner.

The carrier was screaming, blackened teeth bared, its breath rank from the foul garbage it ate to survive. It smelled of urine and feces; the smell was almost overpowering up close. It exhibited no sign of physical handicap.

Quickly Jim appeared over the snarling thing and brought the hammer down squarely upon the back of its head. The impact made a dull thud, like the sound of striking a melon. The thing screamed even louder before turning its attention toward Jim. Jim followed up with another blow of the hammer; this one caught it between the eyes. Though less powerful than the first blow, it was enough to knock the thing to the ground. Dave scrambled to his knees, his head pounding from the impact with the floor as he crawled over to where his hatchet lay.

Incredibly the thing started to rise, the screaming even worse now. Dave felt his blood run cold; it was an absolutely terrifying thing to behold. Gathering up his courage, he swung the hatchet as hard as he could. He buried it into the top of the carrier's head before it could get up again, piercing the skull and driving the blade into the monster's diseased brain.

The screaming abruptly stopped as the body dropped to the floor like a bag of sand, toxic blood pouring from the gaping wound in its head. It twitched a couple of times before finally lying motionless.

Dave looked at his hatchet, still buried in the thing's

head. A thick, infected layer of blood ran down the hatchet's handle, draining into a pool on the hardwood floor. The hatchet was too bloody to retrieve safely, so he decided to chalk it up to a loss and leave it. At least they still had the pistol, plus the shotgun they'd found. He could only hope the shotgun was functional.

Jim turned to Dave. "You okay?" he asked.

Suddenly Jim's eyes grew large as he motioned toward the corner of Dave's mouth.

Dave wiped his face. His fingers came back red.

Carrier blood.

"Shit," he said as he wiped the blood on his pants. He couldn't let Sandy know; she would lose it for good.

"Yeah. I'm fine," he replied. He looked himself over. His head was pounding, he had rug burn on his elbows, a few scratches on his arms, and a knot was forming on the back of his head. No carrier blood was on his cuts, at least none that he could see. He sighed with relief. Still, there was the blood near his mouth…

"Thanks for the help," he told Jim.

Jim nodded.

"Where's Sandy?" Dave asked.

Jim pointed to her; she was still sitting on the floor of the kitchen, sobbing. He and Dave exchanged a knowing look as they walked into the kitchen and helped her to her feet.

"Let's get the hell outta here," Dave said.

Both Sandy and Jim nodded in agreement.

Stepping out the front door and into the snow, they ran.

After escaping from the house, they ran as quickly as they could down the ruined streets of the forgotten subdivision. Signs of lives abruptly halted were everywhere: porch lights that hadn't been lit in years, sandboxes with faded plastic shovels and pails, a dog collar attached to a chain in an overgrown back yard. A rusty bicycle lay on its side on a street corner. Cars sat idle in driveways. It suddenly occurred to Dave that there hadn't been a new car manufactured in the world in three years.

The bodies were everywhere, now mostly decayed into blackened lumps. After seeing so many bodies it was hard to notice them anymore. Dave wondered as he ran how many of the bodies had been victims of the virus and how many had been killed by carriers of the virus. It was impossible to know for sure and he doubted he'd be happy with any of the numbers.

After running a few blocks, the trio slowed to a stop, breathing the crisp, cold air deeply into their burning lungs. Their legs ached from the lactic acid buildup caused by the sprint. Dave's head swam from the sudden exertion, exacerbating the pain from the knot on his head he'd earned during his struggle with the carrier.

The area was apparently clear, so he decided to take the opportunity to check out the shotgun. He fired the unloaded gun once to make sure the hammers were still functional. They were. He loaded the shotgun with two shells before closing up the barrels. He handed Jim the pistol. Dave held the barrel down, cradling the shotgun across his forearm, just as his grandfather had shown him while rabbit hunting as a boy.

They continued walking.

As night continued to creep in, the darkness began eating up the scenery around them. They needed shelter, not only from the wind and the cold, but also from the carriers. After the attack at the house they were all reticent about flippantly strolling into just any random house. As they walked they scoped out houses that looked safe, mostly those with unbroken windows and tightly closed doors. These were less likely to be squatter homes for carriers seeking shelter from the bitter cold. Of course there were no guarantees.

Finally they happened upon a small house on the corner of the street on which they walked. Dave and Jim circled it with Sandy in tow, ensuring it appeared reasonably safe. It did. They walked to the front door, ready to pry it open with Jim's claw hammer. On a whim, Sandy decided to check under the doormat for the house key. Surprisingly enough, she found it. She even smiled at her stroke of luck; something she hadn't done much of in a long time. Dave smiled back, stroking her cheek. It occurred to him that sometimes, even in the most dismal of all days, luck had a way of showing itself to the tenacious.

Taking the key from Sandy, Dave unlocked the door to the house. He slowly pushed it open, peering carefully inside. Meager sunlight shone in through the murky windows, revealing a scene that looked more like a museum than a house. Dust layered the horizontal surfaces, even clinging to the walls. The smell of mildew permeated the air. Children's toys still sat on the floor, covered in dust, undisturbed for years. Sandy stared at the toys, but she didn't utter a word. Dave knew what she was thinking; he just hoped she could keep her spirits up.

With daylight fading, Dave and Jim checked the rest of the house. It was clear. There was no basement, and Sandy was visibly pleased about that. She also made sure to lock the front door, promising she'd never forget that task again. Dave browsed the kitchen and found a meat cleaver to replace his hatchet, along with a book of matches.

When dark finally fell they used the feeble light of the flashlight to navigate through the darkness and climb into a bed in one of the house's bedrooms. They all slept in the same bed, slipping under the blankets and capitalizing on their combined body heat. The sheets smelled of mildew after being locked up airtight for three years, but they'd slept in conditions far worse. After all, a musty bed was still better than no bed at all. The house had no fireplace, so they had to rely on the blankets and their shared body heat to keep them from freezing.

As the trio began to warm up they dozed off into dreamless sleep. Dreamless for all but Dave, who dreamt he was the captain of a large ship, navigating icy ocean waters. It wasn't until just before he awoke that he realized the ship was the H.M.S. Titanic.

The following morning the group awoke, their bellies rumbling to remind their owners of their relentless need for energy. Sandy was still silent and aloof. She spoke very little as they all shared two cans of Spam and water from a single canteen. Dave attempted to coax some conversation out of her, but he was unsuccessful. It was becoming increasingly difficult each day to keep her engaged. Still, he kept at it.

After their meager breakfast they combed the house for supplies. Since the house hadn't been touched after the outbreak they were able to accumulate some useful items. Most of the food in the house had long-since rotted, but a pantry full of canned food still remained. They also found packages of stale crackers, cookies, and powdered milk. Bottles of water still sat in the pantry; they collected a few of those as well. Along with the foodstuffs they retrieved some candles and lighters. A check of the garage provided Dave with a replacement hatchet, albeit a little dull. A rough stone would solve that problem, somewhere safer where carriers wouldn't hear the sounds and come running for dinner.

After replenishing their bellies and their supplies, they stepped carefully out of the house and into the bright daylight. The day was still cold, but the sunlight helped to warm things up. If nothing else it gave the impression that the temperature wasn't as cold as it really was. They walked in a line along the ruined subdivisions, constantly on the lookout for attack. Though untested, Dave felt a bit safer with the new shotgun.

After walking for a while longer they eventually rounded a corner, entering another subdivision street. There they ran into four oncoming travelers sharing the same route. Both groups stopped short. Dave instinctively stepped in front of Sandy; his grip tightened on the shotgun. A man with a short, red beard stood in the lead. He was thin, his skin weathered, his hair receding. He wore large, thick glasses taped on one side.

"Not infected," the red-headed man said.

A teenage boy and girl walking behind him both answered the same way. "Not infected," they both said. A woman bringing up the rear replied with the same announcement.

In his hand the man held a handgun. He paused, his fingers tightening on the handle. Dave realized he was waiting for a response from them. "Not infected," Dave replied. He looked back at Sandy and Jim, raising his eyebrows. They responded accordingly.

The man's fingers relaxed on the trigger. Both groups gave each other a wide berth as they passed.

As the family walked away Dave stopped. "Be careful," he told them. "We ran into some carrier trouble back that way."

The man stopped and looked back at them. He nodded once before continuing on with his family.

They traveled in this fashion for the rest of the day, stopping periodically for small meals and water. They drank all the bottled water they'd found, forcing them to melt snow in their canteens by placing it near their bodies and allowing the temperature to rise. Eating too much snow could lower their body temperatures to dangerous levels. Despite near-continuous walking they were barely staying warm as it was.

Along the way they ran across two infected deadwalkers, both well over a hundred yards away and wandering aimlessly. The three travelers walked past the carriers, being careful to keep them in sight while themselves staying quiet. They saw no more carriers the rest of that day, besides the usual bodies that littered the streets. The sun was brightest around midday and in it they almost felt warm.

By the evening, however, the light and the heat were beginning to wane. It would be another cold night. Dave remembered a time not long ago when he could watch the six o'clock news to know what to expect from the weather; now he had to do it the old-fashioned way. Most often that meant just waking up and seeing what the day brought.

They walked for hours with almost no conversation.

Sometimes Dave wondered why they continued to walk at all. He often considered holing up inside of a house and just staking claim there. That would definitely reduce some of their risks. Eventually their supplies would run out though, and they'd have to venture out again. At least while traveling they could always find new sources of food and water, even shelter when they needed it.

He also supposed that it did Sandy some good to keep moving. It gave her a goal, something to work toward, and made her feel less overwhelmed by their plight. Staying in one place meant accepting their inevitable doom; moving allowed her to continue believing otherwise. She'd had a tough enough time dealing with life even before the world had come to an end.

Dave wasn't sure about Jim. Jim followed. He didn't say much, and he didn't want to lead. He was good to have around; he came through when needed. He also had a way of calming Sandy down, along with an apparently immeasurable amount of patience. That was a quality Dave didn't always possess.

He thought about the family they'd passed earlier in the day, the family with the red-headed father. He supposed that Jim was a part of their family now. They surely all relied upon each other now like family. He wondered if maybe he should have invited the other folks along; after all there was strength in numbers.

Suddenly, two men appeared from behind one of the houses. They placed themselves in front of Dave and his companions, blocking their way.

In their hands they held pistols.

Chapter Six

Trish froze when she heard the sound of her remaining captors returning. She stared at the door to the room, listening to the sounds getting louder, unsure of what to do next. Her stomach felt as though it was twisting into knots and she felt even sicker than she already did. She had to think fast if she was to have any chance of making it out alive.

Darnell was big, really big. She also knew he still had his strength. She didn't. The other guy was a toss-up; she never really saw him during any of her lucid periods. She had to assume he was stronger than her too. There wasn't time to make much of a plan; she decided she would just have to move quickly and be ready when the time came.

She removed the canteens strapped over her shoulders, gently placing the pillowcase of food down on the floor before quietly moving behind the door. She hoped she could ambush them from behind with the knife. If she could cut Darnell's throat then maybe she could stab the other one before he knew what was happening. It wasn't much of a plan, but it was all she had. She just felt so weak; if only she still had her gun. Unfortunately that was long gone.

She looked at Trey's body lying on the floor, his dark blood pooled around it. Her spirits, already plummeting with doubt, dropped further. Once the other two caught sight of Trey's body she'd lose the element of surprise. She rushed over to the body, put down the knife, and attempted to drag Trey's bloody remains out of sight.

Although Trey's body was light Trish was very weak and moving him proved incredibly difficult. She kept slipping in his blood each time she tried to get a foothold. She was making only inches of progress and the footsteps on the other side of the door were getting louder.

She had no choice but to abandon the effort. She had to find a quicker alternative. Trish searched the wall and found a coat hanging on a large hook. She pulled the coat off the hook and laid it on Trey's body, covering it as best she could. It covered his upper body, but left his legs exposed, his pants still around his ankles. It would have to be good enough; she was out of time.

She picked up the knife before walking quickly to the chair where Trey had done his most diligent fingernail work. There she blew out the lantern, casting the room in total darkness.

As the light went out the door to the room opened. She didn't have time to hide behind the door now, so she backed against a wall in the shadows and stood very still. She clutched the knife tightly in her hand, butterflies racing through her stomach.

Darnell paused after he opened the door, peering into the darkened room. Trish saw the light from the open door make its way almost to Trey's body. She held her breath, her nerves on fire.

"Trey!" Darnell called out. "Trey! Where the fuck you at?"

He entered slowly and walked carefully across the room, navigating the near-darkness. He made it to the lantern and pulled out a match from a matchbook in his shirt pocket. Striking a flame, Darnell touched the burning match head to the wick. The flame rose, burning brightly before leveling out. He blew out the match and held the lantern up to get a better look around the room.

Trish's breathing stopped as the light from the lantern spilled upon the edge of Trey's covered body. The sight immediately caught Darnell's attention, but he strained in the dark to identify what he'd seen. He leaned forward, trying to get a better look. When the light from the lantern fell upon the covered corpse Darnell had no problem identifying the body. His eyes grew wide as he opened his mouth to speak.

Trish struck before Darnell could form a single word. She lunged forward with what little strength she still had left, stabbing at his face. Though surprised, Darnell was quick enough to deflect the knife. A split-second later and the knife would have gone through his eye socket and into his brain.

His reflexes, however fast they were, weren't fast enough to avoid the blade completely. It continued its trajectory, slicing his left eye open like the belly of a fish. Darnell felt warm liquid run down his face as the worst pain he'd ever felt in his life took hold of his eye. He dropped the lantern, screaming at the top of his lungs as his eye dripped. The flame extinguished when the lantern hit the floor, covering the room in a blanket of darkness, now lit only by the light trickling in through the open door.

Seeing her opportunity, Trish darted toward the door. She was almost through when she was violently yanked backward by her hair. Even with his eye ruined, Darnell wasn't going to let her get away easily. She hit the ground hard, but she somehow managed to hold on to the knife. Pain radiated through her body as she struck the concrete floor. She rolled to her stomach before forcing herself to her hands and knees. It took all of her effort, but she managed.

"YOU WHORE!" Darnell screamed as he stood over her. His left hand desperately covered his damaged eye, but he managed to raise his right arm and deliver a smashing blow to her head. Shaken, Trish gripped the knife tight, plunging it deep into his foot. The blade went through the meat of his foot, stopping only when it hit the concrete floor. He screamed again, now in even more agony than before.

Leaving the knife in Darnell's foot, Trish scrambled to her feet. Disorientation and nausea raged, but she fought it, taking a step toward the door. As she did, a huge fist landed on the small of her back, sending dull pain all the way down to her toes. It was like being hit with a sledgehammer. Even when injured Darnell was still incredibly strong.

She fell to the floor again, dazed and reeling from pain. Shaking off the pain and disorientation, Trish pulled herself back up to her knees and crawled through the door.

She barely noticed she was crying.

Once through the door she rose to her feet as quickly as she could. She stumbled and fell into a wall before righting herself. She found herself in a long, narrow hallway. The walls spun around her for a second before coming to a stop. Once upright and balanced she ran as fast as she could away from the room and from Darnell.

She didn't look back.

Darnell continued to scream from the room behind her as he pulled the knife from his foot. She didn't listen to see if the third kidnapper was in the building. She didn't stop to find Tim's class ring. She didn't stop for her pillowcase of food. She didn't look for her gun. She simply ran, bleeding from her head, leaving tiny red droplets behind as she did.

She ran through the hallway toward the first door she could find. She made it through the door and into a large loading area of what she assumed was a warehouse. Bright sunlight shone through the high windows, forcing her to squint in order to see. She looked quickly around for an escape route. To her left were loading docks, to her right were storage shelves.

Then she found what she was looking for: a door leading to the outside. A nonfunctioning EXIT sign hung above it, with bright, white sunlight spilling through a wire-reinforced window within the door. Freedom was now less than a hundred feet away.

"YOU FUCKING CUNT! I'M GONNA RIP YOUR GODDAMN HEAD OFF!" Darnell screamed from behind her. Trish ran across the warehouse floor as quickly as she could, hobbling and limping before slamming her battered and bruised body into the exit door.

It didn't budge.

Her heart sank. The door was locked.

It took a second or two for her to realize she'd just missed the panic bar. Her elation running high again, she pushed hard with her hips. The door opened.

Halfway through the doorway she turned around to see the large black man right behind her, his missing beret revealing a shortly cropped afro growing around a large, visible scar. His hand still covered his damaged left eye. Blood ran between his fingers and down his arm, dripping to the floor. He limped as he ran, leaving a bloody footprint behind with every other step he took.

Without thinking, Trish slammed the door closed as hard as she could, just as Darnell met the doorway. The heavy metal door struck him squarely in the face, driving two of his fingers into his already wasted eye. He fell to the floor, kicking and flailing wildly as his eye continued gushing blood and fluid.

Trish wasted no time; she turned and she ran into the icy air, her eyes slowly adjusting to the bright sunlight. As she ran, the screaming behind her faded away. She thought of Tim as she ran, and how proud he would have been to know how hard she'd fought to live.

Once she'd gotten far enough away to feel relatively safe she slowed her hobbled running to a walk. The icy air bit into her lungs and she developed a stitch in her side that wouldn't go away. Her body ached all over. She found it difficult to even breathe.

Despite being able to see well in the sunlight, she wasn't exactly sure where she was. Most of the snow was gone; melted away while she had been held captive. She couldn't see the Howard Johnson's where she'd been kidnapped, but she did find the highway.

There was that, at least.

She walked along residential streets, parallel to the highway. She kept it in sight to keep her bearings; at least it provided her something to navigate by. She walked around the bodies on the ground, some decomposed so badly it was difficult to make out what they even were anymore.

Up ahead, about a quarter of a mile away by her estimates, she saw some large buildings. They were old stores, all located within what had once been a strip mall. She saw what was apparently a Wal-mart or possibly a Target store; the sign long since destroyed to the point of being unreadable.

If she could make it there she might be able to get supplies, at least some water. Maybe she could hide out for a while. It was a long walk though, and every step she took was agonizing. Her entire body ached with excruciating pain. She'd never been thirstier in her entire life.

She continually looked behind her as she walked, afraid that Darnell or the other unseen kidnapper would be there, ready to finish the job they'd started. She reminded herself that Trey was dead, and she could reasonably assume that Darnell was probably dead by now too. The third kidnapper was a mystery; she just hoped she had enough of a lead that he'd never be able to find her.

All she had left was to keep walking.

And so she walked, slowly and painfully, treating each step as a small victory.

One step at a time, she told herself.

One step at a time.

Chapter Seven

Ed Brady stood between two abandoned cars on a desolate highway, watching his children sleep beside a dwindling fire. He had gotten a few hours of sleep while Zach and Jeremy relieved him of guard duty, but it seemed he rarely slept anymore. Even when he did sleep he never slept soundly.

He still had concerns about the carrier blood back at the store. The goggles had stopped most of it; the mask seemed to have stopped the rest. Just a droplet of blood in an exposed area and it was all over. Even a sneeze could be deadly. The fact that he and the boys hadn't been infected yet surprised him. It seemed as if they were exceptionally lucky. The masks, goggles and other gear must have been protecting them so far. Wearing their gear was nothing short of habit for them now.

Especially after Sarah.

Back at the sporting goods store Ed had been able to kill the carrier without using the pistol. Blood spatter from the strike of the baseball bat was dangerous, but not as dangerous as being cornered by twenty deadwalkers responding to the sound of shots fired. It was also a stroke of magnificent luck that the thing had been alone.

Ed watched his children sleep. They slept quietly and peacefully, as if the world hadn't fallen apart at all. It was likely they were all chasing a pipe dream; the world had changed and the cities were gone now. For a quarter million years humans had survived as nomads, farmers, herders, and hunters. They became enlightened, and for a galactic millisecond they formed cities and molded the world in their image.

Now those cities were gone. Only empty buildings remained, standing like ghostly sentinels, towering reminders of all that had been gained and lost.

He wondered what he would do once they got to the city. What if they found it was just like everywhere else they'd been? Would his children's spirits be broken, or would it be off to another promised land, along another dangerous road, constantly on the run like prey animals? How long could they expect to keep that up? How long before their luck ran out?

He put his hand in his front pocket, his fingers making out the painfully familiar shape of the magazine holding those three terrible bullets.

Things would have to get much worse before it came to that.

He noticed Jeremy stir, followed shortly afterwards by his brother. Their eyes opened. Both boys had green eyes.

Like their mother.

"Hi, Daddy," Jeremy said.

Zach smiled.

Ed's already broken heart broke again. How many more times could he live through that pain?

As many times as it takes, he thought.

The cold held out for another week. Ed and the boys kept traveling, building camps and fires each night, usually between stranded cars on the defunct highway. It was just too cold to stay in the cars without some source of heat.

They saw no visible signs of carriers along the way; that was one of the fortunate things about traveling in the more remote areas of the highway.

As the temperatures eventually began to rise and the snow melted, their sled became more difficult to pull. Once they'd exhausted most of the supplies it contained they stuffed the remaining items into their backpacks. They abandoned the sled along the road, leaving it to lie silently among the useless cars and blackened corpses, its useful life now spent.

A day after they dumped the sled another highway exit came into view. Ed felt both hope and trepidation, for while the exits provided stores and houses that might still have some useful items, they often brought them into contact with more of the infected. Both infected and uninfected still vied for the same resources, after all. A week without any carrier interaction couldn't allow them to let their guard down.

They spoke very little as they walked, spending most of their time on alert. Even on the highway, carriers, thieves, and wild animals were very real threats. It was a lawless, cruel, and indifferent world now. Only the careful and the clever survived.

Just before arriving at the exit they stopped to regroup. After a cursory check of their surroundings they inventoried their supplies. Ed removed everything from their backpacks and arranged it on the ground while Zach and Jeremy kept watch. He took a mental note of their supplies before repacking everything into their backpacks, placing their most-used items on top. He worked quickly; should they have to make a quick getaway he didn't want to have to leave behind anything temporarily unpacked.

Ed and Zach carried two 9 mm pistols they'd found a couple of years earlier. They also carried a few boxes of ammunition for these pistols, both precious and valuable. A couple of other pistols had found their way into Ed and the boys' backpacks, but none with ammunition to come along. They took them anyway, just in case. With rampant runs on every gun store during the outbreak, both guns and ammunition were hard to come by. Most of the guns taken during panicked raids had ended up in houses for defense against an unstoppable enemy. Unfortunately those houses very often sheltered carriers now. Many of those houses were also now exposed to the elements, with broken windows, open doors, and rotting roofs. Rust was taking its toll on what weapons were left.

But the biggest problem both then and now wasn't so much a lack of guns as it was a lack of ammunition. Most of the uninfected who'd gotten their hands on a firearm quickly exhausted their supply. There were so many infected at the beginning of the pandemic that there just weren't enough bullets to put them all down. After burning through their arsenal, many survivors had saved the last bullet for themselves. Others had not and their end was much more grisly.

Ed and Zach carried the loaded pistols, but Jeremy had none. Not until they found ammunition for the guns they had or another gun complete with ammunition. This was always one of their top priorities. Unfortunately it was proving more difficult than Ed had foreseen. He'd never thought that in America he'd have trouble getting a gun. More cruel irony.

After repacking their backpacks, the three of them then sat down in the middle of the road and ate some beef jerky, drinking water from their canteens. Before the outbreak Ed hadn't owned a canteen, or a flint, or even a knife, for that matter. They'd never survive without those things now. They ate enough to survive, but there was always more than enough hunger to go around. They were all incredibly thin, but not quite starving…at least not yet. Ed knew that if they didn't find some food soon it wouldn't be long until they were starving. They were always on the verge, it seemed.

They had to do some scavenging off this exit because Ed wasn't sure how long until the next one. They could calculate miles by the map, but the time it took to actually walk those miles was difficult to estimate. There were also other things they needed; boots, coats, pants, and socks, to name a few. They needed to find a department store, if possible, or maybe another sporting goods store.

Ed stood up and gazed at the multitude of buildings off the exit, determining their options. He noticed a somewhat dilapidated Target department store that might be able to provide some of what they needed, provided it hadn't already been cleaned out. He could also make out what appeared to be a grocery store, a couple of gas stations, some fast food restaurants, and some other stores he couldn't easily recognize. The grocery store might still have some canned goods left and the restaurants might have some packaged food they could take along with them. Both decent prospects.

Some of the buildings looked very run down; it was likely that they'd been raided or had just succumbed to the elements after several years of neglect. Nature worked quickly and efficiently on Man's empire, retaking the land stolen from her with ferocious intensity. Behind the commercial buildings were rows of residential area, subdivisions with hundreds upon hundreds of houses. Ed treated houses as a last-ditch option if the stores didn't play out. They were just too dangerous. Given that, the Target store seemed the likely candidate.

Ed looked back at the boys. They were both sitting on the ground in their mismatched winter garb, arms folded, waiting for their instructions. He smiled to help ease their fear. They smiled back, and Ed was struck by just how lucky he was to still have them.

"Let's go."

"Okay, Daddy."

Ed felt his stomach tighten into a knot as they walked down the exit ramp toward the strip mall, dodging abandoned cars and bodies along the way. Visibility was good. The undergrowth was dormant due to the cold weather, but once summer came it would take off like wildfire. He wondered briefly how many years it would take for the road to disappear completely back into the wild.

The large Target building sat at the back of an even larger parking lot that was half-full of cars. They were all parked haphazardly in the lot, many with their doors and trunks still open. Ed and the boys walked through a four-way intersection toward the store, the unlit stoplight swinging back and forth in the cold breeze. Road signs squeaked as they moved in the wind.

Ed and Zach drew their pistols and walked along either side of Jeremy. Jeremy carried the machete. They had their goggles, masks, and gloves on, as usual. They walked slowly and carefully toward the building, looking everywhere for movement. Ed wasn't comfortable being so open and exposed in carrier-friendly locations. If they were attacked they'd likely have to use their guns and that would only attract more of the killers. Out there on the lot there was nowhere to hide. Getting in and out of the store as quickly as possible was imperative.

As they crossed the Target parking lot they passed scores of bones and darkened lumps that had once been human beings. They skirted these without much thought while walking steadily. Ed hated that the boys had to see things in such a disastrous state. They had seen so many dead bodies; it was entirely commonplace now. He wasn't sure if he should feel thankful for that or disturbed by it. Truth was, he was a little of both.

Ed stopped the boys when they arrived at the front doors. The glass in the doors was broken and the place looked raided hard. Chances were there was little left. Still, little was better than nothing.

"Keep your eyes peeled," he told them.

They nodded, their eyes glowing bright green through the lenses of the goggles.

Ed peered into the store through the broken windows. Aisles were ransacked while trash and other debris littered the floor. The weather seemed to have only gotten in just past the broken doors though, so Ed hoped much of whatever was left would be in reasonably good shape. It was worth a shot.

They adjusted their goggles and masks to make sure they were properly seated. Ed chambered his first round. Zach did the same. Ed took the lead into the store as the boys fell in behind him. The door creaked a little as Ed pushed it open, but otherwise it opened without issue.

Once inside, Ed quickly glanced left and right. On both sides were scores of blackened, desiccated bodies. Many were lying down; others were sitting with their backs against the wall. Sitting just as they'd died, their darkened skin stretched tightly across their skulls. Many were partly eaten, either by animals or carriers.

"Ignore the bodies," he told the boys.

Zach and Jeremy nodded, but he saw their eyes dart to and from the bodies as they walked. It pained him to know those images would stay with them their whole lives.

Much of the store had been raided, but they were still able to find at least some of the things they needed. They picked up some light and compact food such as beef jerky, potato chips, and some chocolate bars. To save space they compacted the chips by opening the bags, crushing the chips and then rolling the bags up tightly. They also found some cans of tuna, sardines, and Spam along with two jars of pickles. The glass jars could be useful after they consumed the pickles. It wasn't as much as Ed had hoped, but it was definitely better than nothing.

The floors were littered with the empty packages of supplies opened by survivors who'd used the building for shelter. No doubt many had holed up in large department stores shortly after the infection began to spread. Others had used the place as a rest stop on their way to the coasts. Many others had simply come there to die. This was clear due to the multitude of decaying bodies near the entrance.

Despite the food aisles being mostly picked over, they made out well enough to at least get them to the next exit. There they might find nothing, as often happened. If so, they'd have to deal with that then. Ed still held out hope though; he had little choice otherwise.

They moved on to the clothing aisles, but found only a single boot in Jeremy's size. There were some coats left over, and Zach was able to replace one of his outer layer coats with a new one. Dust covered the unused coat, but otherwise it was in perfect shape. Zach discarded his old, worn-out coat as Ed ripped the tags from the new coat and placed it on his son. Ed placed a hand on his son's head, admiring the way the coat looked on the boy. Zach smiled. Ed looked away as he felt a tear form in the corner of his eye. He remembered school shopping for his son, buying a new coat for the coming winter. He'd never imagined then he'd be where he was now.

Pushing the feeling back, Ed attempted to stay focused. They found Jeremy a new stocking cap to replace his old one, and they found some wool socks to replace the ones with holes in them. Spending their lives walking made short work of socks.

During their search they ended up near the electronics section. Dozens of now-useless digital cameras sat on the display shelf. Behind the digital cameras he found a rack of disposable film cameras. Although it was likely that the film had been damaged by exposure to extreme temperatures over the past few years, Ed lined his sons up side by side to snap a photo of them.

"When was the last time we used one of these?" he asked them.

"A long time ago," Zach replied.

Jeremy nodded in agreement.

Ed smiled. "Say cheese."

Both Zach and Jeremy smiled their best and repeated the phrase. Ed brought the camera to his eye and snapped the picture. Surprisingly the flash still worked. He rolled the film forward before dropping the camera into his backpack. He doubted the film would ever be developed, but it was more a gesture of hope than anything else. An old ritual that brought comfort.

"I wish Mommy was here for the picture," Jeremy said.

Ed looked at his youngest son and smiled. "Me too, buddy."

They spent a little less than an hour in the store, gathering what they could. They found many items they had no use for, but they'd found at least enough to get them by for a while. They remained vigilant, always keeping an eye on the front door and other exits. The near miss in the sporting goods store more than a week earlier was still clear in their collective memory.

Being on the go meant they had to be able to carry everything on their backs. There was no snow in which to pull a sled, and a cart slowed them down too much to be useful. Ed tried not to think about the things they had been forced to leave behind in the past simply because they couldn't carry it all. In the end though what was gone was gone. Living in the present was all they had; it was what kept them alive.

Having gathered about all they could reasonably carry, they headed back toward the store entrance. Ed was feeling increasingly exposed the longer they remained in the store. Bottom line: he wanted out of there. He was considering taking a quick look in the grocery store they'd seen, just to see if they could shore up their food supplies a bit more.

He never got that far.

As they neared the front doors of the store, Ed noticed movement off to the side. Immediately he drew his gun, flipping the safety off as he ushered both boys behind him. His body buzzed with the surge of adrenaline; his pupils dilated, his heart raced, and his senses focused.

He caught sight of the movement again. A female carrier, lying on the floor, rolled onto its stomach as it attempted to stand. Slowly it rose to its feet, balanced precariously on unsteady legs. Ed noticed the body was in good shape; the infection must have been recent.

The carrier took a step forward and Ed leveled the gun, lining the front sight on the thing's chest and the back sight with the front sight. If it charged he'd have to shoot;

there was no time for the bat. His finger squeezed on the trigger.

Then it spoke.

"Help…please," she said, before collapsing to the ground.

Ed removed his finger and lowered the pistol. This wasn't a carrier; this was a survivor.

And he had almost killed her.

He stood with his children, gun still in hand, watching the girl, unsure what to do next. They couldn't help her; they didn't have enough supplies to share and she appeared to be ill. Was she infected? He wasn't a doctor, so how could he know?

He had no other choice but to leave her behind and stay focused on the boys.

But that would be tantamount to murder.

How could he leave this young woman behind after the boys had seen her? Even if he wanted to leave her it was too late to do that without them knowing. He'd taught them it was wrong to kill and that it was wrong not to help people. They'd never be able to understand how it was necessary to leave her behind in order for them to survive. He wasn't exactly sure how he'd explain it to them without them losing their faith in him. He looked down at them; they were both watching him closely, waiting for his decision.

Watching and learning.

"We have to help her Dad," Jeremy said from behind him.

"I don't think we can, buddy."

"But we have to try."

"We don't have the supplies. She's sick, and we don't know what's wrong with her. She might be infected with the virus."

"But we can't just leave her. She'll die here," Zach said.

"I think she might die anyway." *She'll also slow us down*, he thought. *She could be the death of us all.* He hated himself for thinking that, but truth was always truth.

"What if it was Mommy?" Jeremy asked.

Ed sighed.

He knew the decision had already been made.

Ed and the boys found some long boards among the garbage lining the floor. They used these boards, along with a thin, sheet metal shelf to create a makeshift stretcher. Ed used some rawhide shoelaces from their packs to tie the entire apparatus together. The structure proved reasonably strong and lightweight.

Ed told the boys to stay back before slowly approaching the unconscious girl. It was impossible to tell if she was infected with the virus, so they had to be extremely careful around her. They'd know within a day or two if she had it. The masks and gloves would be used until then. After determining she wasn't a threat, Ed and the boys placed her upon the makeshift stretcher they'd built. With Ed on one end and both boys on the other end, they carried her out of the store. They had to shove the door open wider to fit the girl and the contraption through, but they made it. She moaned occasionally as they carried her, but made little other movement or sound.

Ed wondered if the girl had a fever. If so, she at least needed some fluids and rest, and probably some antibiotics. Ed had used up the last of the antibiotics they had six months earlier when Jeremy had run a high fever. Ed had anguished for days until the boy's fever finally broke. He felt in his gut that she wasn't infected with the virus. If she had been, she wouldn't be unconscious, she'd be raving mad. Regardless, he forced Zach and Jeremy keep their face masks and goggles on, just in case.

If what the girl had was bacterial he could do some good with the antibiotics, provided he could find any. If it was viral it would have to run its course. Any antivirals were surely gone, raided after the pandemic started. They proved useless, but many had tried all the same.

At a minimum they needed a place to keep her until she either got better or until she died. Ed recalled passing a few farmhouses just before the exit. In this part of the

Midwest the highway cut right through mile after mile of farmland, so farmhouses weren't that hard to come by. All things considered, he thought it was their best option.

He and the boys carried the girl almost a mile on the stretcher. The lacing between the bars and the board loosened along the way, but in the end it held. Progress was slow, and they had to take a few breaks along the way, but eventually they spotted a suitable farmhouse and headed toward it.

Here the highway was level with the ground around it. In fact, everything was level. Ed marveled at just how flat it all was. They maneuvered the stretcher with the girl on top over a fence before trudging through the frozen, brown vegetation underfoot. The frozen plants crunched with each step they took. The plowed terrain of the farmland was bumpy, filled with dirt clods, dips, and divots. Jeremy fell once, but Ed and Zach were able to keep the stretcher relatively steady until he could regain his footing. The girl stirred along the way, but never woke. She was sleeping very deeply; Ed wasn't sure if she'd even make it through the rest of the day.

As usual, they scanned their surroundings for carriers while they walked, but thankfully saw none along the way. Ed tried not to think about what they would have to do if they did run across any. The thought of leaving the incapacitated girl behind to be devoured alive felt inhuman. The boys wouldn't understand that they might not have any other choice. The best he could do was shield them from it and hope they kept their sanity. He couldn't dwell on those thoughts though; if they had any hope of bringing this girl back from the brink of death they had to first get her stabilized.

The farmhouse sat about a quarter of a mile from the highway, so it didn't take Ed and the boys long to get there. They reached the front yard of the farmhouse and gently sat the girl down on the ground.

"Get behind me boys," Ed told them. "Zach, get your gun ready." Ed drew his own gun, chambering a round.

"What about the girl, Dad?" Zach asked.

"She'll be fine there until we get back. We have to check this house first."

"But what if any carriers come while we're inside?"

Ed looked at Zach, raising his eyebrows. Zach seemed to not understand.

Jeremy did. "Hurry up," he told his older brother, nudging him into the house.

Ed was leery of bringing the boys inside; he had no idea who or what he would find in there. Leaving them outside in the front yard, however, felt more dangerous. He had them walk behind him as he walked to the front entryway, facing backward to keep a lookout. The house's wooden front door was ajar, the screen door torn from its hinges. Besides one broken pane of glass the windows in the door were intact.

He rapped three times on the door before stepping back onto the porch, pistol ready. Zach had his pistol drawn. Jeremy held the machete. Ed heard nothing, so he knocked again, this time more loudly. Still he heard nothing from inside. If there were any deadwalkers in there they would almost definitely be stirring by now.

Murderers and thieves, however, would not. He tried not to think about that.

He motioned for the boys to come forward. "Stay close," he told them as they carefully walked single file through the front door and into the farmhouse. Zach and Jeremy both glanced at the helpless girl lying on the stretcher before following their father inside.

The inside of the house was in good shape overall. It had been raided at some point, but since the roof and most of the windows were still intact the weather damage was minimal. Aside from some warped floorboards by the broken windows, the place was still structurally sound.

They checked every room, including the upstairs bedrooms and the cellar, before determining the house was clear of threats. When they got back down to the stretcher Ed noticed the girl hadn't moved at all, another good sign she hadn't contracted the virus. Another day or two might prove otherwise.

Ed knew they'd never get her up the steps on the stretcher, so he picked the girl up and tossed her over his shoulder. Being so thin she was light enough to go up the steps, but he doubted he could have carried her for a mile this way. He wasn't as strong as he used to be. None of them were.

He carried her to the top of the steps and into one of the bedrooms with the boys following close behind. Once in the bedroom, Ed placed her gently on the bed. The bed was still made; undisturbed for the past three years. He finally checked her forehead with the back of his hand. Although she was still very hot Ed noticed goose bumps on her skin. She was definitely feverish.

He covered her with the blankets from the bed before taking the boys back downstairs to check the kitchen faucets. Not surprisingly, they were non-functional. Peering through the windows above the sink and into the deep back yard, he spied a lever-style water pump. He summoned the boys before grabbing a pitcher from the kitchen and walking to the pump.

Sometimes you're good and sometimes you're just lucky, he thought to himself.

After almost five minutes of priming, the pump began producing clean water. Ed gave the boys a high-five as he rinsed and filled the pitcher he'd brought with him. He sent Zach and Jeremy back inside to fetch more containers. They drank some of the water straight out of the well and Ed thought it might very well be some of the most refreshing water he'd ever tasted.

They washed and filled as many containers as they could find before returning to the house. They brought a cup of water upstairs for the girl. She moaned and her eyes fluttered when Ed attempted to give her a drink, but he managed to get a little down her before she closed her eyes again. After the water he checked the girl's pulse.

She was still alive, for now at least.

Ed sat with the boys on the front porch of the farmhouse, watching the desolate highway. Groups of abandoned cars littered the road here, just as they did everywhere. There was no movement near the road apart from some birds searching the cold ground for food. It was eerily quiet with only the sound of the cold wind breaking the silence.

He sat, wondering what he was going to do with the girl. She was very sick; he didn't need to be a doctor to see that much. The problem was that he really didn't know what was wrong with her, provided she didn't have the virus. The fever smacked of infection, but Ed didn't know if the infection was viral or bacterial. Without access to a doctor or any other medical professional, administering an antibiotic was the only course of action he felt might be able to save the girl. The problem was that he didn't have anything remotely resembling an antibiotic.

He could likely find it though, if he decided to try. If he could find a drug store that hadn't been completely raided it was a real possibility. With a Walgreens or a CVS on every street corner of America it became an even better possibility. Unfortunately he couldn't surf the Internet for store locations like in the old days. He had to do it the hard way: on foot.

But leaving the farmhouse to search for drugs would mean leaving the girl alone while he and the boys searched. It would likely take them a day to find and retrieve the drugs, provided they could find them at all. She'd be without water and protection that entire time.

Of course the reality was that she'd been worse off lying on the floor of the Target. There was no denying that. Truth was truth, after all. At least this way she had a slim chance of survival. And in this cruel and terrible world, that was more than most had.

It was too late in the day to start the search, as night would be falling soon. Should he decide to take this task on, they could begin the following morning at the break of dawn. That would give them the better part of the day to find the drugs and return. It was still winter, so they had less daylight available to them. For now, he could at least provide warmth and water to the girl, provided she made it through the night at all.

Ed watched his boys playing on the porch; Zach with his toy car and Jeremy with his army men. Watching them, he wondered if he'd made the right choice, bringing the girl to the farmhouse. He was putting himself and his boys in harm's way to help a girl who might very well die before they returned.

But in the midst of the waning daylight, the time he most often considered the choices he'd made so far and the choices he still had left to make, he felt it was the right thing to do. Suppose he left the girl there to die. Sure, they might live to die another day, but if he and the boys were to die, would he want to die knowing he'd lost his humanity, turning his back on someone so desperately in need?

Was there a more noble cause to die for than that of humanity?

He thought of Sarah. He remembered how she'd been in the end, so sick and so desperate. He couldn't let another innocent person suffer as she had. Maybe things would turn out differently this time.

He decided they would leave in the morning to look for medicine, the three of them as a team. In the end, they had to hold on to their humanity. It was far better to die as men than to live as animals.

Chapter Eight

Brenda Peterson and Tammy Koch painstakingly made their way through an overgrown field toward an undecided destination. To their right, the highway was barely visible through the overgrown brush, but they kept it in sight to make sure they weren't getting too far off track. The highway was their lifeline. Brenda felt the decision to follow it had been one of her best. She even met Tammy along the same highway.

In her earlier life, before humanity had gone virtually wholesale into the shitter, Brenda worked in a head shop. Before that, she worked the counter at Dunkin' Donuts. Before that she ran the drive-thru at Taco Bell. Before that…just more of the same.

She'd always struggled with her weight; once an ex-boyfriend had even referred to her as 'a fat little hobbit'. She tried liquid diets, carb-counting, detox diets, and a slew of other diets that never worked. Her problem was that she drowned her sorrows in beer and food, and in the old days there was more than enough of beer, food, and sorrow to go around.

Now, however, there was very little of any of those things in her life. Once she got on the road she dropped the weight like a bad habit. The drinking went right behind it. Not surprisingly, the sorrow went with it too. Now she was short, lean, and fucking mean.

Sometimes, even though she knew the world had ended for most, she wondered if maybe it had just begun for her. She'd been coasting in life before the Walking Death arrived, drifting from goofy job to goofy job and from bad guy to worse guy. She'd always chosen the worst ones, the assholes, the ones like her stepfather. Sometimes she wondered if it had ever really been a choice; maybe she was just wired that way.

No focus, no purpose, no direction; that had been her life before the virus. Now she had to focus to simply stay alive. Once she was forced to drop the bad habits and the asshole boyfriends it seemed as if she'd awoken from one long, bad dream. True, she'd traded one nightmare for another, but now she had a purpose, a reason to keep going. Grit and determination had replaced self-loathing, food, and booze as her best friends.

So had Tammy.

Tammy was rough around the edges, at least by most standards. She was a kindred spirit though, another person trapped in the trappings of society. Tammy had seen her share of struggle, and she knew what it was like to make all the wrong choices in life. She knew what it was like to have the wrong parents, to choose the wrong guys, and to work at the wrong jobs.

She also knew what it was like to be a survivor.

They'd both been left behind when everyone else fled to the coast; tossed out like trash or the pets no one could afford to take with them. They wandered independently for a few months, eventually meeting each other inside a Conoco station along the highway. They traveled together after that, scavenging for supplies and avoiding the infected. They became a team.

Brenda had decided very early on to follow the highway. In the times before the Walking Death the highway had been a lifeline for travelers, built with an infrastructure to support them. Brenda figured there was no reason it couldn't still be used this way, even if the highway was defunct.

Despite this conviction she feared the openness of the road itself. It was very exposed. Not only was it open to the infected it was also open to the uninfected. The uninfected could be worse; at least a carrier was clear with its intentions. Two women, even tough women, were prime targets for both. So she avoided walking on the road when she could, but in the long, empty stretches that provided an easier path with good visibility for threat she made an exception. Sometimes the payoff was worth the risk.

How she and Tammy had survived at all was a mystery. She supposed that like almost everything else a lot of it had to do with luck. She concluded that in the end it didn't really matter exactly *how* they survived; whatever they were doing was working, and it would continue to work as long as it did. What would be, would be.

The two women trudged through the undergrowth of the field, Brenda walking in front of Tammy. Both women carried loaded backpacks. Brenda carried a small .22 pistol she'd found inside an abandoned house a couple of years back. Though she really wanted something larger, she'd found so much ammunition along with it that the decision to keep it made itself.

Over her shoulder Tammy carried a rifle she found at an old farmhouse. She had a single box of rounds; not enough to feel confident about. She wanted to check some houses in the subdivision they were approaching for more guns, ammunition, or both. Houses were dangerous though; they'd had some close calls in the past with some carriers that had holed up inside them. Of course everything about life was dangerous now.

The two women came to the edge of the field and stepped out into an open area filled with houses. A concrete street ran along the houses. They found themselves in a subdivision, a subdivision that had been built within a former cornfield. They stepped out onto the street and scanned their surroundings.

Although the front yards of the houses were overgrown, the streets of the subdivision were still mostly keeping the vegetation at bay. Weeds grew up around the edges of the street, some growing in cracks within the street. There were also lines of tall weeds in the seams where the large, individual concrete squares that made up the surface of the street butted together.

Most of the houses lining the street were large, two-story homes with two-car garages. Broken windows snarled at them like mouths with jagged teeth. Storms had done considerable damage to these structures sitting exposed in the open and flat fields. Shingles hung from the roofs and siding hung in long, bent strips. Garage doors stood open, and cars were still parked in driveways. Most mailboxes still stood, some with the flags raised, waiting for a mail carrier who would never arrive.

"You wanna pass through, or do you wanna look in some of these houses?" Tammy asked.

Brenda considered the question. If they ran into carriers here it was likely they could escape back into the overgrown cornfields. That didn't exactly make it safe, but it mitigated the risks.

"Let's go through a few of them," Brenda answered. "We could use some more food, and I know you need more ammunition. Maybe our luck will play out."

"Has so far," Tammy replied.

Brenda smiled. "True."

Brenda and Tammy walked the row of houses, peering from the street into broken windows and open doors. Eventually they ran across a one-story brick house with boarded windows. Intact or boarded windows were a good sign; it meant the contents inside might still be pristine. They approached the front door, hoping it was locked.

Unfortunately they found it to be opened, the interior ransacked.

Deflated, they left the house and continued on, walking the subdivision street and looking for better possibilities. All the houses they passed appeared to have been raided at some point. It was looking increasingly like the entire subdivision would be a lost cause.

The subdivision street ran in a circle, leading both to and from a larger street. It doubled back with a ninety degree turn, forming a sort of horseshoe shape. As the two women followed it they rounded the bend and walked back toward the direction they'd come from, this time on the other side of the subdivision.

That was when they spotted the figure in the distance.

It was walking away from them, along the same street they walked, perhaps a hundred yards away. Both women froze. Whoever, or whatever it was didn't seem to notice them; it just continued walking slowly and methodically away from where they stood.

Brenda and Tammy looked at each other. Brenda slowly pulled her pistol from her belt while Tammy quietly removed the rifle from her shoulder. The figure continued walking at the same pace. Brenda thought there was something strange about the way it walked. This figure didn't walk with the meandering gait that carriers typically possessed. Though not unheard of, this figured suffered from no obvious paralysis either. It's walk seemed purposely directional.

Before Brenda could contemplate any further, the figure stopped walking. Suddenly the figure turned around and faced them. Tammy raised the rifle, placing the butt of the gun against her shoulder. She drew a bead on the figure's head, aligning the notch at the end of the barrel with the groove just above the chamber. Knowing that the noise would attract other carriers, she held her fire.

The figure now faced them, staring. Brenda kept the pistol in her hand, finger off the trigger, waiting to see what happened. The pistol would be useless at that range, but she wanted to be ready all the same. She looked behind them to ensure they weren't being pursued by anyone - or anything. A cursory glanced proved they were alone. Alone, of course, with the exception of this strange figure standing motionless in the road in front of them.

Both Brenda and Tammy stood this way for what seemed like an eternity. Neither moved while they watched the figure watch them. After a few moments the figure simply turned around and continued walking away from them. Tammy sighed and lowered the gun from her shoulder, pointing it toward the ground. She looked at Brenda with a confused expression. "That *is* a carrier, right?"

Brenda thought for a moment. "I think, but I can't say for sure. It didn't look infected. Whatever it is, it's pretty far away. Tough to tell."

"Ever have one see you and just turn away?"

"No. Carriers don't do that. They always come running."

"Weird," Tammy replied. "Really weird."

Brenda turned to leave. "Let's double back, and head the other direction. Either way, I really don't wanna follow it."

Tammy kept her eyes on the figure. "I don't think we have much choice," she said. "It's coming back."

Brenda turned back around to see the figure walking toward them.

"Should I shoot it, you think?" Tammy asked.

"Not yet. Let's see what it does. I don't want to draw any unwanted attention."

The women watched as the figure slowly made its way toward them. It stared straight ahead, directly at them, but somehow Brenda felt it was looking *through* them. It continued walking, very gradually gaining ground. As it came closer Brenda was increasingly convinced this wasn't a carrier. But if it wasn't a carrier, she wondered, then who was it? And what did he want?

Suddenly the figure sat down in the middle of the road.

"What the fuck?" Tammy said. "What is this shit?"

"I don't know exactly. He's not infected, I'm pretty sure of that, but I'm clueless as to what his game is."

They watched the man for some time. He remained in a sitting position, staring at the ground, rocking gently back and forth. They both wondered aloud if he was injured or maybe sick with something other than the deadwalker virus. There wasn't much they could do for the poor bastard either way.

Despite all this, Brenda was curious. She couldn't seem to shake it. There was something about this person that compelled her to find out more.

"Let's go see what his deal is," Brenda said to Tammy.

Tammy's face became a mask of incredulity. "What? Are you for real?"

"Sure I am. Draw a bead on him; if he tries anything, put a bullet in his head."

Tammy wasn't convinced. "I don't think this is a good idea."

"Maybe not," Brenda replied, smiling.

The two women carefully made their way toward the sitting figure. As they neared him they noticed he had no backpack or bag. In fact, he had no possessions aside from the clothing on his body. He was simply sitting on the ground, staring straight ahead, his face covered in dried blood.

"Where do you think all that blood came from?" Tammy asked.

Brenda shook her head. "Let's ask him."

They came within thirty feet of the man then stopped. Now both Brenda and Tammy were sure he wasn't infected. They still weren't sure, however, if he was safe. Being covered in blood wasn't helping his credibility with either of them.

"Who are you?" Brenda asked the man. She kept the pistol partially raised, ready to fire if necessary. Tammy had the man's head directly in her sights.

The man spoke, never looking up. "Who are you?"

Brenda and Tammy both looked at each other with confused expressions.

"What's your name?" Brenda asked.

The man continued staring at the ground.

Brenda repeated the question. "What's your name?"

The man looked up. Brenda could see now that both his hands and face were covered with *a lot* of blood.

"What…is…your…name?" she repeated slowly, sounding out each syllable.

"They're gone. I don't know where they are," the man finally replied.

"Who's gone?"

"They're gone," he repeated. "I lost them."

"What is your name?" Brenda asked yet again.

The man didn't reply. Neck craned, he searched the sky, as if he were searching for the answer there. Eventually he spoke. "Dave," he told her. "My name is Dave."

"Now we're getting somewhere," Brenda replied. "One more question, Dave; why are you covered in blood?"

"I'm not," the man replied.

Brenda raised her eyebrows. "Dude, you are. Take a look at your hands."

Dave raised his hands to his face, studying them. "I didn't know I was."

"Well, you are. Looks like you took a bath in it."

Dave stared at his hands while Brenda formulated her next question. "What are you doing here?" she asked.

"Why would I have blood on me? Is it mine?" Dave asked, seemingly unaware of Brenda's prior question. He touched his face, inspecting his fingers as he pulled them away.

"I don't know if it's yours. I don't know you," Brenda replied. Dave seemed very confused, but she decided to try again. "What are you doing here?"

"I don't know," Dave replied.

"How'd you get here?"

"I don't remember."

"Whose blood is that on you?" Tammy asked.

"I don't know."

Brenda looked at Tammy, perplexed, before addressing Dave again. "Well, what *do* you remember?"

Dave thought for a moment. "The outbreak…a border town. We got kicked out; we've been on the road for a while now."

"Who's we?" Tammy asked.

Dave turned to look at her. "My wife, Sandy, and our friend. His name is Jim. I don't know where they are. I lost them. I was supposed to protect them, but I lost them." Dave returned his gaze to the ground as he began rocking back and forth.

"This guy is fucked," Tammy said. "For all we know he killed and ate those folks he 'lost'."

"Maybe," Brenda replied.

"We should leave him here," Tammy said.

"You might be right."

"What do you mean, I might be right? Of course I'm right. Are you fuckin' nuts?"

Brenda took a deep breath and exhaled. "I don't know. For now, sure, leave him here. I'm not sure what to do with him just yet."

Tammy raised her eyebrows. "That doesn't make me feel any better."

Brenda looked back at her friend. "Me neither."

"Fine. We'll leave him for now then," Tammy said. "Let's go check out some of these houses. I suppose if he's still here when we get back, we'll figure out what we wanna do."

"Deal," Brenda replied.

The two women searched four houses after leaving Dave where he sat. They found some more canned food, some matches, and a few other items they thought might be useful. Brenda also found a pair of insulated gloves and a school backpack. On a whim she kept them for Dave, just in case.

Each time they walked out of a house they peered

down the street to see if Dave was sitting where they'd left him. Each time he was. They spent almost an hour pilfering through the houses they thought might prove fruitful. Dave sat the whole while in the street, rocking back and forth, even after they finished.

Tammy and Brenda walked back down to where Dave sat, keeping their guns trained on him should he make an aggressive move. He didn't. He sat, simply rocking back and forth.

Brenda looked at Tammy, raising her eyebrows and shrugging her shoulders.

Tammy shook her head. "I say we leave him. Maybe this guy's crazy, or maybe he's crazy like a fox. Either way, having anything to do with him is a bad idea."

Brenda considered Tammy's opinion. Tammy was right; it *was* dangerous to bring Dave along. They didn't know anything about this guy, save for his name. Keeping the gun pointed at him, she tossed the backpack and the gloves down on the ground beside him. Maybe he was dangerous, but that dazed look he had…there was something hauntingly familiar about. She'd seen it before.

Just as Brenda was about to explain, Tammy cut her off. "Here comes trouble," she said, pointing.

Brenda followed Tammy's finger. Coming from the end of the subdivision street were three carriers, moving slowly and aimlessly. Brenda's skin crawled at the sight of them. Considering the deadwalker's level of disinterest she was reasonably certain they hadn't been spotted yet. Or at least she hoped they hadn't been spotted.

"We gotta get out of here," Tammy said in a low voice.

Brenda protested. "But our friend here-"

"What about him? He's not our friend. We don't even know him. We have to leave him." Tammy's impatience and frustration came through loud and clear.

Brenda glanced from Dave back to the three carriers. "But they'll tear him to fuckin' pieces."

"That's his problem, sister, not ours. He's a big boy. He can run."

"I suppose…" Brenda replied, trailing off. She looked at the approaching carriers and then back down at Dave. "You said your name is Dave, right?"

Dave looked up at her.

"Listen to me. You need to run. Deadwalkers are heading this way."

He nodded at her.

"I mean it," Brenda told him.

Dave only nodded again.

Both women turned to walk away. As they did, Brenda again glanced down the street at the carriers. They were still well in the distance and they were still meandering. It wouldn't take long, however, before the creatures spotted the three of them making a fuss so close by. And she didn't want to be around when it happened.

Brenda looked back at Dave. He was still sitting where they'd left him. "He's not moving," she said to Tammy.

"That's not our problem, Brenda."

They continued walking, Brenda still watching Dave. He looked directly at the carriers before returning his gaze to the ground. Then he continued rocking as if they weren't even there.

Brenda stopped walking. "Wait," she said to Tammy.

Tammy stopped. "Fucking leave him, Brenda!" Nervous frustration coated her voice.

Suddenly the carriers spotted the girls and bolted toward them, screaming. Two of them were slow, possibly injured or weakened, while one was significantly faster than the others. The fast one bore down on Dave with frightening aggression and speed.

"I have to do something," Brenda said. "We can't just leave him here."

"Yes, we can, Brenda. The only thing we *have* to do is run."

"But they'll kill him, and that'll be on our conscience," Brenda countered.

"That's not our problem anymore. We can't save the fuckin' world, Brenda. If we stay here they'll kill us too."

Brenda watched the carrier in the lead; he was closing the gap quickly.

"C'mon!" Tammy pleaded. "Move your ass!"

Brenda stood, motionless, contemplating. If she left this stranger here she was complicit in his death. Could she live with that? She wasn't sure she could trust Dave, but she felt confident that he wasn't himself. And he was still a human being, after all. Besides, hadn't she been left behind when the virus hit? How had that felt?

"I'm going back for him," Brenda said as she ran toward Dave.

"Shit!" Tammy yelled. She knew once Brenda had made up her mind it was almost impossible to change. Tammy watched the carrier in the lead as it gained on Dave and now Brenda. Brenda would never make it to Dave before the carrier made it to them. Knowing she was Brenda's only hope, Tammy raised the rifle, sighting it in on the carrier in the lead.

It was moving fast.

Brenda ran toward Dave. When she reached him she grabbed his arm, just under the armpit and yanked him up. "Get up!" she yelled.

Dave simply sat, unmoved to act.

"Get up!" she yelled again, hitting him twice in the side of the head as hard as she could. That seemed to snap him out of his fog. Slowly, he stood.

Suddenly Brenda looked up to find the two slower carriers still in the distance while the faster one, the runner, bore down upon her with determined fury. It was less than forty yards away and closing that gap fast.

"Run, you idiot!" she yelled.

Before Brenda could glance at her attackers, she heard the report of the rifle shot. Tammy had fired at the running carrier, but she missed. It was moving so quickly now it was almost upon Brenda and Dave.

Too late Brenda saw this and reached for her pistol. Before she could pull it, another shot sounded. The deadwalker in the lead dropped in its tracks like a stone. It lay on the ground, blood pouring from an exit wound in the thing's back, pooling in the street.

Brenda yanked on Dave's arm. Again he resisted her efforts. "Do you want me to hit you again?" she yelled at him. She yanked harder, feeling him budge a little. She yanked one more time, harder than ever, and he finally began to run. It didn't take long to catch up with Tammy.

"You know you're batshit crazy, right?" Tammy said.

"Yeah," Brenda replied, breaking a slight smile. "I do."

She looked toward the two remaining carriers in the distance. They were slow, but were still closing in. Just as the two women thought there would be nothing more to contend with, from behind one of the houses a hundred yards or so away, another carrier appeared. It was followed by another.

"Dammit!" Tammy yelled. "I didn't want to have to use the rifle, but you didn't leave me much choice, you know."

"I know," Brenda replied. "Just run."

Chapter Nine

In a time before cellular phones, Ed would have used a phone book to look up the number of his local pharmacy before dialing it on a landline phone. Then the cell phone came along, rendering both landline phones and those paper books into useless relics.

As it turned out, the Walking Death had rendered cell phones useless relics now too.

Being that as it was, he still needed to find a pharmacy. They had exactly one day's worth of daylight to find one and hopefully get the antibiotics to the girl they'd found. If they failed, they'd have to hole up somewhere during the night and wait it out until dawn. Ed wasn't sure if the girl would make it through the night without at least some care and water.

He and the boys set out at the break of dawn, right on schedule. They were able to get some water down the girl before they left, but she remained asleep. They left a full jug of water by her bedside along with a glass should she wake while they were gone.

Without a phone book, or a map more detailed than the one they carried, they were on their own searching for a drugstore. Ed figured the place to start would be the exit where they'd found the girl. He didn't remember seeing a drugstore there, but he hoped he could at least get his hands on a phone book he could use to track one down.

They had little difficulty covering the mile or so it took to get back to the exit. The empty road bore no ill-mannered travelers, nor did it host any rabid carriers. Apart from a few squirrels and some birds they saw no other movement.

They arrived at the exit and made their way down the ramp in the same fashion as they'd done the first time through. Ed felt the familiar sense of trepidation return. This time, however, they passed up the Target and walked to the center of the parking lot for a better view. They looked around for a drugstore, a Walgreens, a CVS, or anything else. Unfortunately, they saw nothing.

It looked as if they were going to need a phone book after all, but procuring one in the aftermath of the virus could prove difficult. Like many other exits along this area of the highway, the residential zones butted up against the commercial zones, providing Ed and the boys plenty of houses to search just on the other side of the shopping center. Ed hoped there would be at least one phone book among them.

"Let's go, guys," Ed said.

The boys followed.

It took a little less than ten minutes to make it over the parking lots of the defunct stores and into the adjoining residential area. They walked through an old subdivision, keeping their eyes open for any infected. The bodies of the dead littered the streets here, just as they did everywhere else they'd been. It worried Ed just how little he noticed anymore.

They searched six houses before they found their first phone book. Luckily folks were fairly predictable, and the phone book had been right where Ed expected it to be:

beside the telephone. On the wall just above the telephone was a framed photograph of a couple well into their seventh or eighth decade. Ed was doubtful they'd ever owned a cell phone between them and for this he was thankful.

Ed scanned the yellow pages for pharmacies while the boys acted as lookouts. He found a CVS and a Walgreens; both looked to be within walking distance from where they were. As near as he could figure the Walgreens was closest, about a mile and a half away. He ripped out the page from the phone book, stuffed it into his front pants pocket, and exited the house with the boys.

They traveled quietly and carefully through the side streets. It was their modus operandi. The streets remained eerily silent as they walked. Around them, trees grew unabated over sidewalks while weeds grew through cracks in the street. The grass was mostly brown, but had gone to seed everywhere since the outbreak. Broken glass lay all around, glinting in the sunlight. More bodies in varying states of decay lay all around them.

It took less than an hour for them to make it to the pharmacy. It sat on the corner of the street, looking familiar yet out of place set within all the neglected homes and streets. Ed noted wryly that even at the end of all humanity he could still count on a Walgreens being on every street corner.

They approached the front doors to the building slowly. The locks appeared to be broken, but otherwise the door was mostly intact. Two bodies lay outside the front doors, almost in the parking lot. Ed and the boys suited up as Ed drew his gun and brought the boys into a single file line behind him.

"We're gonna do this just like the others," he whispered to the boys through his face mask. "Jeremy, you watch our back. Zach, you watch our sides. I'll watch our front. In and out."

Both boys nodded.

"Okay then. Let's go."

The sun shone brightly from directly above them, and once inside the store they could see reasonably well. The inside of the store was wrecked. Shelves were overturned, cash registers broken, and all the food that had been on the shelves was gone. Glass, leaves, and other garbage littered the floor. Seeing all that looting didn't bode well for the pharmacy supplies, but Ed tried not to get discouraged.

Luckily for Ed most Walgreens stores were the same, so he knew exactly how to get right to the pharmacy. They walked cautiously through the aisles, stepping around the larger debris as they made their way toward the pharmacy counter. Try as they might to be quiet, they couldn't avoid stepping on smaller pieces littering the floor, creating a miniature racket of crunching and crackling.

They made a beeline to the pharmacy counter; one glance told them it had been wrecked along with the rest of the store. Despite this, it wasn't completely empty, so Ed still held out at least some hope. Once they found any sort of antibiotic they would grab it and get the hell out of the store.

When they arrived at the pharmacy counter they hopped over it, their feet landing in plastic pill bottles, scattered paper, leaves, sticks, and rodent droppings. To their left they saw the broken drive-through window; a chilly breeze blew unimpeded through the window. Rain and snow had entered the building through it as well, damaging the woodwork and staining the floor.

They removed their backpacks so they could move more easily, placing them on the counter. The baseball bat stuck out of Ed's pack like the mast of a ship. Ed had Zach search through all cabinets and drawers for any kind of drug reference guide. He wasn't even sure if such a thing existed, but if it did it could prove helpful.

While Zach was searching the drawers and cabinets, Ed and Jeremy were searching the shelves and the floor for the drugs they needed. Since the incident back at the sporting goods store, Ed was feeling more nervous than usual inside the store. It was still fresh in his mind how close he had come to losing his oldest son. Now here they were again, inside another store. The experience was too similar, causing warning bells to sound in his mind. He told himself it was probably nerves, but he couldn't deny that it was still very disconcerting.

After searching all the drawers and the shelves, Zach could find no drug reference guide of any kind. Unable to afford wasting any more time on it, Ed had Zach help his brother search for the drugs they needed. Without a reference guide, Ed was limited to his own remedial knowledge of prescription drugs. Having been prescribed these drugs in the past, however, he was familiar with at least a few antibiotics: penicillin, amoxicillin, Cipro, and Zithromax. His knowledge went no further than this. It wasn't much, but it was all they had.

Still under Ed's direction, Zach and Jeremy searched for medications beginning with A, C, P, or Z, piling the boxes and bottles in front of Ed. He sifted through what they found, tossing away the non-matches. They searched this way for twenty minutes with no results. Ed almost began to give up hope until he noticed a small, white box given to him by one of the boys. He flipped it over, almost ready to throw it to the side then saw what he'd been looking for: Zithromax. Another box lay near it in the pile, so he grabbed them both.

He called the boys over and hugged them, telling them what a great job they'd done. They beamed with pride.

Nearly a half-hour inside the store had set Ed's nerves on fire. They'd been making significant noise as they sifted through the debris, enough to alert anything within earshot to their presence. They needed to get moving and fast. The longer they stayed inside that store the more exposed they were. They also needed to get back to the girl, provided she was still alive.

Ed slid the Zithromax boxes into his backpack before helping Jeremy and Zach get their backpacks on again. As he picked up his own pack, Jeremy reached out a hand and grabbed his father's shoulder, stopping him abruptly.

Jeremy's green eyes were wide as he whispered: "Dad, I just saw something move at the front of the store."

Ed's blood ran cold as all the color dropped out of his face. The warning bells that were sounding in his head were now a full-blown alarm. His hands were sweating and his body was adjusting to an onslaught of adrenaline as he frantically searched the store for movement. At least they had the pills they needed, but now they needed to get out… somehow.

Ed suddenly noticed movement reflected in one of the cracked surveillance mirrors lining the top of the walls. Something was inside the store, but what it was he didn't know. He considered his options; exiting through the front of the store was likely impossible now that whatever was in the store was blocking the way. He raced through more options before turning to inspect the broken drive-through window. Jagged shards of glass surrounded the edges of the window frame, but Ed thought he could lift the boys through without cutting them. Once they and their gear were clear he'd break the shards and climb out quickly. That was the noisy part. It was also the dangerous part.

Now that Ed had his plan it was time to execute.

They heard a loud crash as the intruder knocked something off a shelf at the front of the store. The boys jumped but didn't make a sound. They knew the rules; it was why they were still alive. No doubt the intruder was a carrier; Ed found it difficult to believe that a thief would announce his presence so flippantly.

Ed whispered to the boys: "Take off your backpacks."

They did as instructed. Once the backpacks were off, he glanced back toward the front of the store again. He saw no more movement, but could hear scraping sounds as the thing wandered through the store.

Ed returned his focus back on the boys. "Follow me to the window," he said. "Backpacks go first and then I'll lift both of you out. Once you're outside put your packs back on and be ready."

"Where will you be, Dad?" Jeremy asked.

"I'll be coming through next," Ed replied.

"Then what?" Zach whispered.

"Then we run."

The three of them walked as carefully as they could toward the broken window. They were quiet, but inevitably they made some noise. There was nothing to be done about the noise. Once they made it to the window, Ed checked the store. No movement or sound. He gently lowered their backpacks to the asphalt outside the window before motioning for the boys to approach him slowly.

Suddenly another loud crash sounded from the front of the store causing them all to jump. They had to move fast; there was no telling how long they had left before they were detected.

Ed lifted Zach first through the window, being careful of the jagged shards of glass that surrounded the edge like a deadly picture frame. The boy was heavier than he'd expected, or maybe Ed was weaker than he realized, but he managed to get Zach out and onto the asphalt without injury or issue.

Next, Ed lifted Jeremy through the broken window. Another loud sound erupted from the front of the store. It took all of his effort to not jump through the window right then, along with Jeremy, broken glass or not. Once Jeremy's feet touched the ground outside he joined his brother on the other side. As instructed, they both immediately began to strap on their backpacks on their backs.

Now, the moment of truth. Ed knew he couldn't make it through the window without breaking the shards around the bottom edge and that was going to make one hell of a racket. There would be no disguising that sound. Once he swung the bat it was a race against time.

Taking a deep breath, Ed asked Zach to hand him the baseball bat from his backpack. Zach handed the bat to his father through the window.

"I'm going to break this glass here at the bottom," he whispered to the boys. "When I do, that thing is going to come running. Once I'm through the window, we run together."

The boys nodded.

"Look at me," he said to the boys, his face becoming alarmingly serious. "If I don't make it out then you run and you don't look back."

"Don't say that, Daddy," Jeremy pleaded, tearing up.

Ed shook his head. "You run, and you don't look back. Understood?"

Both boys nodded again.

"Stand back."

Taking a deep breath, Ed swung the baseball bat. It hit the jagged glass with a dull thud, not the sharp sound of a window breaking that he'd been expecting. He struck again, working quickly to clear a small area he could step over. Just enough to get out without slicing himself open.

Behind him the carrier screamed, wise to their presence.

The clock was ticking.

Ed felt goosebumps break out all over his body as the scream ripped through the quiet store. The sound was horrific. A commotion erupted near the front of the store as the carrier clamored toward the pharmacy counter. It knew precisely where they were. Ed swung the bat again, breaking off two more large chunks of glass. He inspected the windowsill and decided it was good enough to climb over. He didn't have any more time to make it better.

Handing the baseball bat to Zach, Ed swung one leg over the edge, feeling with his toes for the ground below. His boot touched the ground and he shifted his weight in order to drag his other leg out.

Behind him, the thing screamed again. Halfway through the window Ed glanced back into the store. He watched in horror as the carrier came into view from behind one of the shelving units. It was female; still wearing the tattered remnants of a dress. Various shades of brown and black from untended urination and defecation stained the dress. He could smell it as it approached. Its eyes were wild; mad with rage and delirium. It was so emaciated that it looked like a walking skeleton.

Ed swung his other leg over the windowsill and attempted to pull away. As he did something kept him there. He tugged madly, unable to move. He looked down to see that his coat was caught on a shard of glass. Furiously he pulled on the coat in an attempt to dislodge himself.

Behind him the thing charged, closing the distance, its right arm hanging uselessly beside its body. The left arm swung wildly in the air, fingernails like claws, searching for a warm body.

The carrier hit the pharmacy counter just as Ed came loose from the window. Slowed only slightly, it crawled on top of the counter, falling off the other side and onto the floor below. It quickly rose to its feet and made one last dash toward them, closing the short distance with alarming speed.

Ed fell to the pavement outside just as the carrier rammed its body through the window, catching itself around the waist on the broken glass and slicing its stomach open. Blood dripped through the darkened fabric of the dress, pooling onto the asphalt below as the thing screamed madly. It reached out with its good arm toward Ed; its long, yellow fingernails only inches away from his face. Ed pulled back in the nick of time, narrowly avoiding the thing's grasp.

Suddenly Zach brought the bat down directly upon the thing's head. It wasn't enough to kill it, but he knocked it senseless. Summoning all his might, he brought the bat down again, harder. The second blow put the creature in a nearly docile state. It lay in the window, its upper body hanging out, dripping blood and moaning in pain and rage.

Ed took the bat from Zach. He lined the fat end against the base of the thing's neck before bringing it down with severe force. The carrier's body slumped forward, the moaning cut off like a switch.

"Good work," Ed told Zach, out of breath.

His son nodded.

"Dad?" Jeremy said, tugging on his father's sleeve.

"Yeah," Ed replied.

"Behind us."

Ed spun around to see three more carriers approaching from the street. Two of the things picked up speed once they noticed Ed and the boys weren't among the infected. *So much like animals that they recognize their own kind,* Ed thought as he drew his gun and leveled it on the carrier running toward him. He tracked it as it ran, breathing in, letting half the breath out before gently squeezing the trigger. The shot struck the thing in the chest, knocking it down in its tracks.

The second carrier continued running. Ed brought it down with a single shot in the same fashion. The third carrier appeared too sick to be a threat, prompting Ed to leave it. Better to save the bullets and limit the gunfire.

"Follow me," Ed said to the boys. They ran up the street they had originally come from, staying together, keeping each other within sight. The pharmacy building shrank behind them as they fled the scene. Unfortunately, they had a mile and a half to go before they reached the highway - and safety.

Suddenly two carriers, attracted by the gunfire, appeared on the street fifty yards in front of them. The deadwalkers caught sight of Ed and the boys, dashing toward them with a vengeance. One was slow and sick, but the other was frighteningly fast. It began the chase with a guttural growl, increasing in volume and intensity as it built up speed, quickly closing the distance between them. It chilled Ed to hear that horrific sound.

Ed stopped running in order to level the pistol at their attacker. He fired a shot, but missed. Struggling to control his breathing, he carefully squeezed off a second shot. That second attempt put a bullet in the thing's shoulder, bringing it down hard. With the runner down, Ed fired another shot at the second attacker, bringing it down with a direct hit to the chest. Ed watched as the first carrier he'd shot in the shoulder attempted to rise again. He placed a single bullet in the thing's head, putting it down for good.

He counted six shots so far. His magazine held sixteen

shots plus one in the chamber. They were doing well so far. Maybe they had a chance of getting out alive after all.

"Dad," Ed heard Zach say from behind him. He looked backward, feeling his newly bolstered spirits drop. More than a dozen carriers approached from behind.

"Zach, shoot anything that gets close," said Ed.

Zach nodded. "Okay, Dad."

Two more carriers charged from the street ahead of them. Ed shot them both, this time with relative ease. He counted eight shots in his head. Ed listened as Zach fired two shots from behind him. He turned to see a single carrier drop to the ground.

The area was getting crowded. There were just too many of them to take down. Aware that carriers remained determined only when prey was in sight, Ed thought their best chance was to find a place to hide out. A house that wasn't compromised would be best; they could hide there and wait for the carriers to disperse. At the least they could buy themselves some time to think.

"Zach, take out as many as you can. Shoot the runners first," Ed told his son.

"Got it," Zach replied.

Ed and Zach shot as many able-bodied carriers as they could. They managed to kill several of them, but there were still too many more left. It was time to make a run for it.

"Now! Follow me!" Ed called to his sons, pointing down a small side street.

The trio dashed off down the small street while Ed searched desperately for a house that was empty. It was so hard to tell from the street, especially while running from dozens of carriers. He would have to make a guess and hope for the best. Sometimes it just came down to luck.

Eventually, he spotted a house that appeared viable. It was small with no broken windows and a closed door. A perfect candidate.

"Over here!" he yelled, pointing the house out to the boys. They all ran up the sidewalk and onto the front porch. Ed scrutinized the front door; glass panels made up the top of the door, easily breakable. He used the butt of the gun to break out one of the panes before holstering the gun and reaching through the empty panel to unlock the door from the inside.

Three carriers suddenly appeared at the end of the street, all still in hot pursuit. Ed removed his hand from the empty window and shot them all quickly. He could afford to have none left alive to compromise his hideout.

With the carriers down, they rushed inside the house, hoping it was empty. They had little choice either way. He closed the door behind them, locking the deadbolt. He had the boys sit with their backs against the door, facing inside, watching the house for movement. This served the dual purpose of preventing them from seeing what was coming for them from outside.

"Don't look out this window," Ed told the boys. "Zach, if anything in this house moves, shoot it."

Zach nodded in quick acknowledgment.

Ed surely hoped it wouldn't come to that. If there was something - or someone - in the house…he couldn't imagine how that could end well.

Ed got down on his knees and peeked through the window in the door, pushing aside a decorative, nearly translucent window treatment. He watched the street in front of the house closely, being careful not to make any sudden movements that might draw the deadwalker's attention.

As he expected, they all came running. A dozen showed, quickly becoming two dozen and then three dozen. It wasn't long until he stopped counting. The deadwalkers rambled about in the street, pacing back and forth, screaming in agony, frustration, or both. Some limped, while some dragged themselves along the road, their legs completely paralyzed by the virus. Ed couldn't imagine how they were still alive. Some dashed back and forth from one side of the street to another, slamming themselves off the hoods of cars, screaming at the top of their lungs.

Ed watched, his pulse strong in his temple, sweat

dripping down his nose. The deadwalkers continued to amble about, with no direction or purpose, until one of the things broke off from the group and began wandering around by itself. Ed watched, fists clenched as the carrier stumbled onto the sidewalk leading to the house in which Ed and his boys were hiding. His heart beat faster as he adjusted his grip on the pistol. The walker approached the door, staring inquisitively. Ed tensed, his pulse rising. He felt as if his heart might jump out of his chest. The thing continued, walking closer and closer, sniffing the air and staring at the door. Ed swallowed hard as the deadwalker's hand came within inches of the windows…

Suddenly a fight broke out on the street, and the miserable creature raced away from the door and down the sidewalk in a mad rush to join in. Ed sighed with relief. That was way too close.

The deadwalkers stumbled about while Ed and the boys remained inside the house for another half hour. Eventually, the decrepit crowd began to disperse and after an hour only a few carriers remained. The stragglers wandered off after a few more minutes leaving the street silent and empty.

The knowledge that Ed had brought his own boys into the middle of this infestation made him ill. He felt irresponsible, almost reprehensible. It had been a close call on that street, and they were lucky to have made it out of that situation alive.

Still another part of him felt it was the right thing to do. The boys had agreed. They'd chosen to risk their lives for someone else, showing courage far greater than their years.

The decisions were becoming more difficult to make. There was no more black and white in their world, only gray.

Although they had successfully evaded the deadwalkers, they weren't out of harm's way just yet. Those things were gone for the time being, but Ed knew they'd be back with the slightest provocation. They still had some daylight left and if they hauled ass it was highly probable they could make it back to the farmhouse before night fell.

To make it, however, they'd need to leave soon.

Ed turned around, sat down, and leaned against the door beside Zach and Jeremy. His knees ached from kneeling for so long; he hadn't realized how much time had passed. He looked at the boys, quickly noticing they were both staring into an adjacent bedroom. A quick glance revealed what they'd seen.

A body.

The corpse was small and badly decomposed, the body of a child, no older than Zach and Jeremy. Despite all the bodies his boys had seen over the past three years this one was one of their own. Another child, one who, unlike them, didn't make it. It resonated with them. Children could very easily understand mortality, especially when constantly surrounded by death.

Ed knew he needed to shut the door to that bedroom or else they would continue to stare. Instructing the boys to stay put, he rose to his feet. His knees screamed in protest. Once standing, he slowly approached the small room.

What he saw invaded his soul and destroyed him from within.

Despite the state of decomposition, Ed knew he was looking at the body of a child. Footballs, baseballs, and soccer balls adorned the peeling wallpaper. A teddy bear rested on the pillow beside the body. Surrounding the body were army men, Hot Wheels cars, a toy train and a stack of baseball cards, still held together by a rotting rubber band.

A pistol lay on the bed near the boy's knees, a shell casing near the foot of the bed. A black stain screamed from the wall behind the headboard.

Ed stood in the room, mortified. He tried to blink away the tears, but they came all the same. He wept silently in the bedroom of a boy he was too late to help.

Once he'd regained a fraction of his composure, he noticed a box of shells on the nightstand beside the bed. Part of him didn't want to touch the shells, nor the gun. But a functioning gun with ammunition was exactly what his youngest boy needed. A boy who was still alive and very much in need of protection.

Ed searched the room for a blanket, quickly locating one in the closet. He retrieved the pistol from between the boy's knees, gently placing it on the nightstand. He carefully covered the boy's small body, still dressed in his pajamas. The blankets gently drifted down upon the body, covering it from the world.

I wish someone had been able to help you, he thought to himself as he stared at the tragedy before him. *Rest in peace, buddy.*

Ed picked up the shells and the pistol before walking out of the room and closing the door behind him. He walked to where Jeremy and Zach sat by the door and loaded the pistol. He placed the box of remaining ammunition into Jeremy's backpack before handing him the gun. "Don't use it until I tell you," he told him.

"Okay, Dad," Jeremy replied.

"That was a boy in there, wasn't it?" Zach asked.

Ed nodded.

Zach nodded in return. They said no more about it.

Ed zipped up Jeremy's backpack. He wanted to tell them he'd protect them, no matter what, that nothing bad would ever happen to them on his watch. He wanted to tell them that the city by the river was safe and that they'd live there happily ever after. He wanted to, but he knew he couldn't promise any of these things.

And he knew that his boys knew it too.

"We gotta move," Ed told the boys. "Once we hit the street, run. Don't stop until I tell you."

The boys nodded.

Ed unlocked the front door and opened it. Slowly he peered out the doorway, looking up and down the street. He saw no movement.

He took a deep breath. "Go!"

They ran without looking back. They didn't stop until they reached the highway.

Ed and the boys arrived at the farmhouse well before

nightfall. Once inside, they walked directly up to the room where they'd left the girl. Ed instructed the boys to wait outside the room while he tended to the girl.

Once in the room, he removed his gloves and held the back of his hand under the girl's nose to check for breathing. He left it there for a few moments. Her breathing was shallow, but it was there. He glanced at the water and noticed that she had drunk the entire glass sometime throughout the day. That was a good sign; at least she'd woken up once.

He refilled the water from the jug in the room before removing his backpack and placing it on the floor beside the bed. He rummaged through the bag, retrieving the antibiotics. He removed two capsules from the box and placed the first capsule into her mouth, closing her jaw shut with his hand.

As he turned to reach for the glass of water the girl's eyes suddenly opened wide. She spat the pill out, staring frantically at Ed in the surgical mask and goggles. She recoiled and screamed pushing him away.

He felt the pistol slide freely from the holster on his belt.

The girl sat up, eyes wide, swaying unsteadily. Her eyes fluttered. Speaking in a low and determined voice, the girl pointed the pistol at Ed.

"Don't...fucking...move."

Chapter Ten

"Move your ass!" Brenda yelled, giving Dave a hard shove. He ran. Tammy fired off two shots, taking down the two closest carriers and removing their most potent threats. She ran quickly to catch up with Brenda and Dave. Once together they ran hard, away from the carriers and back the way they came. Periodically Brenda looked behind to see how many deadwalkers were still following them. She counted eight, but was relieved to see they were all relatively slow.

They crashed into the dried cornstalks, Brenda in the lead with Dave in tow, Tammy bringing up the rear. At one point Brenda realized she was literally dragging Dave by the sleeve of his coat. At least he was complying, but he seemed not to understand the gravity of their situation.

Behind them, they heard the familiar and terrible sound of carriers screaming, but as they made their way through the dense cornfield the screaming became noticeably quieter. Before long the sounds diminished altogether. They continued running for a few more minutes to be sure they left them far enough behind.

Eventually, they slowed to a walk. A few minutes later they emerged from the cornfield, finding themselves near a fence. Another ten yards past the fence sat the highway. As exposed as Brenda felt on the road, it was still a welcome sight after the run-in they'd just had with the deadwalkers.

She walked to the road, stepping onto the concrete, scanning left and right. The road was open for miles, providing clear sight for threat detection. She decided she'd utilize the road for travel, but first, she needed to secure their new friend.

Panting, she turned to Tammy. "Cover him."

On command, Tammy pointed the rifle at Dave. "What are you gonna do?" she asked Brenda between breaths.

"I'm going to give us a little peace of mind," Brenda replied, placing her backpack down upon the ground and fumbling through it. A few seconds later she retrieved a length of rope. Removing her knife from its sheath on her belt, Brenda measured out a foot or two of rope and cut it, placing the remainder back into the bag.

"Hands behind your back, Mr. Dave," she said, turning toward their new companion. Dave complied without speaking, his breathing labored from the run.

"Nothing personal," she added as she walked behind him, binding his wrists with the rope. Though not an expert in knots, she felt confident enough her tie would hold. She gave the rope a tug to be sure.

"Too tight?" Brenda asked Dave. He stared forward without answering, his eyes still glazed. Brenda took his shoulder and gently shook him, looking him in the eye. "Dave, is this too tight?"

He shook his head from side to side to show it wasn't.

"Good." She walked back around in front of him. "Once we get to know you better we'll talk about untying you."

She looked for a response, but he looked right through her. Shaking her head, she turned to Tammy. "We gotta get that blood off his face. It's creeping me the fuck out."

After happening upon a small stream, Brenda washed the blood from Dave's face. If the cold water bothered him it didn't show. He remained vacant, staring off at nothing in particular. He was following orders well enough though, so that kept Tammy from complaining too much about the situation Brenda had gotten them into. Brenda was relieved for this, if nothing else.

After Dave was properly washed up the group continued walking. They didn't speak for some time, quietly treading the miles, one after another. Dave offered no conversation, nor did he complain about the walking. He never asked for a break, for food, or for water. He walked where he was directed and didn't stop until he was told.

The group walked like this for most of the day along the highway, stopping periodically to rest. Dave took water when offered, but he ate nothing. He was no more conversant during the breaks than he'd been during the walking. An hour or so before sunset the girls decided to make a camp for the night. It was still cold out, but at least the temperature had now risen above freezing. This pleased Brenda as she hated the cold. She hoped the rise in temperature meant spring was on its way, but if not, even a short reprieve from winter was welcomed.

The girls made their camp off the road, in a spot fifteen feet into the woods. They decided to build a fire despite the temperatures being milder than they had been the past few days. The fire would warm them, and as Tammy pointed out, it would allow them some light to keep an eye on their new friend. Brenda could tell Tammy still didn't trust Dave. She also thought that was understandable.

There were plenty of dead tree limbs lying around, so they gathered up enough to keep the fire burning most of the night. Some dried tree bark and crispy leaves served as tinder, catching the spark from Brenda's flint nicely. It wasn't long before they had a warm fire going.

They sat, silently leaning against leafless trees, watching

the fire for some time. It gobbled up the wood, hissing, and crackling as it consumed the fuel. Dave remained silent, choosing to stare vapidly into the flickering flames rather than speak. Brenda and Tammy sat across from him, a few feet apart. They watched him closely.

Tammy finally broke the silence. "Why is he here?"

Brenda looked at Tammy before moving her gaze to the fire. She paused, unsure of how to answer the question.

Tammy continued, clearly insistent on an answer. "You know, he's the not the only uninfected person we've come across in all our time on the road together. I mean, you never took any special interest in anybody we ran across in the past. Hell, we avoided them." She stared at Brenda. "Tell me, what's so different about this guy?"

"A feeling," Brenda replied.

Tammy furrowed her brow. "A feeling?" She waved her hands around in an attempt to get Dave's attention. He stared into the fire, seemingly oblivious. "Do you see this? He's fucking gone to Pluto."

"I'm not so sure about that," Brenda replied. "I think he's still in there…somewhere."

"What makes you say that?" Tammy asked. "And don't say 'a feeling' again."

"I think this might be a stress reaction."

"A stress reaction? You mean like shock?"

"More or less, yeah."

"How would you know what shock looks like?" Tammy asked.

"I've seen something like it before, is all."

"Where?"

"I guess I sorta went through it myself."

"What do you mean?" Tammy asked.

Brenda took a moment, inhaling deeply before continuing. "You remember me telling you about all those douchebags I used to date, right?"

"Yeah, I remember. They sounded like real winners."

"Well, some years back, before the outbreak, there was a particular douchebag I dated who answered to the name of

Duane Cummings."

"I don't think I remember you ever talking about him."

Brenda shook her head. "I know. I never told anybody about Duane, not even you. It was a rough period in my life, probably the worst." She paused. "No, on second thought, it was definitely the worst."

Tammy listened in silence as Brenda continued. "I met Duane just after high school. He was older than me, and from the way he told it he could walk on fucking water. My mom and dad were drunks, so there wasn't a whole lot of time left for me, you know? I had no friends and Duane seemed to be the only person in the world who could see me. Problem was, Duane was crazier than a shit-house rat. Fucking paranoid jealous. I wrote it off at first, just ignored it. Then we moved in together and it all got worse. A lot worse. Eventually, I had enough, and I knew I had to leave him."

Brenda paused, watching as the yellow-orange flame slowly consumed the tree limbs they'd piled on. She instinctively looked around for carriers and saw none. She barely noticed the habit anymore.

"What happened?" Tammy asked.

"Finally, one day he damn near killed me."

"Fuck me," Tammy said.

"I don't remember what started it. Probably something stupid. He was always so mad, just mad at the fuckin' world, you know? I suppose I was just another thing to be mad at that day."

Brenda paused again, collecting herself. Tammy remained silent. "Things escalated and got way out of hand. Before I knew it, he'd bitten my tongue halfway off, fractured my eye socket, and broke three of my ribs."

"Oh, honey…"

"He smashed my face through a wall, Tammy. Luckily I missed the wall stud by like two inches. If not, I'm not sure I'd be alive today. After Duane beat the shit out of me and left me for dead, I just sort of…checked out, you know? I got into my car and I guess I just drove. I had blood gushing from my mouth, covering my shirt. I was a bloody mess. Cops said I drove to a McDonald's about a mile down from the house and then walked into the lobby. I stood there just asking what time it was." Brenda chuckled. "Freaked everybody out, that's for sure."

Tammy said: "So you think this guy went through something similar? Is that what you're saying?"

"Maybe. I mean, at first I didn't remember any of it; Duane beating the shit out of me, driving to McDonald's, or the first day in the hospital. It took a couple of days before I got my wits back. First, I realized that my tongue hurt like hell and then I noticed I was in a hospital room. But after that, it all started coming back. Well, most of it at least."

Brenda glanced over at Dave before returning her attention back to Tammy. "The thing is, Tammy, I think our new friend here's got the same thing, or something like it. Something happened to this guy, something bad, and I think he's just checked out for the time being. Like I was."

"So you don't think he's faking?"

Brenda shook her head. "No, I don't. That's why I couldn't leave him back there, you see? He's not himself. I don't think he even knows where he is right now. He can't make decisions and I know what it's like to go through something like that.

"Tammy, I asked myself back there, what would I want someone to do for me if the shoe was on the other foot? And then I wondered what would my grandma would think if she knew I just left him there to be shredded by those monsters? That kicked my ass into gear. I guess I couldn't bear the thought of Nanna's disappointment, even fourteen years dead. She was more of a mother to me than my own mother was."

Tammy examined Dave closely, as if she were trying to figure out what he was. "How long do you think he'll be like this then?"

"It's hard to say. I came out of it after a couple of days. He might do the same, but it could be longer. Or never. Either way, if he does come to his senses, I want him tied up. When he remembers whatever it was that happened to him, I don't know how he's gonna react. He might go nuts, he might not. Hands bound is how we want him to stay."

Brenda stared into the crackling, orange fire, watching the embers glow. The warmth felt good against the slight night chill. "I'll take the first watch," she said. "Try to get some sleep. I'll wake you up in a couple of hours."

"You gonna be okay with him?" Tammy asked.

"Yeah. I'll be fine."

"I'm taking you up on that offer then." Tammy stood, retrieving the bedroll from her backpack. "Brenda?" she said.

"Yeah?"

"Thanks for taking first watch. And sorry about all that Duane shit."

"Thanks."

"Whatever happened to him?"

"Cops picked him up a few hours later. Eighteen years, no parole. The state got him on attempted murder. Apparently he'd been bragging to his cousin about how he was going to kill me. I found that out later. You know, I always thought blood was thicker than water. Not this time, I guess."

"Well, I hope that cocksucker starved to death in his cell after the virus hit," Tammy said.

Brenda nodded. "Me too."

"Put your hands in the air," the man on the left said. He held a pistol in his hand. He was short, squat, and balding.

No one moved.

"DO IT!" the other man yelled. He was taller than the first man, with lighter hair. Both men had beards of considerable length.

And both carried pistols.

"Drop the goddamn guns," the balding man ordered.

Dave considered their options. If he provoked these two they might all be killed. If he complied, they might live. Even so, robbed and left with nothing was almost the same as death.

Dave raised the shotgun. He thought he would be more afraid than he really was, but he was surprisingly calm. The men in front of him tensed; he could see uncertainty in their eyes. "No," he told them. He kept his eyes on the two assailants. "Sandy, get behind me."

Sandy stayed where she was, frozen.

The second man scowled. "Listen hero, I'll blow your brains out, fuck your little girl up the ass then blow her brains out while your friend here watches."

Dave glanced at Jim only to find his friend's hands empty. He'd not even had time to pull the pistol. Jim shot a helpless look back.

Dave knew it was all up to him now.

"How do I even know that gun is loaded?" Dave asked the balding man. "Maybe you're bluffing."

"You want to take your chances?" the man replied.

Despite his fear, Dave still felt calm and confident. He had these two right where he wanted them. "I'm willing to bet that if I pull both of these triggers at the same time the two of you will disappear." He was sure they'd back out of this standoff, maybe throw out some four-letter words along with some empty threats before walking away.

He couldn't have been more wrong.

It happened so fast he almost didn't hear the first shot. Just a small crack, and Jim dropped to the ground like a box of rocks. Dave heard a second crack and felt a warm spray cover the side of his face, dripping into his left eye. Out of his peripheral vision, he watched as Sandy fell, her hands going instinctively to her neck before she tumbled to the cold ground.

Before he could process what was happening Dave heard a loud boom, barely feeling the massive recoil of the shotgun as both barrels went off in his hands. The light-haired thief's chest turned red as hundreds of small buckshot tore through his skin and into his chest, knocking him to the ground. He was dead before his body touched the ground.

The balding man screamed, grabbing his shoulder. A significant amount of buckshot had penetrated the man's skin, producing dots of red through his coat. Despite being shot, the man raised his gun. In a detached and dream-like state, Dave felt himself run toward the man, tackling him to the ground before the thief could squeeze off the shot.

It wasn't until later Dave realized he'd been screaming the entire time.

Dave landed on top of the balding thief and felt a hot pain as the man punched him in the kidneys. Dave straddled the man's chest, bringing the butt of the shotgun squarely down on the man's nose. The nose exploded in a fine, red mist. Streams of dark, red blood ran from the man's nostrils, down his cheeks and onto the ground below.

Dave brought the butt of the gun down again, shattering the thief's eye socket. Barely alive now, the man's eyes widened as he watched the butt of the shotgun rise high into the air above him. Another impact from the butt of the shotgun and the man went limp, his face a devastated mess.

The man didn't move again.

Dave lost count of how many times he smashed the shotgun into the thief's face. When he finally stopped the man's face and head were unrecognizable as being human, now just a mess of tissue, blood, hair, and bone. What had once served as the thief's eye sockets was now a single deep cavity filled with a pool of dark, red blood. The eyes remained open, staring blankly into the sky.

Dave dropped the shotgun to the ground. He scrambled off the man's body to tend to his wife. As if still in a dream he crawled to her, moving in slow motion. When he reached her, he saw she was holding a gaping wound in her neck. Blood poured through her fingers as she struggled to breathe. Hot tears formed in Dave's eyes as he watched his wife fight a losing battle for her life.

Sandy's eyes were wide but unfocused. He couldn't tell if she could see him at all. He consoled her as best he could, holding her head and rocking her gently. Only once did her eyes meet his, and in this instant they shared all they could.

Her eyes quickly lost focus again as she made her last attempt to draw a breath. Dave heard a sickening, sucking sound as she struggled to draw air into her lungs. She exhaled once more before her body relaxed and her hand fell away from her neck. Below it, the entire left side of Sandy's neck was gone, ripped away by the thief's bullet.

He placed his forehead on his wife's as he wept.

Jim had died instantly, or as near to instantly as Dave could figure. He was in such a fog he could barely think. The rational part of his mind, barely noticeable at this point, had simply stopped functioning. He was numb all over, physically and emotionally. He was covered in drying blood, the blood of his dead wife. He could feel it hardening on his face and hands in the cold air like a death mask.

Dave sat motionless on the ground for what he thought might have been a very long time. He could no longer tell. Time was passing slowly for him; each moment felt like an eternity. He sat between the bodies of his wife and his friend, staring at the ground. Eventually, his legs went numb and his fingers and toes began to freeze. A distant part of his brain considered he might have frostbite, but that hardly mattered anymore.

Eventually, he stood up, or he tried to at least. He fell. His legs felt like jelly from having been folded under himself for so long. He lay on the ground staring at the gray sky, as thousands of needles stabbed his legs all over. Once the pain subsided, he stood, staring into the distance.

He looked at the body of his wife. He'd wanted so much for her to be happy again. This fucked up, terrible world had finally gotten her, and he hadn't been able to protect her at all.

Until death did they part.

Dave dropped his backpack to the ground and began to walk, leaving behind his wife and his only friend. Lying dead on the frozen ground, their bodies mingled with all the possessions they'd carried.

Dave carried nothing now.

He needed nothing.

He felt nothing.

Now he too was the walking dead.

Dave stood up beside the campfire.

Brenda pulled the gun from her front pocket. "Hold it now, hoss. Stay right where you are."

Dave looked over at Tammy, still asleep by the fire. He stared at Brenda.

In the light of the fire, Brenda could see recognition in Dave's eyes. He was coming back to them. She tightened her grip on the pistol.

Dave opened his mouth to speak, but said nothing. It was coming back now, all of it, all at once, like a tidal wave of recollection. An emotional earthquake. He dropped to his knees beside the fire, his hands still bound, a spate of emotion engulfing him, dragging him out to a melancholy sea where he knew he would surely drown. "Oh God," he said, shaking his head. A tear ran from the corner of his eye. "It was all my fault."

Chapter Eleven

The girl pointed the gun at Ed, shivering as the fever raged within her body. She opened her eyes wide, her mouth pursed. She was afraid, and that frightened Ed even more. "What the hell are you trying to put down me?" she yelled.

Ed kept both hands visible. He spoke softly and slowly in an attempt to keep the girl calm. "My name is Ed, and what I just gave you was medicine. You've got a fever; it's an antibiotic."

This explanation appeared to have no effect on the girl. "The hell it is," she said. "You know what, asshole? The last time somebody crammed a pill down my throat, they raped me for days. What makes you think I'd ever let that happen again?" She thrust the gun toward him, breaking into a violent coughing fit.

Ed stepped closer, thinking he might wrangle the gun away, but she recovered quickly, raising the pistol and leveling it at his head.

"Stay where you are, prick," she ordered. "You take another step toward me and I'll put a hole in your head."

Ed backed up, raising his hands higher in the air. “Okay,” he said, nodding.

“Daddy, what’s going on in there?” Zach called from the hallway.

Ed could hear the concern in his son’s voice. “It’s okay buddy, just stay where you are,” he replied as calmly as he could manage.

“Why is the girl yelling?” Jeremy asked from the hallway. “Is she okay?”

The expression on the girl’s face changed from what appeared to be fear to something resembling curiosity. “Who the hell is that out there?” she asked.

“Those are my sons,” Ed said. His heart was racing as he struggled to show a calm exterior. The last thing he wanted to do was spook the girl. Her mental state seemed erratic, provoking it could be lethal.

“Those are your kids?” the girl asked.

Ed thought he saw her firm grip on the pistol relax just a little. The curiosity on her face now seemed to outweigh the fear. She looked more confused than frightened.

“I have two sons,” Ed explained. “Zach is ten; Jeremy is eight. We found you unconscious inside a Target store, about a mile away from here. We carried you here and then we got you the antibiotics.”

The girl’s eyes fluttered. She closed them.

Ed waited. No response. “Nobody here is going to hurt you,” he said, attempting to reassure her.

The girl lowered the gun. She swayed. Suddenly her eyes opened again and she raised the pistol, eyes wide. “I can’t believe anybody anymore,” she said, her voice cracking.

She looked into Ed’s eyes and he could see her indecision clearly now. She needed a reason to believe, and she needed it now.

“How do I know you’re not lying?” the girl asked, the confidence and anger now all but gone from her voice.

“You don’t. You can’t know that with any certainty,” Ed told her, hoping like hell that had been the right thing to say. She was still listening, so he continued. "Look, I'm going to level with you. I've got two boys out there who need me. You've got a gun pointed at me, and that is making me very nervous. I need you to put that gun down so we can talk. I don't care if you keep it, just don't point it at me. I'll show you the pills I'm giving you, and I'll tell you everything that's happened so far, but I can't do it with that gun pointed at me."

"Daddy, are you okay?" Jeremy called from the hallway.

Ed knew his boys and he could tell they were growing increasingly concerned. The last thing he needed was them breaking into the room and Zach pulling his gun. That would escalate things way too quickly.

"Everything's just fine," Ed called back. "I'm just talking with…" He looked at the girl, raising his eyebrows. "What's your name?"

She answered, a confused look on her face. "Trish."

"Trish," he finished. "Our new friend is Trish. Say 'hi', guys."

Both boys reported from the hallway. "Hi, Trish," they both called.

Ed could still hear a hint of fear in their voices. They were following his directions to the letter, though, just as he'd taught them to do.

Ed turned to Trish, looking directly in her eyes. He lifted his hands into the air. "Just lower the gun, that's all I ask. Please."

The girl stared back, the gun still raised and pointed at Ed. She lowered it once, but raised it again. Once more she lowered it, keeping it there. She lay back down slowly on the bed, curling her body into the fetal position. She let go of the pistol, closing her eyes.

Ed stood there for a moment, waiting. A few moments later he walked slowly over to the bed, retrieving his gun.

"Where am I, Ed?" Trish asked, her eyes still closed.

"You're in a farmhouse, just off the highway. You've been here for about a day and a half."

She nodded, her eyes still closed.

Finally, Ed's pulse was returning to a reasonable rate. He felt the situation was contained. "You want to meet the boys?" he asked.

"If you're going to kill me just do it. I can't go through what I went through again."

"Nobody here is going to kill you. We just want you to get better." Ed called the boys in, guiding them to the side of the bed. They tromped into the room and stood, staring at her.

Trish opened her eyes and stared back at them. Ed thought he saw the slightest smile appear on her lips.

"We got you medicine," Zach said. He was beaming with pride at the announcement.

Jeremy nodded in agreement. His eyes were wide with excitement. "Did you take your pill yet?" he asked her.

"No. Not yet," Trish replied.

"You should take it now then," Jeremy advised her, as if prescribing medicine was a common thing for him. This time, there was no doubt of Trish's smile.

"Trish accidentally spit it out when I gave it to her," Ed told the boys. "Help me find it."

Zach and Jeremy complied, searching near the nightstand, under the bed, and on the floor. Finally Zach located the pill near the edge of the bed. He reached down, picked it up and brushed it off before handing it to Trish. "Take this," he told her. "Dad says it'll make you feel better."

She took the pill from him. "Thank you."

Ed pointed to the box on the table beside the bed. "You ever heard of something called a Z-pak?" he asked.

Trish didn't reply.

Ed continued, unabated. "Well, it's an antibiotic. You take it for five days. I'm hoping it'll knock out whatever's causing this fever and sickness." He picked up the box and showed it to her. She examined it briefly before closing her eyes again. "You need to take two pills right now," he said. "After that, one a day. The sooner you start, the better."

"Help me then," Trish said.

Ed lifted Trish's head as Zach handed the glass to his

father. Ed helped Trish swallow both pills before gently placing her head back on the pillow. "You need to sleep now," he said. "That's very important. We'll be across the hall if you need us."

Trish nodded as she closed her eyes.

Ed patted both boys on the back. "Let's go guys. Trish needs to rest."

Jeremy reached out and touched Trish's shoulder. "I hope you get better soon," he told her.

Trish smiled wide. Ed smiled too; the boys had that kind of effect on people. Ed and the boys walked out of the bedroom and into the hallway, closing the door to Trish's room behind them.

Trish survived the night. Ed checked on her the following morning while she was sleeping. Though her sleep was restless, she was still sleeping, and that was important. Ed helped her drink some water and helped her up to use the toilet. Now that she was drinking water again the necessity to use the restroom was returning. It turned out the bathtub was easiest for that.

The first day Ed changed her out of the clothing they'd found her in and into some pajamas he'd found in a drawer in the bedroom. The pajamas had to be more comfortable than what she'd been wearing, and it was easier to get them out of the way when nature called.

She didn't say much that day, so Ed kept the boys out of her way. He knew she needed the rest; it was essential to her recovery. The boys played in the bedroom across the hall most of the time. Ed offered her some food, but she refused, claiming she wasn't hungry. He wasn't surprised; she still felt hot with fever. He gave her another pill that evening, along with more water. While he couldn't swear to it, he was confident she didn't feel as hot by the end of the second day.

Ed and the boys remained in the same adjacent room, each one again taking turns on guard duty while the others slept. The next two days followed in a similar fashion.

Trish slept most of the hours during the day, getting

up periodically to pee in the tub. She was gradually drinking more water each day, and by the third day Ed and the boys had to go back down to the pump and get more. Ed and the boys ate their rations like usual; consuming the bounty they'd picked up at the prior highway exit as well as what they already carried with them. Each day Trish refused any food offered, her appetite still suppressed. She took the antibiotic obediently enough, and that was what Ed was most concerned about.

On the fourth day, Trish appeared remarkably better. When Ed checked on her that morning her eyes were open and bright. He thought for a moment he'd seen the tiniest smile flash across her face as he walked in. He sat across from her in a chair he'd brought up from the kitchen. She finally accepted some of the beef jerky he offered her, chasing that with the water they'd drawn from the pump out back. She took a bite of the jerky before looking up at Ed. Her eyes were no longer laden with dark circles as they had been when he and the boys found her.

"How long have I been out?" she asked.

"A few days or so."

"I feel better. Not great, but better."

"Good. Your fever seems to have broken now too. The coughing isn't as bad either."

Trish closed her eyes and took a deep breath. She opened them and looked around the room before focusing back on Ed. He could see sincerity and honesty in her eyes. "So you're one of the good guys, huh?" she said.

Ed paused, his conscience reminding him that his first reaction had been to leave her where they'd found here. Though guilty about that now, he reminded himself that he'd ultimately opted to bring her back to the farmhouse. Or, more accurately, the boys had, and he'd complied. He hoped it amounted to the same thing. "I suppose," he said.

"Well, you saved my life. Sounds like a good guy kind of thing to do."

"I guess you could say that," he replied, smiling.

She stared directly into his eyes, commanding his

attention. "Thank you," she said.

"Don't mention it."

Trish reached up and took hold of his hand, squeezing it with what strength she could muster. "Seriously. Thank you."

He felt his face flush hot. "You're welcome," he said.

"Tim told me there were people like you still left, but I didn't believe him. I guess I was wrong."

"Tim?" Ed asked.

"I'll tell you about him sometime; once I feel better."

Ed nodded. "Fair enough."

"Where are the boys?" she asked, changing the subject.

"In the other room, playing."

"Would it be okay if I saw them?"

"Sure. Don't see why not." Ed called for the boys. A few moments later they came clamoring into the room.

Trish looked at Ed apologetically. "I'm sorry, I forgot their names."

"It's okay. You weren't feeling well. I wouldn't expect you to remember." He pointed to the boys in order of oldest to youngest. "This is Zach, and this is Jeremy."

"Hi there, boys," she said to them, sending them both a big smile.

"Hi, Trish," Jeremy answered, looking pleased with her improved condition.

"Are you feeling better?" Zach asked.

Trish nodded. "I am."

"Good," he told her.

Jeremy turned to his father, the look of elation never leaving his face. "Looks like the medicine worked, Daddy, just like you said it would."

Ed smiled. "Looks like it did just that, buddy."

Jeremy turned to Trish. "Guess what?" he asked.

"What?"

"We walked to a drugstore, and then we found the medicine there. We had to run from a lot of carriers, though 'cause they were everywhere. Then we hid in a house until they all left. We found me a gun there too, see?" He held up his gun to show her.

"Keep that thing pointed to the floor, bud," Ed reminded him.

"I will, Daddy," Jeremy replied, his exuberance slightly dampened.

Trish looked at them all. "You guys really took some risks for me, huh?"

"We wanted you to get better," Zach told her.

"Well, I appreciate it so much, all of you."

Ed cut in. "Okay guys, let's let Trish get some rest. She's getting better, but she's still got a ways to go. You guys go on back to the room and play now."

"Can we stay a little longer?" Jeremy pleaded.

"Later. For now, Trish needs to rest."

"Okay," both boys replied, nearly in unison, their tone despondent. They walked out of the room, gently closing the door behind them.

"Could I have some more of that jerky?" Trish asked.

Ed handed her the rest of the package. He stood up to leave. "You get some rest now. Yell for us if you need anything."

"I will," Trish told him.

Ed walked to the door, opening it.

"Ed," Trish said from behind him.

He turned to face her.

Her eyes locked on his. "Thanks again," she said, a smile spreading across her face.

Ed smiled back before shutting the door.

The following morning Ed left the boys in the bedroom across from Trish's. He walked to her room and knocked on her door.

"Come in," she replied.

Ed walked in to find her sitting up in the bed, her back resting on the pillow. "Good morning," he said. He walked over to her and felt her forehead. It felt cool. The dark circles under her eyes had all but disappeared. She was still thin though, incredibly thin at that, but she exhibited an exuberance she hadn't possessed before. "Fever's down," he told her. "I think it's almost gone."

Trish smiled at him. "I'm hungry, too."

"That's good. You up for some Spam? Fresh out of the can."

"I'd love some," she said, smiling.

Ed pulled a can of Spam from his backpack, removed the lid and produced a metal fork from the pack. He handed it all to her.

"Thanks," she said. The smile seemed to never leave her face now.

"Don't mention it," Ed replied before walking out of the bedroom and leaving her to her meal.

Ed sat on the front porch of the farmhouse watching the highway. Zach and Jeremy played quietly beside him. He had a good view from the porch, hopefully good enough to see trouble coming from a distance. They locked the back door then jammed some old two-by-fours they found under the door handle, nailing them to the wooden floor.

As he sat, Ed thought about Trish. He tried to imagine what she must have gone through before they'd found her. She said she'd been raped, and he had seen the bruises on her thighs while caring for her while she was sick. She also had cuts on her head and large, bluish-black bruises on her back and shoulders. She looked as if she had been hit by a car. No wonder she'd almost killed him.

Now that the fever had almost passed and she'd gotten some rest, Trish was beginning to come around. She was talking, and she showed none of the previous signs of aggression or fear. They hadn't had much conversation over the past several days, but they had enough for Ed to feel comfortable with her mental stability. Bringing her to the farmhouse had been a good idea after all. They couldn't stay forever though; supplies were running out. They'd need to get back on the road soon to restock.

And there was the big conundrum: what were they going to do with the girl? He couldn't just leave her, not in the condition she was in. She'd be a sitting duck. Taking her with them concerned him as well. Ed had traveled with only the boys for such a long time. They had a system, they relied on each other, and they were family. They were a team. Taking on someone else meant they would need more supplies and he would now be responsible for yet another person. She might slow them down, maybe even get them all killed.

However, despite his initial misgivings, Ed was beginning to like her. So were the boys. He remembered Sarah, how pitiful and tragic she had been toward the end. He vividly remembered how helpless he had felt then, how completely useless his efforts to save her had been. In the end, he did manage to stop her suffering, but he couldn't save her life. This time around he had a second chance to get it right.

Of course all this internal dialogue was predicated on the assumption that she *wanted* to travel with them. For all he knew she might want to go it alone, exactly as she had been doing when he and the boys had found her inside that Target store. He had to consider that possibility. It would be as much her decision as it would be his.

Sudden movement near the road caught his eye, ripping him from his thoughts.

It was a carrier.

"Get down," he whispered to the boys, pointing toward the thing. He slowly moved from the front steps to where the boys sat. They all crouched down behind a porch swing, hoping it and the thick slats supporting the front railing would be enough to keep them concealed.

"Don't move," he told the boys. "If it spots us, go into the house immediately. I'll be right behind you."

The boys nodded in acknowledgment.

They all watched as the carrier continued to make its way slowly along the highway, dragging one of its legs behind it. It was slow and meandering, almost confused in the way it walked. To Ed, it looked near death, but that didn't mean it wouldn't charge if it saw them, no matter how sick it was. They couldn't afford to take any chances with it.

After several more minutes of watching the carrier walk away, Ed assumed the coast was clear. They couldn't sit on the porch anymore. It was too dangerous. Ed began to question the decision in the first place. Maybe it had been a bad idea all along.

Ed shuffled them all back into the house before closing and locking the front door behind them. He turned to his boys, his face painted with consternation. "We need to get moving soon."

Trish sat upright in the bed, eating another container of Spam. By now the color had returned to her face and the fever had all but disappeared. She was finished with her antibiotic treatment and was on her first day without them. Ed felt that she was progressing well and Trish herself admitted to feeling better than she had in weeks.

Ed didn't tell Trish about the carrier he'd seen from the front porch. Mostly he didn't want to upset her while she convalesced, and besides, there was nothing she could do about it anyway. He decided to instead bring the boys up to her room so they could all spend some time together.

The boys told Trish all about their time spent on the road. She listened intently to their stories, nodding where expected and asking questions the boys were keen to answer. They all seemed to get along well. Ed wished the boys had something else besides the road and the virus to talk about, but the truth was they didn't. And no amount of wishing was going to change that.

After recounting the story of Zach's run-in with the carrier at the sporting goods store some weeks back, Zach appeared uncomfortable with the discussion. Jeremy, on the other hand, told the story with zealous conviction. He beamed when he got to the part where his father had stormed in and killed the carrier with the baseball bat.

Noticing Zach's demeanor, Ed stepped in and brought things to a halt. "All right guys," he began, "how about you two get back over to our room and play for a while? Trish has heard enough stories for today."

"Do we have to?" Jeremy asked.

Ed nodded.

"C'mon," Zach pushed. "Dad said we need to go."

Jeremy shot his older brother a disapproving look before both boys walked out of the room, Zach in the lead.

Ed pulled up the chair from the kitchen and sat down beside the bed. "How's the Spam?" he asked.

"Good," she replied, watching him.

Ed looked down at his hands. An awkward silence followed.

"Something tells me you're not all that interested in how good the Spam is," Trish said.

He looked up at her and smiled. "You're pretty observant."

She smiled back as she stuck the fork in the remaining Spam, placing the can down upon the nightstand. "What do you want to talk about then, if you don't want to talk about Spam?" she asked.

Ed wasn't sure where to begin. He decided the best thing was to just come out with it and see where the chips fell. "We'll be leaving soon, maybe sooner than you might expect," he said.

She nodded.

"It's completely up to you, but this farmhouse is just a temporary stay for the boys and me. We're running low on supplies, so we're gonna have to get moving again soon."

Trish looked at him, a slight smile forming on her lips. "And you want to know if I want to come with?"

"You *are* observant," he said, chuckling.

"I don't know," she replied. "I guess I hadn't given it much thought."

"Somehow I doubt that," Ed said.

Trish laughed. "Well, maybe I've given it a little thought."

Ed finally decided he'd beaten around the bush long enough. He just needed to come out with it. She was either going to come with them, or she wasn't. As he prepared to ask, he was interrupted.

"Carriers!" he heard Zach yell as his son came barging into the room. Zach's eyes were wide with concern. "Out front!"

Jeremy raced in behind him. "Lots of 'em, too," he added. "They're headed toward the house!"

The humor in Ed's face washed away. He was hoping to leave on his own terms, not like this. "Can you walk?" he asked Trish.

She nodded.

"Can you run?"

"I think so."

Ed turned to Zach. "How close are they?"

"I don't know exactly, pretty close," Zach replied, his voice shaking.

Ed turned back to Trish. "Get dressed as quickly as you can. We're getting out of here."

He didn't wait for a response. He raced into the bedroom he and the boys had been using, peering out the front window and into the field between the house and the highway. There he saw dozens of carriers descending upon the house, just as the boys had described.

Ed bolted toward the back of the second floor of the farmhouse. From a window at the back of the house, he could see as many carriers in the back as were in the front. They were flanking them from both sides, closing in like a pack of wolves.

The doors and windows were secured, but Ed knew that would only buy them a fraction of the time they needed. Eventually, the whole lot of the filthy things would come crashing down upon them. The only question was how long that would take.

As if to answer that question, Ed heard a loud crash from downstairs: the unmistakable sound of a window breaking.

Options. What were their options? His mind raced. They couldn't stay in the house; there was no hiding from that many carriers. The horrific things would eventually sniff them out. They also couldn't make the jump from the second floor for fear of breaking an ankle. That left them with only one option: they would have to shoot their way out.

"Boys, get your packs on and follow me," he commanded. They did as instructed. He walked over to Trish's room, the boys in tow. She was still struggling to get her coat on, but was otherwise dressed. Ed helped her with the coat. "I think at least one is in the house," he told her. "Probably more by now."

"Shit. I heard a window break," she replied. "What's the plan?"

Her calm exterior surprised Ed. She *had* been through a lot already though, he reminded himself. "We're going to go out through the front door then we're going to make a break for the highway."

Trish's eyes widened. "Are you crazy? How are we going to get through all the carriers downstairs?"

"Shoot anything that moves," he replied.

Zach and Jeremy stood behind him. Their masks covered their faces; their goggles covered their eyes. Ed put his mask and goggles on as well. Seeing Trish had none, Ed looked around for an impromptu substitute. He drew his knife, cutting a thin line of fabric from the bed sheet. He handed it to her. "Tie this around your mouth; it'll have to do for now."

As Trish tied her makeshift mask to her face, Ed continued giving instructions. "Stay together in a single line. Don't separate. Once we get downstairs, we head straight for the door. Like I said, shoot anything that gets in your way. Understand?"

The boys nodded, their eyes wide with anxiety.

"It'll be okay," he told them. The words felt hollow on his tongue.

They walked to the top of the steps and paused, gathering their courage. Ed looked at both Trish and the boys and nodded. It was now or never. The commotion downstairs was clearly audible as the invading carriers wrecked the farmhouse. The boys drew their guns, and they all started down the steps.

Before they could make it three steps down, a carrier appeared at the bottom. It quickly caught sight of Ed and his group, stopping to watch them. They all stood this way as the seconds passed like hours. The carrier watched them, scrutinizing them, determining if they were one of its kind. A few moments later it opened its mouth and screamed through rotten teeth, alerting the others.

The deadwalker scrambled up the steps in an impatient fury, ready for the kill. Halfway up the steps Ed put a bullet in the thing's chest, knocking it backward. It tumbled down the steps, landing hard at the bottom, its eyes wide open. Alerted to their presence now, Ed heard another deadwalker scream from somewhere on the bottom floor of the farmhouse. It was soon followed by more screams.

A few moments later Ed and the others arrived at the bottom of the steps, making a ninety-degree turn when they hit bottom. The room reeked of urine, meat, and feces, the stench nearly overpowering. Once down the steps, they sprinted toward the front door of the house. They ran in a tight group, just as they discussed. Ed saw three carriers already in the house, all positioned between them and the door. He shot them all, spending four bullets to do it. The carriers fell to the ground, two of them screaming from gutshot wounds.

Ed heard a shot from behind him. He turned to see a carrier go down, dropped by a shot from Jeremy's new pistol.

With all the carriers inside the farmhouse apparently down now, the living room appeared clear. They darted toward the front door.

Suddenly Trish screamed. "Ed, to your right!"

Ed turned quickly as a carrier charged from their right side. Ed brought it down with a lucky shot to the throat. Trish turned away, covering her face with her hands, trying to avoid any blood spatter.

After what seemed to them like an eternity, they

arrived at the front door. The chair Ed had placed under the door handle now blocked the way, their protection from the outside now a roadblock. They stood there, feeling more exposed than ever while Ed wrangled the chair out from under the door knob. The seconds ticked by like hours.

Finally, the chair came free and Ed tossed it to the side. He opened the door, peeking his head through to check the porch for carriers. There were five carriers on the porch with a handful more walking aimlessly in the front yard. He looked at Zach and pointed toward the two carriers to their left, silently communicating a plan. They heard more glass breaking behind them as more of the deadwalkers poured into the house. Their combined screams escalated, melding into a horrific cacophony of nightmarish proportion.

Ed charged through the door and out to the front porch, firing into a crowd of three carriers. They fell quickly. Zach turned, firing shots into the carriers his dad had assigned him. With the porch clear, they had only a few seconds to make the dash through the front yard and to the highway.

"This way!" Ed shouted, pointing.

Ed, Trish, Zach and Jeremy ran down the front steps and into the front yard. The carriers ambling around the yard took notice of their presence, descending upon them. Ed and his group ran hard, making a beeline toward the highway, shooting any carriers that got too close.

By the time they'd made it through the center of the crowd there were a dozen dead or wounded carriers in their wake. They ran as fast as they could, across the farmland between the house and the highway, navigating the bumpy terrain. As Ed looked behind them, he saw three healthy and fast carriers in pursuit.

Runners.

"Keep going!" he yelled to Trish and the boys, stopping short. As instructed, Trish and the boys ran on. Ed dropped to one knee, steadying the pistol with both hands before firing off five shots. The shots brought two of the carriers down, but the third one ran, unfazed.

Ed sighted in the charging carrier, squeezing the trigger, only to hear the sickening sound of the firing pin striking an empty chamber.

He quickly shoved the gun back into the holster before drawing the baseball bat from his backpack, like a sword from a sheath. Just as Ed made it to his feet, the carrier leapt toward him. Ed threw himself to the side, avoiding the carrier's grasp, rolling with the baseball bat still clutched in hand.

The carrier struck the ground hard. Slightly dazed, but not unpersuaded, it attempted to rise.

Ed regained his footing, just as the carrier got to its hands and knees. He took three steps toward it before bringing the baseball bat down on the back of the thing's head. The deadwalker dropped to the ground, blood pouring from the wound on its head. Its body twitched and jerked in the brown grass of the field. Ed didn't stop to see if the thing was dead. Immediately he raced toward the highway and ran, catching up with Trish and the boys who'd been nervously waiting for him. He wiped the bat on the grass before placing it back into the sleeve on his backpack.

A glance behind revealed two more carriers in pursuit. "Run," he told them.

They ran.

As they ran in the darkness, Ed kept his fold in check, ensuring no one fell behind. He picked them out in the dim light, first Zach, then Jeremy.

Trish was nowhere to be found.

He glanced backward as he ran. Behind them, lying on the ground, a dark silhouette in the dim light, was the shape of a body.

Trish had collapsed.

Chapter Twelve

Brenda and Tammy traveled with their new companion along the silent highway. His hands were still bound, but as an act of compassion Brenda tied them in front of his body to give him more freedom of movement and make him more comfortable. Dave knew it was also a good faith gesture on Brenda's part and he appreciated that.

Two days had passed since Dave's memories returned. He'd spent a fair part of the first day introverted, the tears coming frequently. The girls had given him the necessary space in which to grieve for his loss. By the second day most of the tears had dried up. He spent the time lost in thought, contemplating while they walked along the barren highway.

As Dave walked he replayed the events of the shooting in his mind, like a terrible highlight reel on the evening news. He blamed himself. Convinced there had to be something he could have done differently, Dave anguished over the death of his wife and their friend. He been so sure of himself, so convinced that the men before them posed no real threat, but by the time he'd realized his error both his wife and his friend were dead. He wondered if, in the end, his confidence had been what killed his companions.

He continued replaying the events, searching for different outcomes, searching for answers, but by the end of the third day bitter reality took hold. No matter what *should* have happened, nothing could change what had *actually* happened. Maybe he could have done things differently, maybe he couldn't. There was no guarantee things would have turned out differently.

The cold and hard truth was that he'd never know. He'd probably always feel some responsibility, but nothing would bring his wife and friend back. They, like himself, had been thrust into a horrific situation over which they had little control. They died. He lived. Survivor's guilt wouldn't help anyone.

If he'd made mistakes, he'd made them in good faith. All he could do was accept reality and honor the memory of his fallen loved ones.

And never make the same mistake again.

At the end of the second day the trio set up a camp. The weather wasn't particularly warm, but it was holding above freezing. That suited Brenda just fine. They passed a two-story farmhouse earlier in the day and Dave could have sworn he saw people through the second floor windows. He pointed them out to the girls as they passed, but they simply ushered him along.

The prior night at camp all three had slept under blankets with no fire. Brenda shared a blanket with Tammy, and they gave Dave their extra. Neither of the girls trusted him enough yet to get close to him. The girls also alternated guard duty among themselves only, with part of their guard duty being that they keep an eye on their new companion. Given the circumstances Dave found he couldn't really argue with their logic. In their shoes he'd likely do the same.

On this night, however, the three of them sat in a small circle in the dark, speaking very little. As he sat, Dave thought about everything that had happened up to that point, how the girls had saved him, and how they were still keeping him around despite not knowing his background. The knowledge that Brenda had cleaned blood off his face - his dead wife's blood, no less - without knowing to whom that blood belonged, moved him. These women had put themselves out for him, even risking their lives to save his. It was his turn to make them understand that they hadn't made a mistake.

He decided he couldn't stay withdrawn forever; he had to come forward at some point. He cleared his throat, and the girls turned their attention toward him.

"When the plague hit Sandy and I had just gotten married," he began. "She was really a wonderful person." He stared off into the dark forest. "We weren't exactly kids when we were married, but we were still pretty young. Maybe too young, but who the hell ever really knows?"

The girls didn't speak, but they watched him, listening to his story. Tammy lit a cigarette from a crushed pack in her front pocket. She took a deep drag from the cigarette before blowing smoke into the crisp air.

Dave continued. "We were happy at first, at least I was, but Sandy never seemed to be able to find that same happiness. She was really depressed, even saw a few different doctors about it. They medicated her and put her into therapy and that kinda helped, I guess. We got by.

"Then the outbreak hit and we went right to one of the border towns. We already lived close to the coast, so we made it there without much of a problem. I know now we were the lucky ones."

Dave paused. He felt as if he were tearing the scab off of a wound.

"Go ahead," Brenda said in the dark.

Dave trudged on. "The problems for us started afterward, after the virus lingered for so long and life didn't go back to normal like they all said it would. We lived there in the border town for a while, maybe a year and a half. At first it wasn't so bad, but then things changed. Our town was taken over from the inside by a...I don't know exactly what to call him. A con artist maybe? He called himself a preacher, but he wasn't, at least not like the preachers I grew up with as a kid. He was a crook and a murderer. He controlled the weak ones through scripture. They were all just so desperate to believe anything."

Dave recounted the story of how he and his wife had befriended Jim and how they'd been framed before being tossed out of town, beyond the protection of the fence.

"Sometimes I wish they would have just killed us outright instead of tossing us out there to suffer. It would have been more humane. Despite it all we survived, by our wits and luck."

Tammy took another drag from the cigarette before blowing more smoke into the cool, evening air. Brenda listened closely. The acrid smell of cigarette smoke hung in the still air.

"We wandered for a long time, bouncing from house to house. Like I said, we got by. Until the day Sandy and Jim were killed. It all happened so fast. These men, they stopped us. They had guns. I thought they were bluffing, but they weren't." He looked at the two girls. "Before I knew it Sandy and Jim were dead and I had killed both of the men who did it. After that I guess I sort of blacked out. Maybe I went into shock, I don't know. All I know is I dumped all my stuff right there and just walked off. I wasn't thinking straight. I still don't remember what happened after that; it's all just a blur until I ran into you guys in that subdivision."

Dave stared at the ground for almost a full minute. No one spoke. Night had fallen and black shadow draped everything like a cloak.

"If you'd left me there I would have died, so this is where I say 'thanks'. Really. I owe you two my life, or whatever's left of it."

"It was mostly Brenda," Tammy said. "I was gonna leave you there."

"Well, whoever it was, I'm still grateful. I thought you should know it."

"No biggie," Brenda said in the dark. "And Dave?"

"Yeah?"

"Welcome back."

The group traveled together for another two days in the usual fashion. The girls kept Dave's hands bound, mostly due to Tammy's insistence. They camped each night in the woods without a fire, speaking very little. After telling his story Dave didn't feel much like talking for a while. He was content to sort through his thoughts for the time being.

Despite the catharsis of telling his story Dave still felt the pain and guilt of his wife's death. He supposed those feelings would never fully disappear. He could only hope it would fade after some time. As the days rolled on, he found himself growing more accustomed to his new life without Sandy. He supposed it was one of the things that made humans so resilient, the ability to move on after something so tragic. Still, it didn't seem fair to her.

He thought often about Sandy while they walked. He remembered her in the beginning, when they first met, and how her eyes sparkled. He remembered how her blond hair fell in big curls around her thin shoulders. Her pale skin and pink lips, and the smile she always had on her face when she saw him. No wonder he'd fallen in love with her.

In life she'd suffered so greatly. He could only hope that now, in death, she'd found some peace.

It was time he bury his dead.

Two women he'd never met before had saved his life. He supposed it was more accurate to say one woman saved him. A short little black-haired girl, covered with tattoos and sporting a tougher-than-shit attitude. Saved by a girl who looked more at home in the post-virus wastelands than she probably ever had in the world that came before it.

Dave thought Brenda seemed tough, but she was also sympathetic. She'd come back for him when there was no requirement to do so. There were no police, no laws, and no witnesses anymore, nothing to force her to do anything. It was a selfless act.

And Tammy?

Well, he'd just have to wait and see about her.

Brenda, Tammy and Dave walked. The wooded areas were becoming sparser now, morphing into neglected farmland. Most of the residential areas were now behind them. Though they kept him bound, the girls shared their food and water with him and he took it willingly. He thanked them and walked wherever they instructed without any sort of protest. For the time being it was an amicable relationship.

But as time passed their rations ran low, and they all knew that if they were to keep going they would have to resupply.

After miles of walking, a road sign came into view, proclaiming an exit ahead. Two gas stations appeared to be all the exit had to offer.

"We should get off this exit," Brenda suggested to Tammy.

She nodded in response. "Sounds good."

Dave offered no argument. He was as hungry as the girls were.

As they neared the exit the girls followed the road as it veered off from the main highway. Just before they reached the end of the exit Dave simply stopped walking and waited. The girls continued on until they noticed Dave had fallen behind. They both stopped, turned around, and stared.

"What?" Tammy asked, her tone sharp.

Always with the attitude, Dave thought. *Kid gloves with this one.*

"Look, I know we need to stop here. I'm not arguing that."

"Good," Tammy said.

Dave continued, ignoring her. "But we all know what might be there waiting for us. Carriers or even worse."

"And?" Tammy shot back. "We already know this. This isn't our first time around the block, you know."

"I know," Dave replied, pushing down his frustration. "But I'm still tied up over here, which means I can't defend myself. I can't help you guys either, not like this."

Tammy chuckled. "No offense buddy, but we don't need your help. As a matter of fact, you're slowing us down."

"Tammy, c'mon," Brenda said. "Give him a break."

Tammy appeared incredulous. "What? It's true. Hey, he needs us more than we need him."

Kid gloves.

"You may be right," Dave said, "but if there's something nasty waiting for us in one of those gas stations I can't do shit with my hands tied."

"So you expect us to untie you?" Tammy asked.

Dave shrugged. "Yeah, I do."

"You can forget about that."

"I'm telling you right now I have no intention of hurting you two, bottom line. Look, you guys saved my life, and I owe you, but I need to be able to protect myself if something goes bad. At this rate you might as well just feed me to the deadheads because I'm helpless."

"Fair enough," Brenda said.

Tammy's face went red. "What? We're not untying him."

"Yes, Tammy, we are."

"But-"

"He's right. If he was going to try something he'd have already tried it. Besides, he might prove useful."

Dave smiled.

Tammy's lips pursed into a thin line. "Fine."

When the group stepped into the parking lot of the 7-Eleven, Dave's first task was to find some sort of weapon. It didn't take long. He chose a car at random and tried the driver's side door. He was pleased to find it was unlocked. He supposed that when death was imminent, locking up one's car wasn't a big concern.

Dave reached below the dash, found the trunk release lever, and pulled. The trunk popped open.

"What are you doing?" Brenda asked.

"Self-defense," he told her.

Tammy shot Brenda a glance, concern flashing across her face.

Brenda shook her head.

Dave walked to the trunk, opened it up fully, and searched inside. A few moments later he produced a tire iron. He turned to the girls, imitating an infomercial host's voice. "A versatile tool, sufficiently capable of changing a flat tire, or bashing in the head of an infected human."

Neither of the girls laughed, so he dropped the act promptly. Truth was, he was nervous and the joking had been a cover up. He couldn't shake the bad feeling he had about the building they were about to enter. In the end he had little choice; they needed supplies pronto if they planned to continue.

"Let's go, wise-ass," Tammy said.

Dave followed without comment.

As they continued through the parking lot, multiple decaying bodies lay all about, requiring they step over or around them. Promptly they arrived at the convenience store's front door. The busted glass door had been almost completely removed from the hinges, hanging askew by the top hinge only. In the time after civilization fell, Mother Nature had blazed a trail into the store through the weakness of the open door, leaving dirt, dead leaves, and plants in her wake.

They stepped inside, Brenda in the lead, followed by Dave, with Tammy bringing up the rear. She kept her rifle pointed at Dave. They stepped quietly around most of the debris, producing very little sound with their gentle footfalls. Brenda allowed Dave to venture off on his own, much to Tammy's dismay. Truth was, he took a little satisfaction in that.

None of them spoke once inside the store. They kept their eyes and ears open for any sounds that might warn of carrier presence. The shelves were mostly bare, the store having been raided hard already. Dave looked under the shelves and in as many crevices as he could. His nerves were electric; places like this always bothered him.

Near the back of the store he found some candy bars and some beef jerky that had gotten lodged halfway down the back of a fallen shelf. He thought he could get to them, but to do so he'd have to move the shelves.

Just as he was about to place his tire iron on the floor and scoot the shelf he saw something that made him freeze.

A female carrier knelt in the corner, chewing on the intestines of a raccoon, entirely engrossed in the activity. It knelt on the floor, covered in black filth, tearing away at the animal's flesh, gulping down innards as if they were candy.

Dave remained as still as a statue. So far the thing hadn't noticed him and this was a distinct advantage he wanted to keep. His stomach flip-flopped as butterflies dashed madly about inside. He was stuck, unable to warn the girls and unable to kill the thing from a distance with a pistol.

There was only one solution. Man up and take the deadhead out before it caught sight of him or the girls.

He took a deep breath, gripping the iron bar tightly in his right hand. In one fluid motion he stood up and ran toward the carrier.

He made it halfway before it saw him. Despite spotting him as he ran, the thing hesitated for a moment before launching into its expected round of screaming. Maybe he'd caught it by surprise, maybe it didn't want to put down the food. Maybe it was just plain lazy. Regardless, Dave didn't care. The hesitation gave him the advantage he needed.

By the time the deadwalker screamed Dave was nearly on top of it. A moment later it made a dash to get to its feet, but by then it was too late. Dave lifted the tire iron high into the air, bringing it down on top of the thing's head with all his might. As the metal impacted upon the carrier's skull Dave could feel the bone split beneath the steel.

"Dave?" Brenda yelled from the other side of the store. "Where are you?"

Both girls came running from the front of the store.

Finishing the job he started, Dave brought the tire iron

down on the thing's head one more time. After the second blow the raccoon fell from the thing's grip. Innards slipped out of its open mouth, sliding out and striking the floor with a sloppy smack.

Another scream sounded, this one from the front of the store. It was a sound of anger and fury. Dave watched in horror and disbelief as another carrier emerged from behind a shelf near the front of the store.

It was a child.

What had once been an innocent little girl now descended upon Dave with only murder on its damaged mind. It snarled and drooled as it ran toward him, arms out, claw-like fingernails and teeth bared. Readying himself, Dave fixed his grip on the tire iron and raised it into the air, waiting. Brenda and Tammy were yelling in the background, but he no longer heard them, his sole focus now on this demented little monster running toward him, ready to tear him to bits.

Growling, the little girl closed the distance quickly. Then it stopped. It stared at the body of the carrier Dave had just killed, head cocked. From its mouth came a sound that froze Dave where he stood.

In an instant the thing screamed again, louder than ever. With only seconds to spare, Dave swung the tire iron, bringing it down squarely on the thing's small head. He felt its neck snap under the force of the impact. It stumbled, reeling from the blow before falling flat on its back. It twitched and kicked, muscles locked in spasm. Bloody drool leaked from its mouth.

Dave wanted to turn away, to run screaming from the building and never stop, but he had to finish what he started. He brought the tire iron down upon the carrier's small head one more time. Its skull and eye socket crumpled with the blow. It kicked violently again before exhaling a final breath. Its head fell to the side. Blood leaked everywhere from the thing, pooling onto the dingy floor beneath it.

Dave looked up, tire iron still clutched in his hand. His eyes met Tammy and Brenda's. No one said anything. They didn't have to.

"Let's get what we need and get the fuck outta here," he said.

After procuring the candy bars and beef jerky from behind the fallen shelf, some additional searching revealed more trapped foodstuffs. They were past the expiration date, but they all felt the stuff was edible. It wasn't a lot of food, but it was enough to get them by for a while. Another search behind the front desk revealed an old baseball bat. Dave helped himself to it. He kept the tire iron too, just in case.

Once they had finished collecting what little the shelves had to offer they headed toward the exit of the building. Brenda and Tammy were the first ones out. As Dave headed toward the door he glanced at the two dead carriers lying on the floor, bloody messes made by his hand.

"You coming?" Brenda asked from the parking lot outside.

Dave stared, barely noticing. From that carrier, the little girl…had he heard what he thought he heard? Surely not.

If so, it could change everything.

"Dave?" Brenda repeated.

He turned to her. "I'm coming," he said, taking one last glance at the bodies before stepping through the door and into the bright sunlight outside.

After they left the 7-Eleven they scavenged through a nearby Shell station. Luckily they met no carriers within. Unfortunately the supplies they did manage to gather were even more meager than the 7-Eleven had been. Combined, they netted very little for their efforts. Like so much in this new world, it hardly seemed worth it. Still, food was food and it would hopefully be enough to last them until the next exit.

Having exhausted the only two convenience stores off the exit, they walked the entrance ramp back to the highway, dodging parked cars and bodies along the way. The blackened bodies littered the ramp, noticeably thinning out by the time they made it to the highway. Dave ignored them.

They walked without speaking for most of the day, stopping once to eat and a few more times for water and bathroom breaks. Dave was happy to be walking for the first time in almost a week without his hands bound. He carried the baseball bat with him, along with the tire tool, slipped through and secured by a belt loop.

He'd expected Tammy to cry foul about his newly acquired freedom of movement, but she didn't. She just walked, as silently as he and Brenda.

As night set in they camped. Without any woods nearby, they took cover among the millions of decaying cornstalks. They built no fire, the temperatures didn't warrant it and they didn't want to draw any unneeded attention. Instead of circling a campfire they simply sat in a loose circle, much as they had the prior night.

"Those weren't the first carriers you ever killed, were they?" Tammy asked.

"No," Dave replied. "I've killed a few before."

"Hand to hand like that, or with a gun?"

"Both, but mostly hand to hand."

"But that one was a kid, at least it used to be. First time for that?" Brenda asked.

"Yeah."

Brenda paused. "You okay?"

"I suppose."

Another pause.

Dave asked: "You two planning on tying me up again?"

"No," Brenda replied. "We don't have a gun for you, but you can keep the bat and the tire iron. You already know how to use them."

"Good," Dave said.

"What you did back there was brave," Brenda said. "You helped us out. I'd say we're about even now. Tammy?"

"Sure," Tammy replied, shrugging her shoulders.

Dave decided to change the subject. "You two ever

wonder why you didn't get infected?"

"Dunno. I guess we're lucky," Tammy answered.

"You think it's just luck? Don't you think that virus was swimming around in the air back there at that gas station?"

"I guess," Brenda said. "But what's your point?"

"When the virus hit, that shit spread like wildfire. It got almost everyone. How did you, or me, or any of the survivors make it this far?"

"Maybe we're just *damn* lucky," Brenda said.

"I'm not so sure. Maybe it's us who are the walking dead, and we just don't know it yet."

"What do you mean?" Brenda asked.

"I'm just saying that maybe we're on the wrong side of the ratio. Maybe the future is them. Like *I am Legend*, or something, you know?"

No one replied. With the conversation now tapered off, they sat, surrounded by the sounds of nature. Chipmunks scurried through the woods while birds chirped their indecipherable songs to one another. An owl hooted in the distance. Wind blew dead leaves along the ground, rustling them as they moved. It occurred to Dave that he couldn't remember the last time he'd heard an internal combustion engine.

"The small one back there at the store, the little girl," Dave said, breaking the silence. "She said something before I brained her."

"Bullshit," Tammy said. "Deadwalkers don't talk."

"That's not exactly true," Dave argued. "I've heard them spout a few words, mostly just gibberish. But nothing with any meaning. Nothing that made me think they were self-aware."

"What do you think it said?" Brenda asked.

Dave remained silent.

"Dave, what do you think it said?" Brenda repeated.

"I think I heard the little one say *Mommy*."

"No way," Tammy said. "That's impossible."

"Is it?" Dave asked.

No one answered.

They spent another eight days on the road, passing abandoned cars and skirting random corpses like piles of manure. They saw a few carriers wandering aimlessly off in a distant cornfield, but the road remained otherwise empty. They stopped at two more exits along the way, one offering very little in the way of food and supplies, the other providing considerably more. Most of what they procured was canned, but they also found some dried food inside a grocery store.

As they walked, they talked. The simple job of walking throughout the day precluded most of the more lively conversation, but the nights spent camping provided much more depth to the talk. They discussed the virus, the aftermath, and the scramble to get to the coasts. Tammy impressed upon Dave the differences in how the wealthy and the poor had been treated after the outbreak. Brenda discussed her transformation from broken and overweight victim to survivor.

Dave spoke of Sandy and Jim, not of their murders, but of their lives. It still hurt, but his guilt had waned considerably. He was now just sad and lonely. Through the course of these conversations they learned that all three of them had lost someone close to them to the virus. It was a common thread between otherwise disparate people.

Each night after they spoke they felt a little closer to one another. Tammy softened as the days passed, to the point of even laughing at some of Dave's jokes. Dave surprised himself by even having the frame of mind to tell a joke. Brenda listened to Dave's stories, commenting and laughing along the way.

They continued the pattern; walking, camping and talking, day upon day, night after night. The deserted road presented no major hurdles, and they met no carriers close enough to be a threat, nor did they encounter any threat from the uninfected. At night they could hear the carriers' pitiful and frightening screams, bone-chilling agony drifting in from far away. It reminded them that they had to remain cautious.

On the eighth day they came upon another exit. The ramp lead down to a very large strip mall, chock full of various businesses. They noticed the bright orange colors of a Home Depot, along with a large grocery store and a Sam's Club. Dave was convinced they should check out the Sam's store, as a discount warehouse was likely to have survived the worst of the looting. There was so much there, he figured, that there just had to be something left. Brenda and Tammy agreed and so it was decided.

It took another twenty minutes to reach the exit. Once there, they made their way off the highway and headed toward the Sam's Club. After crossing the barren wasteland of the store's gigantic parking lot, the trio reached the front doors. Both doors were gone, glass broken, tossed to the side.

Brenda drew her pistol and Tammy readied her rifle. Having no gun, Dave produced the baseball bat he'd found back at the 7-Eleven station. It was hard for him to imagine all that had occurred more than a week ago. He shoved the thought of the small carrier out of his mind. He needed to focus.

"This time I think we should stay together," Dave said as they stood in front of the main entrance. "It's big in there, and we need to watch out for each other."

"Fair enough," Tammy replied.

Dave thought it nothing short of amazing that Tammy would concede anything to him at all. Looked like kid gloves had paid off.

Brenda nodded. She looked at Dave. "Whatever you may or may not have heard back at that gas station, you know it doesn't change anything."

Dave didn't answer.

"I'm serious. It doesn't change anything. Those things want to kill us and eat us, period. That little one back there, no matter what you think she may or may not have said, it was still trying to kill you."

"She's right," Tammy added.

Dave nodded.

Brenda pushed. "Promise me you won't forget that."

"Fine," he said. "I promise."

"You sure?"

"Yeah. I'm sure. I'll be fine."

Brenda shot him a dubious look before dropping the topic. "Let's go," she said.

They walked into the darkened store, Brenda in the lead, followed by Tammy with Dave bringing up the rear. It wasn't lost on him that this was another achievement in gaining Tammy's trust. Before she wouldn't have dared turn her back on him. The light was ample near the front door, but was considerably reduced in the inner regions of the large structure. There were some skylights installed throughout the ceiling, and they were providing enough light to operate by.

They walked past the cash registers and then headed deeper into the store, weapons drawn, cautiously searching the aisles for anything useful. It was obvious that others had already been there before them, but as Dave had suspected those survivors were unable to scavenge it all. There were leftovers, and plenty of them.

Pay dirt, Dave thought, smiling in the dim light.

The plan was simple: find as many essentials as possible, stuff their backpacks and get the hell out. Dave had wanted to fill up a shopping cart originally, but the girls argued that they should only take what they could carry. In the end he bent, partly because he thought they were right and partly because he didn't want to cause any rifts in this new partnership between the three of them. Besides, if they'd put it up to a vote he would have lost anyway. Better to concede as a display of good faith.

They made their way further into the deeper regions of the building. There the light began to peter out. The skylights did their job of allowing in just enough light to see, illuminating most of the store in their dim glow. Dave looked back toward the front of the store; the light passing through the front doors looked like bright dots in the distance. The place was huge and they were very far away from the exits. He tried not to think about that.

They filled up on canned foods wherever they found them. Where possible they took the smaller cans; each one was a meal with no waste. Dave picked up a toothbrush along with two tubes of toothpaste. It had been some time since his teeth had seen a good brushing, at least since he'd been raiding houses with Sandy and Jim. He pushed the pain of that memory away; he could mourn when he and the girls were all safe again.

As planned they stayed together, their weapons holstered while they used their hands to fill their backpacks. They worked as quickly as they could, all three of them well aware of just how quickly this gold mine could become a death trap.

Suddenly, they heard footsteps in the store, followed by the sound of low voices. Although Dave couldn't make out the words, he could tell the sound of a conversation when he heard one. He reckoned those voices were not coming from carriers. Carriers spoke gibberish, or at least he had thought so before last week. These voices included no screams and Dave had never met a carrier that didn't scream. That meant they were dealing with the uninfected and as they all knew, the uninfected could be far worse.

Dave held a finger to his lips, shushing the girls. He held up his hand in the universal gesture for 'stop'. He pointed to their weapons and they removed them, catching his drift quickly.

The footsteps approached closer. Despite the echoes Dave was sure he could hear them originating from an aisle running perpendicular to the aisle in which he and girls stood. That meant they were close.

Dave crept to the end of the aisle to wait for the strangers to pass. Brenda and Tammy followed. Despite the strangers' attempts to speak quietly, their voices carried in the openness of the large warehouse. Their footsteps echoed loudly throughout the structure. They were definitely close now.

"Are those carriers?" Brenda whispered.

"I don't think so," Dave whispered back.

"Thieves, maybe?" Tammy asked.

"Maybe," Dave said. He looked into the distance trying to spot any movement. He couldn't see the voices' owners, but he could still hear them.

"You think we can get out without being noticed?" Brenda asked.

"I don't think so," Dave whispered back. "What do you guys think we should do?"

"Surprise them," Tammy said. "We need to act first."

"I don't know about that," Dave said.

"We don't have time to vote on it. They're almost on top of us!" Brenda whispered as loudly as she could.

"Fine," he responded.

"Don't do anything stupid," Tammy whispered.

"I'd give you the same advice," he shot back.

"Shut up, both of you," Brenda said, silencing their bickering. "They're almost here."

As the group of strangers walked into view Dave inhaled deeply. He released the breath, trying to slow his shaking hands. His heart was racing, his knees were wobbly.

It's now or never, he told himself.

Dave stepped out of the shadows, baseball bat in hand, Brenda and Tammy wielding their guns directly behind him.

"Stop right there!" he yelled. "Don't anybody move a fucking muscle!"

Chapter Thirteen

"Zach, Jeremy!" Ed yelled. "Over here!"

Both boys stopped when they heard their father's call. They turned, saw Trish wasn't with them, and ran back to their father. They all made their way toward where Trish's body lay motionless on the ground.

As they reached her they saw more carriers approaching. Ed picked her up quickly, tossing her small body over his shoulder. "Let's go!" he yelled to the boys.

They glanced once more toward the oncoming carriers before following their father. Ed ran, flanked by both boys, as Trish lay slumped and still over his shoulder. They reached the highway and kept going, running until they could run no longer. Periodic glances behind saw the carriers drop off, too sick to continue their pursuit. Once Ed and the boys hit their exhaustion point they slowed to a fast walk, keeping a periodic lookout behind as they kept moving. Each glance backward revealed no carriers. Still, they walked for some time, desperate to put as much distance as possible between themselves and the carriers they'd narrowly escaped.

Even after running a considerable distance they found

they were still in farm country. Ed motioned for the boys to follow as he veered off the road and into a cornfield, penetrating perhaps a dozen yards before stopping. He wanted a chance to check on Trish before continuing any further.

After instructing the boys to keep a lookout, Ed lay Trish down gently on the ground between the cornstalks. He held his hand under her nose and breathed a sigh of relief when he felt warm breath. Trish moaned, her eyes fluttering. She opened them quickly, looking around at the cornstalks before finding Ed.

"What happened?" she asked.

"You passed out while we were running. You're still pretty weak," Ed told her.

"Where are we?"

"We're in a cornfield, just off the highway. We can't stay here though, we have to keep moving."

"Did we outrun them?"

Ed smiled. "We did."

Trish exhaled a sigh of relief. "Oh, that's good. But I don't think I can walk very far."

"That's okay. You're riding piggyback."

Ed helped her to her feet, steadying her when she became dizzy. "Hold on," he said, kneeling down and lifting her to his back. She wrapped her arms around his neck as she rested her head on his shoulder.

"Thank you," she whispered to him.

He grinned. "Don't mention it."

* * *

Ed found he was able to carry Trish further than he'd originally thought he could. She had always been a small girl, and not having a square meal in so long only made her that much lighter. She held on tightly as they walked, while both boys walked on either side of them, keeping their eyes and ears open for threats.

They walked along the highway at a pace that would put serious distance between them and the carriers from the farmhouse. Ed doubted the ones they left behind had the physical stamina to pursue them this far, but it was better safe than sorry. They walked for an hour or so, stopping periodically for food and water, and for Ed to rest his arms. Because they'd kept their bags packed and ready, they still had all their supplies. As such, they had enough food to keep them going for a while.

Eventually daylight began to wane and Ed knew they needed to set up a camp. His arms were becoming extremely weak from the strain of carrying Trish for so long (along with his backpack that she was wearing), and they all had had one hell of a day. The weather wasn't freezing, but it was still very cold. They would definitely need to sleep in their sleeping bags tonight.

He wished they could have had a couple more days, even a week in the farmhouse. Trish really needed warmth, comfort, and rest to properly recover. She had had that in the farmhouse, but on the open road these things were scarce. *Wish in one hand and shit in the other…see which one fills up first*, he thought to himself.

It was what it was, and there wasn't much he could do about it. And there definitely wasn't a goddamn thing he could do about much of anything in the short time before dark fell. They were committed to the road for the night, regardless of Trish's condition.

Before long they happened upon another section of the road flanked by forest. This patch of woods broke up the monotonous cornfields for almost a mile, at least as far as Ed could tell in the fading daylight. He decided this area would do. He desperately wanted to get off the road and under at least some cover before night fell.

They walked off the road and headed into the woods. The canopy of trees blocked some of the sunlight, but since the trees were just starting to bloom there wasn't the heavy ceiling of leaves there would have been in full summer. Ed calculated at most another thirty minutes of useful light while under the trees, enough to build a rudimentary camp.

They chose a place to stop and he had the boys unroll their sleeping bags. They lay the bags down on the layer of plastic they carried with them to keep the fabric from drawing any moisture out of the ground. If not, it would make for a damn cold night. Once the sleeping bag was unfurled, Ed lay Trish gently down on its soft surface.

"I feel cold again," she said softly.

Ed felt her forehead; it was warm again. The fever was back. For how long, he didn't know. The girl not only needed rest, but she also needed heat. He asked both boys to lay down on either side of Trish before covering them all with the other sleeping bag. Combining Trish's body heat with the kids' would hopefully help to keep her warm, making her sleep more restful. He thought the same might be true of the boys too. They really had taken to her.

"I'll take first watch," he told them. "We'll take turns after a few hours. That schedule should take us through the night."

The boys agreed, snuggling up next to Trish. They were all out cold in less than five minutes.

Ed stood, looking at the three of them sleeping so peacefully together. If the girl died Zach and Jeremy would be beside themselves. He liked the idea of them having a mother figure in their life again, but he worried about it ending badly…again.

The thought of his dead wife brought a familiar stab of pain. Worse, he could barely remember Sarah's face now. Memory could be a real motherfucker, erasing the things one wanted to remember while keeping the things one wanted to forget as fresh and alive as the day they happened. This was Ed's case, at least. What he remembered about his dead wife seemed nothing more than an idea, a concept. Specific details of events in their shared life blended together, birthdays, anniversaries, and day-to-day life escaped him. His time with Sarah was like one long dream, as thin and fleeting as it was muddy and garbled.

Clear and ever-present in his mind, however, was the last image of the thing that had once been his wife. Her eyes were wild as she shook with uncontrollable rage. And the screaming; it went on for hours, terrible screams of both madness and frustration. Her only desire at the end was to kill. It didn't matter if the victims were her own flesh and blood, only the maniacal compulsion remained.

That hadn't really been Sarah. Not *his* Sarah, at least. What she'd become was a monster, a wild animal, a vicious creature that would never be satiated, no matter how many times it killed. In the end Ed had had no choice. With no power to heal, in the end he had only the power to clean up the mess, and that really wasn't power at all. That was just responsibility.

At the time he kept four bullets in a magazine in his front pocket, just in case they ran out of all other options. To end his wife's suffering he used one of those four bullets that day. Since then he continued to carry the remaining three, inserted into the special magazine he kept in his pocket.

That special, terrible magazine.

Just in case the worst should happen.

* * *

Ed felt there was a lot to be said for preparation. That much he could control. He also felt there was a lot to be said for luck. Luck, by its nature, he had virtually no control over. They had their share of good luck along the way and, if Ed had to admit it, he might have to give as much credit to luck as he gave to preparation. Luck and preparation were kissing cousins; complimentary conditions that, when delivered in tandem, often meant the difference between living and dying.

Sometimes it was better to be lucky than prepared.

After dawn arrived Ed took stock of his brood. Trish's fever had subsided, lasting only a few hours the prior night. He took this as a good sign. She still needed rest though, and Ed needed a place to allow her that necessity. With no specific plan in mind, Ed and the boys walked back to the highway, still heading west. Trish rode piggyback again, still too weak to walk long distances.

Within an hour they stumbled upon their gift from an indifferent universe. It came in the form of a large RV, abandoned along the highway. Most of the tires were flat and the windshield had a crack in it, but it was otherwise in great condition. When they reached the RV, Ed lowered Trish down on the ground. She was at least strong enough to stand. He tried the front door to the RV and found it unlocked. He opened it and cautiously peeked inside. The keys were still in the ignition.

He drew his gun, ushering Trish and the boys behind an abandoned car for cover. He stepped carefully into the RV, checking for any hostile inhabitants. The investigation proved it was clear, so he directed both boys inside the RV. He helped Trish navigate the steps leading into the vehicle. After he was inside the vehicle, Ed pulled the keys from the ignition, placed them into his pocket, and locked the door behind them.

He turned, taking in the interior of the home on wheels. The inside of the RV was very large. It was so large that the thing could easily be mistaken for a bus. It was warm inside, but not too hot. The cool weather outside kept the interior of the RV at a reasonable temperature. The air was stale, but breathable, and the interior suffered only from a buildup of dust.

Ed cracked a window to allow some fresh air to flow through. He already felt safer in the RV than he did on the open road. He even felt safer than he had at the farmhouse. He wasn't sure why exactly, maybe because the RV was a smaller structure and it just seemed easier to secure the entry points.

Ed motioned for Trish and the boys take a seat on the small couch in the RV's living room. He strolled through the interior, taking inventory, eventually finding himself in a bedroom at the back of the vehicle. In it was a full-size bed, still covered in sheets and blankets.

After identifying the bedroom, Ed walked back to the couch and helped Trish up. He walked her back to the bedroom and helped her out of her coat. Underneath she still wore the nightgown he'd found for her back at the farmhouse. She slipped into the bed and he pulled the covers up to her narrow chin, covering her shoulders. She smiled at him. Ed felt his stomach flutter a little. Ignoring the feeling, he smiled back. Trish closed her eyes, a slight smile still on her pale lips as she dozed off to sleep.

He walked out of the room, closing the door behind him. As he walked past the RV's back door he checked again to make sure it was locked before returning to the children. The boys seemed content to just sit on the couch and play together, so Ed decided to survey the RV a little more closely and see what they had available to them.

The home on wheels sported a kitchen area near the center of the vehicle. Past that, before the bedroom, was an enclosed bathroom area. Strangely enough the RV almost felt larger on the inside than it appeared on the outside. Ed was amazed by how roomy and spacious it was.

He opened cabinets in the kitchen, inspecting the contents. He nearly gasped after opening the first cabinet. Canned food lined the shelves inside. Next to it he opened the second cabinet and found the same thing. Inside the third and final cabinet he found the remnants of a rotten loaf of bread and a desiccated Bundt cake, along with various kitchen utensils.

Ed walked back into the RV's living room, plopping down to think in a plush chair. The way he figured it they could live in the RV for a week or two if needed, a perfect place for Trish to rest and recover. It was also a perfect place for the boys to sleep in a real bed and feel at least some degree of safety, if only temporary. They would need to leave to get water since he didn't trust the water that had been sitting in the RVs tanks for the past three years.

All in all, this was a wonderful find.

Ed sat back in the chair and watched his two boys. They smiled at him and he smiled back, his eyes heavy with fatigue. He was sure the boys had to be tired too. They'd all been through a lot the past couple of days. Escaping death had that effect on people.

"How about you guys take a nap?" he suggested. "You can share the couch."

"But we're not tired," Zach replied.

"Yeah, we're not tired," Jeremy added, as if to offer credibility to his brother's argument.

Ed thought about it. They had locked the RV, drawn the curtains, and no one knew they were there. He could surely nap safely for a bit. "Fine then," he conceded. "You guys stay on the couch and keep your voices down. Don't talk above a whisper. We don't want anyone who might be outside to know we're in here."

Both boys agreed.

Ed lay back in the chair, placing his head on the plush headrest. The chair was like heaven, cradling his aching body. He felt his muscles relax as sleep began to overtake his waking mind.

This is perfect, he thought to himself as sleep swiftly overtook him.

* * *

Ed's eyes opened quickly.

Something was wrong.

Where was he? Where were the boys? Where was Trish?

He sat up in the chair, breathing heavily, as he tried to shake the fog from his mind. Quickly it came back to him. They were in an RV on the highway. Trish was sleeping in a bed near the back of the vehicle. He looked over at the couch; both boys were out cold, sleeping on opposite ends of the couch. Ed breathed a sigh of relief as he waited for his racing heart to slow.

The light was getting dimmer inside the RV. He wondered how much time had passed since he'd fallen asleep. They'd found the RV around midday, so by his estimates they must have been asleep for six hours or more. He hadn't understood how exhausted he'd been. Apparently everyone else had been as well.

He stood up and stretched, listening to the sound of his knees and his back popping. He was getting old, and living on the road as they did only brutalized his body further. It was the way of the world now, whether he liked it or not.

He checked the kids again before walking to the back of

the vehicle. He gently opened the door and checked in on Trish. She was still asleep, the covers rising and falling slightly in the dim light. He smiled at the sight. He hadn't expected to be so fond of the girl so quickly.

With Trish's and the boys' welfare and comfort tended to, Ed walked back to the living room of the RV and retrieved his canteen from his backpack. He took a long drink of the tepid water before sitting back down in the chair again. He didn't want to wake the boys. If they were hungry they'd wake up and find him.

Glorious sleep quickly called to him again, that irresistible siren song of peaceful escape and rejuvenation. Within a minute he was asleep again.

That day all four of them slept the entire night. It was the first time any of them had slept a full night in years.

* * *

The following morning Ed awoke feeling better than he had in months, maybe even years. Both boys stirred shortly afterward, both complaining they had to pee. Ed did too. The RV provided a bathroom with a functional toilet, so all three made quick use of it.

After they'd answered the call of Nature, Ed checked in on Trish. He found her lying in bed with her eyes open, looking at the wall.

"You okay?" he asked her.

"I'm great. Feeling better. How long did I sleep?"

"Long enough. You're feeling better and that's what matters."

"I am feeling better. And I'm hungry again too."

"Excellent," he said. Ed walked over next to her, placing the back of his hand on her forehead. She still felt a little warm, but not hot. "Looks like your fever has gone down again."

"Well, that's good," Trish said.

Ed nodded. "Sure is. Hey, I'm about to make breakfast. Not sure exactly what's on the menu, but I'm hoping it'll be something better than Spam and beef jerky."

Trish smiled. "We can always hope, can't we?"

Ed walked out of the room and into the kitchen. Both boys were in the living room playing with a deck of playing cards they'd found inside the RV. It looked as if that would occupy them for some time, so Ed left them to it.

After opening the first cabinet and scanning over the canned food labels Ed eventually chose green beans and corn. He also found some spud flakes in a tin. It had been a long time since any of them had had a meal that substantial in one sitting. His mouth watered at the thought of it.

He found some bowls in another cabinet and a can opener in one of the kitchen drawers. Using the can opener, he removed the tops of the cans, dividing up the contents between the four of them in roughly equal portions. He called the boys over to the kitchen and they carried their bowls into the bedroom to eat with Trish. They ate in silence, all of them ravenous and enjoying every last bite of their lukewarm vegetables and mashed potatoes. They washed it all down with the water they had in their canteens, using up most of it. Ed thought it might easily qualify as the best meal he'd ever had.

Once they'd finished eating, Ed had the boys clean up. Trish said she wanted to get out of bed and go sit in the living room for a while, so Ed allowed the boys to use the playing cards in the bedroom while he helped her to the living room. Once there, Ed offered her the plush chair. She accepted, so Ed took a seat on the couch across from her.

For a while they just sat, silent, enjoying the feeling of their full bellies.

Eventually Trish broke the silence. "I'm sorry I almost shot you," she said.

"That? Oh, I'd almost forgotten about it," he told her, smiling.

"I just didn't know if I could trust you then," she said.

"Well, the important thing is you didn't actually shoot me."

She paused, taking a deep breath. "I wasn't sure if I could trust anybody again, not after what happened."

Ed didn't reply.

"Three guys caught me while I was sleeping one night," she went on to say. "They drugged me and they raped me for days."

"That's terrible," Ed said, somber. He couldn't begin to imagine what that must have been like.

"I killed at least one of them, maybe even two of them. Stabbed one of the assholes to death." She stared at the walls of the RV. "The other one I messed up pretty bad."

"What about the third guy?" Ed asked.

"Don't know. I don't even remember what he looked like, they had me so doped up."

"I'm really sorry to hear that. But you got away, right? You escaped and you survived. That's what matters now."

Trish nodded. "The last thing I can remember is walking toward that Target building, thinking that if I could just find some food and water there I'd be okay. After that, zilch. I don't remember anything else until I pulled the gun on you in the bedroom of the farmhouse."

Ed shifted in his seat. He called to the boys to make sure they were okay before refocusing his attention on Trish. Even in the relative safety of the RV they seemed too far away. It was a habit that kept them all alive.

"Have you ever killed anyone, I mean anyone not infected?" Trish asked.

"No," he replied. "I've been lucky so far." He didn't mention Sarah. Not yet.

"I keep thinking I should feel badly about it," Trish continued, "but the truth is I'm glad he's dead. I'd kill him again if I could. Does that make me a monster too?"

"They did horrible things to you. Of course not."

"You know what my only regret is? I didn't get the chance to kill the third one."

Silence followed as they sat.

"It was fortunate our paths crossed," Ed said, smiling.

Trish returned the smile, her eyes wet around the edges. She nodded. "Yeah, it sure was." She changed the subject. "So what's your story, Ed? How long have you guys been on the road? How'd you end up there in the first place?"

Ed took a deep breath. "We've been on the road for a couple years. We spent the first year after the outbreak in a border town along the east coast. After the first year the town ran out of food and people started getting sick. Really sick, stuff unseen in decades. It didn't take long to figure out that we needed to get out of there. We packed up what little we had left and just walked out."

"You and boys?"

A pause. "My wife was with us then."

"Sorry."

"It's okay. It was a long time ago," he told her. That was a lie. It seemed like it was only yesterday to him. But he knew that Trish had her own losses to bear and she didn't need his too.

Trish said: "I lost someone I loved too. I think everyone did."

"Sorry to hear that," he told her.

Trish nodded. "His name was Tim and he was great. I still miss him a lot."

They sat in silence again. Ed liked this girl more and more. She was tough. A fighter.

"So where are we headed?" she asked.

"Which version do you want?" he asked her. "The optimistic version, or the pessimistic version?"

"How about both? That way I can decide which one I like better."

"West, toward Saint Louis." Ed told her about the radio transmission he'd received and the faith the boys placed in the city by the river being a suitable safe haven.

Trish's face was earnest. "What do you think, Ed? Do you have faith?"

"Whatever faith I had I lost a long time ago," he said, "but for those boys in there, I'll believe in whatever it takes."

"Sounds like you still have at least some faith left, Ed Brady."

"The city is all we have left."

Trish fixed Ed in a steady gaze. "Well, if you'll have me, I'm on board."

Ed couldn't help but grin. "We'd love to have you come with us," he told her. That wasn't a lie.

"Then it's a deal." She looked down at her hands, pausing for a moment. "Ed?"

"Yeah?"

"Thanks again, I mean it."

"Don't mention it."

"I really owe you guys. You went out of your way to help me, a total stranger. You risked your lives."

Ed felt his face flush. Her graciousness demanded his modesty. "Don't fret about it, we're square."

"You risked your boys' lives," she said.

Ed nodded. "You need some rest," he told her, changing the subject. "There's a full-size bed back there with your name on it. You go rest up while the boys and I fetch some water. We'll lock up the camper while we're gone."

"Don't you think I should come with you?"

Ed shook his head. "I don't think that's a good idea. You're not roadworthy just yet. It's too dangerous. Besides, I can't carry you anymore. I'm not as young as I used to be, you know." He grinned, pointing to the gray hair around his temples.

Trish laughed, the sound of it like music to Ed's ears.

* * *

Ed and the boys carried their canteens with them, plus six other containers with lids they found in the RV. During the trip out, Ed remembered seeing a small stream about a quarter-mile east of the RV, down in a gully within the woods. He hoped it was fresh enough to suffice for a watering hole. Between the canteens and the containers Ed hoped they could squeeze two days out of the water they were collecting. The safety of the RV was comforting, and the more they stayed inside it the less they exposed themselves to peril.

It took twenty minutes of walking to make it to the stream. They passed the normal collection of random, rotten corpses and deserted cars while they walked the highway. Once, in the distance, they heard the tormented scream of a carrier, but it sounded very far away. Regardless, it reminded them to be quick about their work.

Within ten minutes of arriving at the watering hole they were fully filled and on their way back to the RV. They made the round trip in a little more than an hour. Although the trip proved uneventful, Ed felt more exposed than he usually did. The threat of danger was more palpable somehow, closer and more likely. Maybe it had something to do with the feeling of safety provided by the RV. Though only a respite from the horrors of the outbreak, he'd already grown accustomed to it. He had to be careful about getting too comfortable; the lull of temporary safety and comfort could be dangerous.

For better or worse, they were going to the city. Although it might be a pipe dream, the city was the only thing that could provide long-term protection for his boys.

And that was all that mattered to him.

* * *

The water lasted two days, just as Ed had hoped. Though the stream had been fast-flowing, Ed didn't trust that the water was parasite-free, so they boiled the water they drank. Trish slept most of the days away, usually stirring around lunch and dinner before falling back to peaceful sleep. Day by day her strength was slowly returning, and she showed no signs of fever since the night they'd slept in the woods.

The weather began to warm up, but the mild spring conditions kept the RV's internal temperature at a very comfortable level. They cracked a couple of windows when it got warm, creating a draft that ran through the vehicle, cooling it quite nicely.

Ed and the boys went back out for water every couple of days, using the same stream each time. It remained fast-flowing, the water clean and free of dirt.

With spring came rains, and showers covered them off and on for several days throughout their stay. Besides one tiny leak the RV remained watertight, and the sound of the raindrops dancing on the roof was pleasantly hypnotic.

During the rains they placed multiple receptacles out to catch the rainwater, including all the empty cans from the food they'd been consuming. The rains came hard and fast, and they collected enough to keep them from going back to the stream for an extra day, which would no doubt be swollen with muddy water.

After four days of nearly day-long resting, Trish's sleeping patterns adjusted to that of a normal person and she no longer felt the need to sleep all day. Her appetite had returned in full-force, and the four of them found themselves eating better than they had in years. Watching the boys eat a meal of some real substance, even canned food served at room temperature, made Ed feel good. They deserved so much more than what they had.

Sleeping arrangements had emerged on their own. Trish slept in the bed, Ed in the plush chair, and the boys took the couch each night. Often the boys would fall asleep in the bed while Trish and Ed talked into the night. Once asleep, Ed would then transport both boys, one by one, still sleeping, to the couch so Trish could have the bed.

During their time in the RV their conversations centered on a multitude of topics. They discussed their lives on the road before they met each other. They talked about music and movies, neither of which had been made in years. They hypothesized about the origin of the virus and compared notes on their observations of carrier behavior. Talk of the new world.

Ed didn't talk about Sarah, and Trish didn't talk about Tim.

Often the boys would sit up with Ed and Trish before bed. Zach and Jeremy reminisced about their own young lives before the outbreak. They spoke fondly of school, their friends, and, on occasion, their mother. They loved her and they missed her greatly. So did Ed. He was happy they remembered her so dearly.

The boys would often spend time with Trish, talking about anything and everything important to them. Trish listened closely, keeping up a wonderful dialogue. Ed smiled as he observed this; to watch her with the boys was to believe the two might very well be her own. It had been so long since they'd experienced the maternal qualities of a female.

On one particularly rainy day of their stay, Ed and the boys found themselves washing their filthy clothes in the rain with a bar of soap they'd discovered the RV's bathroom. Though cold, the rain provided them an opportunity to get clean again, prompting Ed to uncover a new appreciation for the phrase *cleanliness is next to godliness*. Trish joined in after some time, though Ed instructed the boys to look away, providing her with at least some privacy. After their refreshing outdoor shower, they all wrapped themselves in towels from the same bathroom while their clothes dried.

Once inside, Trish tended to the boys' grooming, drying their hair, clipping their fingernails, and cleaning their faces. With a comb from the bathroom, she worked the knots out of their hair before trimming it into something presentable. She offered the same service to Ed and he gladly took her up on it. After a quick rinse back in the rain they all looked more presentable than they had in years. It was an immeasurable boost to their worn spirits.

Before bed Trish told the boys stories, a mashup of half-remembered fairy tales and fables from early in her childhood. Occasionally she'd concoct a story or two of her own, something incorporating a character the boys wanted to hear about. She held the boys in rapt attention while she spun tales of dragons, knights, goblins and maidens. They listened with unbreakable concentration as she described werewolves and vampires ravaging the countryside. She stopped short of zombie stories. Reality was enough for that.

Ed watched all this with a mixture of love and trepidation. After so many years on the road, after so many terrible things, after so long without their mother, he still had his sons. And not just in body, but in mind. Their spirits were unbreakable; they saw the worst that nature and humanity could throw at them and they refused to give up.

They deserved someone like Trish and the thought that she could be taken away from them in an instant weighed heavily on his mind. Before the outbreak, back when the world was sane, everything had been taken for granted. The truth was that even then everything was just as fleeting as it was now, just as transient, just as fragile and just as precious.

The only difference was that now he knew it.

And he would never forget it.

* * *

Almost two weeks after they happened upon the RV, Ed found himself sitting in the plush chair he'd grown to love, talking to Trish and watching the light outside the windows dissipate into inky darkness. Trish sat on the couch, relaxed and healthier than she'd been in years. The boys were asleep in her bed, the playing cards they had found either erected into small houses or scattered all over the floor of the bedroom.

Ed could see Trish had put on some weight since they'd discovered her, nearly dead inside a ransacked Target store. But it wasn't just her weight gain or grooming that made her shine. It was her drive and determination returning as well. She was getting back to her old self again. The frightened and desperate creature he'd met was giving way to a strong and defiant woman.

It was time for all of them to move on.

"We need to leave soon," Ed said, looking toward her in the fading light. "This place is great, but it's really only temporary."

She nodded. "I know. We're wearing out our welcome here." She gestured with her hand, her voice taking on a grand tone. "The city awaits."

Ed chuckled. "We can take the rest of the canned food with us; I think we can carry most of it."

"I agree," she added. "I've developed an insatiable appetite for lukewarm green beans, so those have to come with. Of course, I'd kill for a Big Mac right now."

Ed laughed out loud. She wasn't exaggerating; she wolfed down green beans like they were jelly beans. And a

Big Mac did sound good.

"I don't want to tell the boys tonight," he told her. "I'll tell them tomorrow morning."

"Do you think they'll be disappointed?"

"A little, I'm sure. They like this little house on wheels. I think though they'll be less disappointed since you're coming with us."

Trish smiled.

"They like you. When you were sick, they worried. They helped. They need someone like you around. They're better off for it." He paused. "So am I."

Trish smiled. "You know, Ed, I do think you're one of the good guys."

Ed held up a hand. "I'm just a regular guy."

"And modest, too."

They sat together in silence, watching the last fragments of daylight succumb to the darkness of night. Ed felt his eyelids grow heavy. His thoughts were rambling the way they did just before he fell asleep.

"Ed?" Trish called out softly in the near darkness.

"Yeah."

"Can you hold me?"

"You sure?"

"Yeah. I'm sure."

Without speaking, Ed rose. He walked to the couch and lay down behind her.

"Just for a while," she told him. Ed placed an arm around her and she snuggled into his body. Ed felt strangely awkward while also feeling perfectly natural. He wondered if maybe after so many years alone and without his wife, the natural feeling was what caused the awkwardness.

Within minutes Trish dozed off in his arms. Before he knew it, Ed was asleep too.

* * *

The following morning Ed and Trish awoke on the couch together. Ed sat up, looking down at Trish as she stirred, eventually opening her eyes.

She smiled at him. "Did we sleep the whole night

through?"

"Apparently so. I'm going to go check on the boys."

A quick check on the boys revealed they were still sound asleep. Both Ed and Trish used the RV's bathroom. Before long they'd be back to eliminating outside again, a thought Ed didn't exactly relish.

Ed and Trish packed the remaining canned foods into their backpacks. Trish had no backpack, so they used a pillowcase from the bed to hold the overflow. They would eat for a good long while on the canned food they were taking with them.

The boys awoke during the packing. Ed explained to them that they were leaving, and they took the news with no noticeable disappointment. Their city awaited them, after all. They were ecstatic to learn that Trish would be accompanying them to the city. He was sure that helped to offset any of the disappointment they might have felt leaving their life in the RV behind.

After all their things were packed they were ready to leave. Ed left the door unlocked and the key in the ignition, should anyone else find the RV and also consider it useful. The four of them took a last look at their home on wheels before saying their final goodbyes. It was as if they were leaving behind an old friend; a friend for whom they all cared deeply, but knew down deep inside they would never see again.

* * *

With so much food in their packs they passed up the next two exits over the subsequent days. Each day they walked they saw little to no carrier activity. The screams could be heard occasionally, and the bodies still lay in dark piles, but the deadwalkers never showed. This both pleased Ed and worried him. He hoped the deadwalkers' numbers were thinning, but he feared that instead they might simply be congregating elsewhere. And he didn't want to think about what kind of nightmare that could be.

Trish traveled well. She kept up with Ed and the boys and she was able to walk for long distances without tiring easily. She was functioning near full capacity now that her infection was gone. She didn't talk much while they walked; she was mostly focused on keeping an eye out for threats. Ed wasn't surprised she'd been able to stay alive for so long on her own. She had a natural knack for survival.

Ed sometimes found himself, typically at the end of a long day, waxing nostalgic for the safety and comfort of the RV. He shook those thoughts from his mind as quickly as he could manage. That kind of thinking would get them nowhere. It was living in the past, and living in the past was what got a person killed. Focusing on the future was critical to their survival.

Their rations held out for longer than they expected, but they eventually began to dry up. It was time to find a suitable exit and resupply. They walked for another day, sleeping near the edge of the road that night, taking turns with guard duty, and trying to forget what it had been like to sleep in a real bed, surrounded by four walls and roof over their heads.

The following morning they got moving at the break of dawn. Within a couple of hours an exit appeared on the horizon. With their supplies not yet completely exhausted, Ed wasn't convinced it was necessary to stop. However, once he saw the large discount warehouse ahead he decided stopping was imperative. The likelihood of again finding so much in one place, just there for the taking, was slim. It would be foolish to pass up such an opportunity. Trish and the boys agreed.

Another twenty minutes of walking brought them to the exit; another ten minutes brought them to the front door of the warehouse. They huddled together, forming their game plan: stay together always, look for nonperishable foodstuffs, replace worn-out equipment and clothing, and keep an eye out for threats.

And always know the exits.

Ed and the boys suited up, covering their eyes with their goggles and their mouths with the face masks. Trish reused her impromptu face mask Ed had made her back at the farmhouse, tying it over her mouth. It wasn't much, but it was better than nothing. He hoped they could find more masks inside.

They entered the store, guns drawn. Inside it was reasonably well-lit near the front of the store, but became progressively darker near the back. There were skylights that provided enough light for them to see by. The shadows, on the other hand, made Ed very nervous. He knew what could be lurking in them.

The group continued with extreme care. They combed the canned food aisles, taking what they could carry. Quickly they located the clothing aisles. Though dusty, the clothing was otherwise fine. While there they changed their shirts, each person in the group finding their size as quickly as they could. They tossed their old clothing to the side.

After suiting up with new shirts, they headed toward the back of the store to look for goggles, face masks, or other miscellaneous supplies. Instead they found defunct freezers filled with rotten, desiccated food. Undeterred, the group turned around and headed back toward the front of the store to see if they could find the actual hardware aisle. They whispered to each other as infrequently as possible, trying to keep their voices down. The natural reverb inside the large building allowed sound to travel both well and far.

They walked, still whispering to each other when suddenly a man stepped in front of them. Behind him were two women, both holding guns. Instinctively, Ed pointed his pistol directly at the man. Jeremy and Zach trained their weapons on both women in the party opposite them.

"Stop right there!" the man yelled. "Don't anybody move a fucking muscle!"

Chapter Fourteen

"Put the guns down now!" Dave yelled. He stood slightly in front of Brenda and Tammy, baseball bat raised. He wished now he had a damn gun.

Ed didn't reply. He kept the pistol pointed at Dave while he ushered both boys behind him.

"I said don't fucking move!" Dave yelled again.

"You need to calm down," Ed warned.

"You shut up," Brenda said, raising the pistol.

Dave's thoughts raced. He felt transported back in time, back to the place where he'd cost his wife and friend their lives. He couldn't make that mistake again. He *wouldn't* make that mistake again. He took two steps back until he was standing between both the girls.

Zach and Jeremy kept their guns pointed where they were, but Ed could see they were afraid. Their hands trembled lightly as they struggled to keep up a calm exterior.

"Boys, just hold tight," Ed told his sons. "Don't do anything unless I say."

"What's with the masks?" Tammy asked. "You infected?"

"Don't you worry about us," Ed replied.

"She asked a question. Give her an answer," Dave ordered.

Ed stared at Dave, his expression cold. Ed had no doubt he could put a bullet through this man's head in less than a second, but what happened after that was anybody's guess. Unfortunately this wasn't a situation where they could just shoot their way out.

"I said calm down," Ed told him.

"Fuck off. Answer the question," Dave repeated.

Ed paused, formulating his next move. Compliance seemed the best way to diffuse this bomb, or at least to mitigate escalation. "Listen to me, nobody's infected here. We're only here for some food and supplies."

Dave considered the man's answer. Those masks; they all wore them except for the girl, but even her mouth was covered with a strip of cloth. They didn't appear infected, but one never knew. He considered that they might be thieves, but the children… Still, children could be trained to do horrible things. Maybe this guy and the boys kidnapped the girl with them. She sure looked like hell.

"Who's the girl?" Dave asked.

"None of your goddamn business," Ed replied. "Tell those girls of yours to lower those guns."

"He doesn't tell us what to do," Tammy replied. "We don't belong to him."

Defiant to the end, Dave thought. If Dave wanted to be taken seriously he needed a gun. He had to put some fear in them. "Brenda, give me that gun," Dave said.

"I've got this, Dave," Brenda told him.

"Brenda, hand it over."

"Goddammit, Dave, we got this!" Tammy said.

"Give me that fucking gun!" Dave yelled, his eyes wild. Before Brenda could protest, Dave reached out, yanking the gun from her hand.

"You asshole!" Brenda screamed as she took a swing at him.

Dave dodged the swing and pointed the gun at Ed. "Do you hear me now?"

Ed didn't reply. Things has escalated from bad to worse.

"Not this time," Dave said in a low voice. "It won't go down the same way this time."

"What are you doing, Dave?" Brenda yelled.

"Shut up, Brenda," Dave said. "I'm not going to let this happen twice."

Now Brenda was worried. After what Dave had told them after coming out of his stupor, she had serious concern they were on a runaway freight train.

"You all need to calm down so we can talk," Ed told them. The man with the gun was a loose canon, even the girl with him showed concern. Ed wasn't seeing a simple way out of this.

"Talk…right," Dave said. "You come in here, sneak up on us in masks and then you tell me you want to talk. The only reason the three of us aren't dead is because we caught you before you could catch us."

Dave put his finger on the trigger of Brenda's gun. Could he get all three of them before they fired? He could get the man in front, but maybe not the kids. The kids! Could he really kill children? They were only children, for Christ's sake! But would they do it to him if given the chance? The last time he'd been so sure what to do and look how that turned out. His confusion mounted; nothing felt right, nothing felt certain. Now he doubted everything. He wouldn't allow himself or either of the girls to be killed, that much he knew. These girls had saved his life.

He couldn't make the same kind of mistake again and allow anyone else to die.

* * *

Ed stood, gun pointed, considering his options. He knew he had to take action; he couldn't wait forever. The man in front of him could now kill him with a single pull of the trigger. This man, Dave, wasn't responding to reason, so Ed felt his only choice now was to use the only leverage he had: more guns. It would mean involving the kids in a gamble, but if he didn't it could mean that none of them survived. "Jeremy, draw a bead on the girl with the rifle," Ed told his youngest son. He kept his stare focused on Dave. "Zach, cover the other girl."

Ed watched Brenda tense. Her eyes darted back and forth. He'd just gotten a rise, if nothing else. He hoped it meant things were going his way.

"Daddy," Jeremy said, shaken. "They're not carriers. They're not infected."

"Just do what I tell you, son," Ed told him. "Trust me."

As instructed, Jeremy pointed the gun at Tammy. Ed saw no perceptible reaction from her. He focused back on Dave. "Look, Dave. I need you to listen to reason and think this thing through. You have two guns, we have three. Odds are we'll get all of you before you get us." He wasn't sure he believed that himself, but he hoped it sounded convincing.

"Like hell you will," Dave replied.

"You willing to chance that?" Ed asked.

"Are *you*?" Dave returned. "Are you willing to bet your children on it?"

Ed didn't answer.

They stood this way, guns raised, staring at each other. No one moved. Ed's heart raced as the seconds ticked by like hours.

Suddenly, from somewhere in the warehouse, they heard a voice. "Looks like what we got here is a Mexican Standoff."

Ed had no idea who this new voice belonged to, but the last thing he wanted was even more trouble from even more people with even more guns. Then he saw a shadow of a man appear off to his right. The man stood by a pallet of dog food, hands on his hips, with two pistols dangling from holsters attached to a belt around his waist. He looked like something out of a spaghetti western.

"Who the fuck are you?" Dave yelled, his confusion and frustration more obvious than ever.

Ed watched Dave closely. Dave's face grew red and sweat beaded on his forehead, despite the cool air. The guy was running hot and Ed feared anything could go wrong now.

"Name's Mitchell. Mitchell Burdette. Same as my daddy,

but not his daddy before him." The man chuckled to himself. No one joined him.

"What is this shit?" Dave yelled, exasperated. He pointed the gun away from Ed and directly toward Mitchell. "Who are *you*?" he yelled.

"Whoa now, son," Mitchell said from the shadows. His hands never left his hips, nor did he flinch when he saw Dave point the gun his way. "First off, you ought not point that thing at me. I don't have a weapon drawn, so you're breaking the rules of the Mexican Standoff, least as I understand 'em to be." Mitchell spoke with a thick Appalachian accent; not quite southern, but definitely not northern. Somewhere right in between.

"Give me one reason I shouldn't shoot you where you stand," Dave said to the man, pistol still raised.

Mitchell paused a moment. "Well, the first reason is, near as I can figure, I'll get you first."

Dave paused. "No you won't," he said. "I'll put a bullet through your head before you ever know what hit you."

Ed heard the conviction draining from Dave's voice. The guns on Mitchell's hips, along with his confident stance told Ed that Dave might have overplayed his hand.

Mitchell laughed out loud. "Holy smokes, son. That's one bold statement. Keep in mind you just met me; we ain't even got acquainted yet. Let's just say that your skill assessment might be lacking just a bit."

Dave kept the gun pointed at Mitchell, but said nothing.

Mitchell continued. "Even though you might not know it, none of you folks really want to shoot each other. If you did, you'd already done it. You're looking for reasons not to, but you're afraid. I'm gonna help you folks with that. I'm what you might call an 'impartial third party'. So, first off, let's everybody just take a deep breath and relax."

Mitchell turned his attention toward Ed first. "Now, you there with those young boys. What's your name, friend?"

Ed wasn't sure what to do. The entire thing was so bizarre. Should he play along? For the time being he decided to. It was better than a shoot out. "My name is Ed," he replied, his eyes and his gun never leaving Dave.

"What's your boys' names?"

"Zach and Jeremy."

"How about the little lady there? What's your name, missy?"

Trish answered for herself, following Ed's lead and telling Mitchell her name.

"Well, it's nice to meet you, Trish," Mitchell replied. "You too, Ed. And same to you, masters Zach and Jeremy. Now, as a fair and unbiased third party, can I ask why the three of you are wearing those masks?"

"Protection," Ed replied.

"From what? The virus?" Mitchell asked.

Ed nodded again. "Right."

"Fair enough," Mitchell replied. "Not sure how much good they'll do. Mind pullin' 'em down a bit, so we can see who you are?"

Ed shook his head. "I don't want to risk it."

"I don't see much risk, not here at least. I don't have one and I'm okay."

"You say you are, but how do I know?"

"I suppose you don't. I've been here for a while though, months now."

Ed thought about it. The risk was probably low. "Do what he says," he told Trish and the boys.

They followed his directions.

"Those are some handsome young boys you got there, Ed," Mitchell said. "And a mighty pretty lady too, I might add." Mitchell smiled in the dimly lit room, gesturing toward Trish before turning his attention to Dave.

Dave kept Brenda's gun trained on Mitchell, but if Mitchell was afraid, he never let it show. He asked Dave: "Now, what's your name, son?"

"Fuck off," Dave replied.

"It ain't a tough question. Is it gonna kill you to answer? Way things are shaping up here it's looking like it might get you killed if you don't."

Dave paused for a moment. Ed hoped he was

considering Mitchell's veiled threat very wisely.

Finally Dave answered. "My name is Dave."

"Pleasure, Dave. How about the ladies?"

"I'm Brenda, this is Tammy," Brenda replied, gesturing toward Tammy.

"Good to meet you three," Mitchell said. "Brenda, right?"

"Yeah."

"Now, I've got a question for you, honey. What brings you into my little corner of the Badlands?"

"You live here?" Brenda asked.

"That I do. I guess you'd have to call it squatter's rights, but I occupy it all the same. Have for a while now, maybe six months. Hard to remember time anymore, what with the calendars useless and my memory even more useless."

"We're walking the highway, heading west," Brenda replied.

"Along I-64?"

"Right. We stopped off for supplies and then all this happened," she said, waving her hand toward the group.

"I see. How about you, Ed? What's your story? You folks walking the highway too?"

"You could say that. All we want is to pass through, unharmed."

"Sounds reasonable enough on both ends," Mitchell said. "So, if you could indulge me the opportunity to summarize, the three of you were just walking the road," he said to Dave and his group. "And you folks," he motioned toward Ed and his group, "the four of you, you got pretty much the same story. Am I right so far?"

No one responded.

"I'll take your lack of objection as a 'yes'," Mitchell said. "So, since this is obviously just two groups of people, minding their own business, who happened to surprise each other, how about everybody put the guns away?"

Dave replied: "Not until they do."

"Don't count on that, friend," Ed replied.

Mitchell wouldn't be persuaded. "Would it be safe to say

that everybody wants to put the guns down?"

Still no response.

"Well, I didn't hear a 'no', so I'm going to assume the answer is 'yes'. So, let's say, just for the sake of argument, that everybody lowers those guns at the same time. I could give a count, say to three maybe, then everybody puts the guns back into their holsters, pockets, or wherever they choose to keep 'em. Then we all talk. Would everybody be willing to consider that?"

Ed responded first. "I'd consider it, provided they do the same."

"I'd be willing too, provided they follow through," Dave said.

"Well, shit, this thing's about as good as settled. I'm gonna count to three then, just like I said I would. On three let's see all the guns lowered." He took a breath and counted. "One, two…three."

At first, no one moved, but within a few seconds, gun barrels were lowered to the ground. Everyone stood there, silent, waiting to see what happened.

Suddenly Dave sat down on the ground, dropping Brenda's gun to the floor. He placed his face in his hands. The rest of the group remained still. They all stayed this way for some time, as if to test the newly formed truce.

Eventually Mitchell broke the silence. "Whew, that was a doozy. Now, any of you folks drink coffee?"

And with that the standoff was over.

* * *

Both groups sat on opposite sides of the aisle in the warehouse, on top of the wooden boards that made up the surface of the lowest shelf. Dave, Brenda, and Tammy sat on one side; Ed, Trish, Zach, and Jeremy sat on the other. Trish and Ed sat with both boys in front of them. Dave sat between Brenda and Tammy, his face in his hands, Brenda's hand resting on his back. Tammy stared at the concrete floor.

No one spoke.

Mitchell was off getting coffee for his new guests. A few

minutes later he returned with a small propane burner, two coffee pots, and the plastic filter cup from an automatic coffee maker. The cup was lined with a paper filter and filled with coffee grounds. One of the coffee pots was filled with water; the other was empty. He set up the contraption on the floor between the two parties.

"Instructions say not to burn this indoors, but I figure this place is so big and drafty it might as well be outside," Mitchell said as he pulled a lighter from his pocket and turned on the propane burner, touching the yellow flame to the invisible flow of gas. It transformed into a strong, blue flame upon contact with the flow of propane. He adjusted the flame lower before placing the coffee pot full of water on top of the burner to boil.

"Even after the fall of civilization I still have to have my coffee," he mused. "Some things never change, it seems." Mitchell sat on the floor, his back against one of the shelves and his legs crossed. "Carriers don't often come in here, despite how much food there is. Seems like they can't get the boxes open. So, Ed…headed west, eh? How long you been on the road?"

"Two years, give or take," Ed replied.

"Where'd you come from?"

"Border town, along the east coast. It never really had a name, at least not one worth a shit. Once the food ran out we took to the road."

"The four of you?"

"No," Trish said. "I came later. Ed and his boys here saved my life."

Mitchell smiled. "You're a good man, Ed. Too many folks leaving other folks for dead nowadays. It's the way of world now, I suppose, but it's a trend worth bucking." He glanced at Zach and Jeremy. "Those are some fine-looking boys you got there, Ed."

"Thank you," Ed replied.

"It's a miracle you still got 'em, safe and sound, you know."

"I do," Ed replied. "It's about the only thing I know for

sure anymore."

Mitchell nodded, pausing for a moment, drifting off. "Good man," he said, nodding.

Suddenly Dave looked up from his hands, fixing his eyes on Mitchell. "You could have been killed back there. Why did you step in? Why risk it? Why not just snipe us all from a distance?"

Mitchell took a deep breath before exhaling. "'Cause it was the right thing to do."

"That's it?" Dave asked.

"Well, sure. Ain't that reason enough?"

"Things aren't that simple anymore."

"Actually," Mitchell replied, "they are." He took another deep breath. "Look, son, there are two lists in life, a list of things we *can* do and a list of things we *should* do. I work off the second one. Just because you *can* do a thing don't always mean you *should*."

Wisps of steam rose from the water in the coffee pot. Mitchell turned off the burner, removing the pot from the heat just before it came to a boil. He slowly poured the hot water through the coffee grounds, filling the empty pot with the dark and rich liquid. The strong smell of brewing coffee filled the air around them, reminding Ed of Saturday mornings at home, back in his previous life, when he still had the luxury of taking his freedom and safety for granted.

"It ain't so bad in this place," Mitchell went on as he poured the rest of the hot water through the coffee grounds. "It's drafty and cold in the winter, but pretty damn nice right about now. Damn near anything you'd need too, food, supplies, or what have you. I sleep up high, on the tip-top of one these shelves. It's high enough to be out of the way, but also high enough to make me a bit nervous. The deadwalkers don't seem to come in here too much, but every now and then one of those poor bastards will wander around until it finds its way back out again."

"Did you come from one of the border towns, or were you just unlucky enough to get left behind with the unwanted few?" Brenda asked.

Mitchell poured the filtered coffee into the Styrofoam cups, handing a cup to all the adults. He passed over Zach and Jeremy. "Since you boys likely don't drink coffee I think I might be able to round up some juice boxes, maybe even some candy bars once we get through all our jabbering here. Provided it's okay with your dad."

Ed nodded. Zach and Jeremy beamed at the opportunity for sweets.

Mitchell answered Brenda's question. "I never made it to the border. I lived in West Virginia, which ain't that far away from all those towns that sprung up around Virginia Beach right after the outbreak."

Mitchell sat down on the floor, leaned against the shelves and took a sip of coffee. "Back before the government disappeared they were sending folks to the coast in army trucks. I headed west; business to take care of. Turned out that didn't quite work out for me, so I just kept going. I guess I've been on the road for about three years now.

"One thing you got wrong though; there were more left behind than went to the coasts. There were lots of reasons; not enough trucks, not enough money to bribe the army, or just not important enough to take. Most of the ones left behind aren't around anymore to tell you themselves. Lots of unlucky folks that didn't take sick shortly after the outbreak were ate by the ones that did."

Mitchell took another sip of black coffee. "I can tell you this, though; a lot of those deadwalkers are dying off. It's slow, but I think it's happening. That first year, I ain't quite sure how I made it. I guess the good Lord musta been watching out for me. They were everywhere then, and they were in better shape too. A lot of 'em wasn't even paralyzed yet. They were pretty fast, some of them." He chuckled lightly. "I guess I was faster."

"That business you had to take care of; when that fell through why didn't you go back to the coast?" Trish asked.

"I guess I could probably ask you the same question," he replied, smiling.

"Fair enough," she replied.

"Wasn't no sense in it. I was by myself, the borders were already full, so I figured I'd do just as well out here on my own. Seemed I was better off seein' to myself than having someone see to me."

"Amen to that," Tammy chimed in.

Mitchell turned to Tammy. "She speaks!" he said, smiling. "What's your story, young lady? How'd you end up out here in these badlands?"

"Army trucks saved the trailer parks for last," she replied. "And by last I mean not at all. We were kinda like third class on the Titanic; just weren't enough life boats left."

"Sink or swim," he said.

"And I'm swimming," she answered.

Mitchell nodded.

Silence ensued as the adults drank their coffee. Zach played with his toy car while Jeremy played with the three army men he carried everywhere. The light was beginning to wane outside and the skylights were losing their power to illuminate.

Dave spoke, breaking the silence. "Look, Ed, I apologize for what happened back there. I'm not a bad - we're not bad people here. I lost someone close to me in a standoff like that one and it was all just sorta déjà vu back there. I guess I went a little nutty. These girls saved my life, so I wanted to protect them. I didn't want to make the same mistakes as last time and see anybody die because of me."

Ed stood up, gently moving the boys out of his way before walking to where Dave sat. He extended his hand to Dave. "We're good," Ed reassured him. "Nobody got hurt. We can thank Mitchell here for that."

"Here, here," Brenda said, raising her coffee cup and smiling. "And thanks for the Joe."

Mitchell smiled back. "You're welcome, missy. It's nice to have visitors, despite the circumstances under which we made our acquaintance. And seeing those boys just made my day. Reminded me of…well, never mind all that." He trailed off, staring into the distance, lost in thought for a few moments. When he stood up, he groaned as his knees and ankles popped and cracked. He surveyed his guests, clapping his hands together.

"Let's eat."

* * *

They ate a hearty meal, at least by post-outbreak standards, consisting of canned tomatoes and corn, Vienna sausages, and strawberry preserves. As promised, Mitchell allowed the boys to choose from a stack of candy bars. Their faces lit up, smiles miles wide as Jeremy chose a Snickers bar and Zach had a Butterfinger.

The group made idle chat during dinner, with periods of silence falling in between. They discussed the coming spring and shared some anecdotal accounts of their time spent on the road. Though all the stories varied slightly, they all contained long periods of boredom, scattered with intense interaction with the infected. It was very much like war in that sense, Ed thought.

He supposed it was a war, after all.

The light inside the warehouse faded even more quickly than the light outside the building. The skylights were almost completely dark by the time they finished with dinner and discussion. Mitchell produced a flashlight so they could find their way back to where he slept. He told them he had dozens of flashlights along with enough batteries to power them for a what he called a 'good long while'. Just one of the many benefits of shacking up in a warehouse super store.

Mitchell led both groups through a series of aisles until he arrived at the aisle containing the shelf on which he slept. Placed against the shelves was a long, aluminum ladder extended up to the top shelf.

"That's where I sleep," he told them all, shining the flashlight on the top shelf. They could see various items placed on the shelf, one of which was a cot. "I used to pull that ladder up every night, but for a man my age that's a lot of work. Plus, I was afraid that one day I'd just fall right off on my damn head trying to lift it. All that's changed now."

He beamed with satisfaction as he shined the light on a

rope tied to the top of the ladder. It ran through a support joist in the ceiling, the other end lying on the shelf above them.

"Now I use a rope. I pull this rope and it lifts the ladder off the ground. Then I just tie the rope off to the shelf. It keeps the ladder out of reach of those pitiful things out there, should they decide to pay me a little visit during the night. Helluva lot easier on the back, too. They can't seem to climb too well, least not these shelves, but I don't want to make it any easier on 'em by giving them an invitation."

He shined the flashlight up toward his shelf again, looking back at the group. "I could probably fit two of you up there, if you want. It's up to you folks. You'll probably want to bunk in one of these shelves as well, just to keep yourself off the ground. That's my advice, at least. As for me, I'm going up. I hate to be a party pooper, but I ain't twenty years old anymore."

Mitchell shined the flashlight on the group. "You all got flashlights?"

They answered that they did.

"Good. You folks are welcome to stay the night. You're also welcome to stay for a while longer if you like. I do enjoy the company, for what it's worth. 'Night."

The group said goodnight to Mitchell as he climbed the ladder and vanished into the darkness above. Once he got to the top, he pulled a rope attached to the top of the ladder. They watched as it rose into the air, just out of reach.

"Ain't it brilliant?" Mitchell called down to them, chuckling as he said it.

Ed couldn't help but smile. "Ingenious," he called back.

Mitchell then flipped off the flashlight, casting the rest of them in darkness.

Ed liked Mitchell already, despite just meeting him. He really seemed like the real deal. Ed removed his flashlight from his back pocket, turning it on and shining it around in search of a suitable place to sleep. The other group had already disappeared into the darkness where they were also searching for their own place to sleep. He left them to it.

Eventually Ed and his group spotted an empty shelf. It wasn't as high as the one Mitchell used, but it was off the ground. "Trish, you and the boys could sleep here," he suggested. "What do you think?"

Trish walked over to the shelves and looked up as Ed shined the light for her to see. "I think we can fit, but you'll need to give us a boost," she answered.

Zach and Jeremy agreed.

"I can manage that," Ed said, smiling. He handed Trish the flashlight before boosting her up to the shelf. He waited for her to climb in before lifting up both boys. She helped them into the shelf where she sat as Ed tossed up their backpacks. From the packs she removed some blankets before rolling out their sleeping bags.

"How is it up there, boys?" Ed asked.

"It's like a tree house!" Jeremy exclaimed.

"Yeah, Dad, this is cool!" Zach added.

Ed chuckled.

"Are you coming up?" Trish asked. "There's room, you know."

Ed looked over briefly at Dave and the girls. Their dim flashlight bobbed about in the darkness like a firefly in a grassy field. He'd need to keep an eye on their new friend, Dave, just to be sure he wasn't batshit crazy after all. For now they'd rotate guard duty and try to get some sleep.

"I am," Ed replied before climbing up to the shelf to join them.

* * *

The rains came during the night. Water dumped from the sky as if from a broken dam. The falling rain made a surprisingly loud roar as it fell on the roof of the building. The rains continued throughout the night and into the following morning at an almost invariable rate. Ed found it hard to stay awake amidst the lull of the beating raindrops above. It reminded him of rainstorms from his youth, lulling him to sleep in his upstairs bedroom.

The following day each group stayed mostly to themselves. Ed, Trish, and the boys walked to the front of the store to get a look outside and assess the weather. The rain was ceaseless and torrential, so Ed decided they should stay inside, at least until the storm passed. Trish and the boys agreed. They'd all been caught in rainstorms like this before and he didn't want to repeat the miserable experience if they could avoid it. The rain soaked everything and chilled to the bone.

Around midday Mitchell invited everyone to meet with him for lunch. They were served canned vegetables and fruits along with mashed potatoes from re-hydrated spud flakes. Thanks to Mitchell's propane camp stove their meal was piping hot. It was the first hot meal any of them had in longer than they could remember.

With the food and the candy, the boys were beside themselves. The truth was, so was Ed. Between saving Trish's life and finding the RV, and now the wonderful hospitality Mitchell had shown them, life wasn't as bad as it had been during the winter. The weather was improving as well; spring had sprung, and the rains had come in full force, as if to prove it.

Throughout the day Ed watched Dave carefully. He kept his distance to avoid provocation. To Ed, Dave seemed to be behaving normally, interacting with the girls like a reasonably well-adjusted person, or as well-adjusted as a person could expect to be in the aftermath of the world's worst pandemic.

The conversation over lunch had been benign enough. Mitchell spoke of his time in West Virginia, living in a trailer in what he referred to as a 'holler'. Mitchell's opinion was that the world had dismissed his state and its people as insignificant. Ed wondered though if Mitchell didn't also admire this fact just a bit. It did make them an exclusive group.

Dave spoke of the border town from which he'd come, but conspicuously avoided discussion of his wife. Ed could understand that. Watching his new acquaintance closely, focusing on his body language and eye contact, Ed went about the task of analyzing their new friend. Dave didn't seem to be one for eye contact with Ed, but after what had happened the prior day Ed understood that too.

Ed did notice, however, that Dave made plenty of eye contact with Brenda while the other girl, Tammy seemed disconnected. Though not entirely sure what was driving the dynamics of this group's relationships, Ed was keen enough to understand there was something under the surface.

The question was, how was that helpful in determining any of their intentions? Ed didn't have an immediate answer for that one, so it was back to the wait and see approach. For now, he and his family seemed safe enough.

After lunch the groups split up again, each searching through the store for supplies. 'Take anything you folks need,' Mitchell had told them. 'There's more than enough for a geezer like me to live on. God provides, even in the worst of times.'

Ed stocked up on batteries for their flashlight, a necessity in the near-complete darkness of the warehouse after sundown. The four of them found more clothing to replace the tattered and filthy things they were already wearing. They kept their winter coats, however. Those were specialty items; very warm and very hard to come by. Ed even picked up a bottle of propane and one of the small stovetop attachments Mitchell used to heat their food. He thought it would be nice to cook a meal or two for Trish and the boys after they got back on the road again.

They passed Dave, Brenda, and Tammy twice while gathering supplies. Both times they nodded to each other. Ed noticed no tendency toward aggressive behavior from the three. Ed was feeling better about these people as the time passed.

As the second day came to a close the rain persisted. It wasn't the downpour it had been the prior night, but it was still significant enough to drench everyone completely should they venture out. The moderate temperatures wouldn't be warm enough to offset the cold the soaking would bring, so Ed and his group decided to wait until the storms passed, as did Dave and the girls.

As darkness came and stole all the natural light, Trish

and the boys returned to their designated shelf. Ed gave both boys hugs before boosting them up to the shelf and into their sleeping bags. This night, however, they were in new sleeping bags, discovered in the camping section.

Before he gave Trish a boost up to the shelf, she turned to Ed and asked him if he was coming up as well. He looked over at Dave and the two girls, watching their flashlights flicker and bounce in the darkness.

"I will in a bit," he said. "I think I might have a little chat with our new friends first."

"Okay. We're going to turn in then," Trish replied. She touched Ed's shoulder. "You be careful, okay?"

He returned the touch. "I will."

Jeremy and Zach both waved and said goodnight from the shelf above. Ed boosted Trish up and into the shelf where they bedded down for the night. Using the flashlight to shine a path through the warehouse, Ed headed toward Dave and the girls.

* * *

"Need any help?" Ed asked as he approached Dave, Brenda, and Tammy. Brenda shined the flashlight in Ed's eyes, causing him to instinctively raised his hand to shield them from the light.

"Sorry about that," Brenda apologized as she moved the light down from his face. "I think we're good here, but thanks anyway."

"Sure thing," Ed replied. He paused for a moment. "Hey, Dave," he began, "we usually have to rotate guard duty among ourselves while we're on the road. I assume you three do as well. I thought maybe you wouldn't mind alternating along with me while everyone gets some sleep."

Dave looked at Ed. "You sure about that? I mean, after what happened earlier…"

"I'm sure."

Dave turned to Brenda. "What do you think?" he asked.

"Fine by me," she replied. "Thanks, Ed," she added. "We could use the sleep."

"Don't mention it."

Tammy silently continued about the work of preparing their bedding and organizing their supplies while Ed spoke to her companions. Ed took note.

"So, Dave," Ed said, "Wanna shoot the shit? I'm not tired now anyway."

Ed thought he could see the hard lines in Dave's expression lighten, though it might have been the low light of the flashlight.

"Sure," Dave replied. "Why not?"

Ed and Dave found themselves sitting alone at the end of the aisle upon some large buckets of economy-sized laundry detergent. As they sat, Ed turned his flashlight on from time to time, scanning the aisles as far as the beam would penetrate, searching for any activity. He saw no movement, nor did he hear any sounds to announce the arrival of any uninvited guests. Neither man said anything for some time.

"How'd you meet those girls?" Ed asked, finally breaking the silence.

"They found me, actually," Dave replied.

"That so?"

"Yeah. I was in a bad way. Out of my fucking gourd really, if I'm being honest."

"They take you in?"

"They did. Brenda did, at least."

And there it is, Ed thought to himself. The mystery of Tammy was unveiling itself.

"They're rough, I know, but they're good people," Dave added.

"Who's not rough, nowadays? This is a rough world," Ed replied.

"True," Dave agreed. "True."

Ed shifted the subject, lightly probing. "Tammy seems quiet."

Dave inhaled deeply. He put his hands behind his head as he exhaled. "She's a tough nut to crack."

"Three's a crowd, huh?"

"Never thought about it that way, but yeah, I guess you're right."

Ed flipped the flashlight on, scanning the aisles again. They were clear.

"It's getting better now, I think," Dave continued. "She seems more agreeable."

"That's good," Ed said. He made a note to keep an eye on Tammy, all the same.

After another pause, Dave asked: "That girl you found, she said you saved her life."

"The boys and I found her inside a Target store. She was half dead, beat to hell, dehydrated with a high fever. We took her in, got her some antibiotics and then just hoped for the best."

"Looks like your hoping paid off," Dave replied. "She seems like she's doing okay. How long have you and the boys been traveling with her now?"

"A few weeks, maybe. It's hard to keep track anymore."

"Yeah, no shit," Dave agreed. "How about those boys? I'll bet you're damn proud. I never had any. It didn't make much sense, what with the world ending and all."

"I couldn't be more proud," Ed replied.

The two men sat in silence for another minute or two. Ed flipped the flashlight on periodically, surveying the aisles.

"Look," Dave began, "I'm not crazy, and I'm not an asshole. I'm definitely not a killer. I know it might have looked that way, but that shit that happened back there when we ran into you guys…" he trailed off.

Ed waited.

"I'm just saying it was a one-off," Dave continued. "Things are still so raw right now. I lost Sandy only yesterday, it seems."

"I get it," Ed said. "Our past defines us as much as it haunts us." More silence. "Tomorrow's a new day," Ed said, checking the aisle again for movement. He stood up. "We should get some sleep."

"Good idea," Dave said, standing up as well.

Ed walked back toward Trish and the boys.

"Ed?" Dave called out in the darkness.

Ed stopped. "Yeah, Dave."

"Thanks for understanding."

"Don't mention it," Ed replied. He made his way to his family, leaving Dave to his thoughts.

* * *

Ed knocked on the support beam of the shelf to let Trish know he was there. She was still awake. She called down to him. "Ed? Is that you?"

"In the flesh," he called back. "I'm coming up."

"Okay."

Ed climbed the shelving support beams to the second-level shelf where Trish and the boys were bunked for the night. Both boys were fast asleep. He maneuvered around them, being careful not to wake them. They stirred, but remained asleep.

"I thought you'd be asleep already," he whispered.

"I couldn't. I was a little worried. That man…"

"Dave?"

"Yeah, Dave. He flipped his lid yesterday, you know?"

Ed chuckled softly. "You could say that."

"Well, I was worried about you. I wasn't sure what might happen."

It made him feel good to hear that. "Dave's as stable as can be expected, I suppose. He had a loss recently, that standoff triggered something in him. He says he's better now."

"Do you believe him?"

"I do. My gut tells me he's legit."

"What about those girls? They're a bit scary."

"Not sure yet. Dave vouches for them, for whatever that's worth."

Trish paused for a moment. "What about Mitchell? He seems nice. I want to trust him. I get the feeling he could have killed us all if he'd wanted to."

"I get that feeling too. Ol' Mitchell Burdette looked like a wild west gunslinger standing there with those pistols strapped to his hips, didn't he?"

"He seems like a good guy," Trish said. "We should still be careful though, especially tonight. I hope you were planning on one of us staying awake."

"I was. You read my mind." He said in the dark.

"How long do you want to stay here?" she asked.

He thought for a moment. "I'm not sure. At least a day or two, definitely after the rain stops. I'd like to walk out of here with some serious supplies, if nothing else."

"And then we're off to see the wizard?"

"We are."

A pause followed. Trish touched Ed's hand. She leaned in and kissed him in the darkness.

He returned it.

Chapter Fifteen

Finally, the rain stopped. Sometime over the course of the night the slow drizzle subsided to a light sprinkle which was by morning mostly gone. The clouds dissipated and the sun came out in full force, beginning its job of burning off the water from the ground. It was just one more day on a planet already four and a half-billion years old.

After nearly three days Trish and the boys had begun to settle in at Mitchell's, enjoying the routine of hot meals and a warm, dry place to sleep. The boys had grown particularly fond of daily candy bars after dinner and Ed couldn't blame them. They wanted what all little boys wanted. The fact that they'd ever been denied these things was an unparalleled injustice.

Ed knew, however, that complacency bred carelessness. Safety was an illusion. That's why their things were always packed and ready should they need to flee. In the pre-virus world nothing was certain; this was even truer in the post-virus world.

Eventually they would have to leave this place, just as they'd left the RV. Trish and the boys were growing fond of Mitchell. The truth was, so was Ed. By all appearances

Mitchell was a kindhearted man with a paternal nature and a knack for saying the right thing at the right time. His convictions were simple and right. He was religious, but not over the top with it. Ed thought he was the kind of person you wanted to have around when the going got tough and that would make it all the more difficult to leave.

As much as Mitchell complained of his advanced age Ed knew that was a kind of humble ruse. Mitchell was fifty at most, but Ed was willing to bet that he could move like a man half his age. He had only alluded to his skill with a gun, never explicitly bragging about it. It had been Ed's experience that those who possessed exceptional abilities never needed to brag about them.

Though he was feeling very positive about Dave and the girls, Ed kept his eye on them all the same. Dave had become a helper to Mitchell, fetching the water and food and taking care of the trash. After the conversation they'd had, Dave was beginning to seem less like a loose cannon and more like a man who really had just been pushed too far.

Ed could understand that.

He understood it very well.

* * *

Mitchell asked them to stay for dinner and for another night, despite the rain all but ceasing. Everyone agreed. Upon their first encounter, Ed had thought of Mitchell as a loner, a recluse holed up in a world he'd created for himself. Now, however, he was seeing this man differently. Mitchell was lonely, plain and simple, and now that he had company he didn't want to lose it just yet.

They all had lunch together, but this time they didn't disperse to their separate groups directly afterward. Ed sat near Trish, the boys playing nearby. Dave, Brenda and Tammy sat across from them. Ed couldn't help but notice the distance between Dave and Brenda was far less than the space between Brenda and Tammy. There was a storm brewing there, that was for sure.

Before long a conversation arose, prompted by Trish. "So how did you two meet up?" she asked Brenda and

Tammy, taking a sip of coffee.

Brenda looked at Tammy. "Go on," she said. "You tell."

Looking reticent, Tammy complied. "Um, well, we met in an old gas station," Tammy said. "The army guys left me behind, so I decided that I'd just strike out on my own. Better to die on my feet than live on my knees and all that, you know? In those days I was carrying a baseball bat with a nail through it. I walked in and saw Brenda, then I just about buried that nail in her head. Luckily I didn't. Not much more to tell."

Brenda continued the story. "We decided we were stronger together than apart, so we joined up. We've traveled together ever since. What's it been, two and a half years now?"

Tammy nodded.

Brenda fired the question back at Trish. "How about you? What's your story?"

Trish sighed. "I was in high school when the virus struck. Tim was my boyfriend. We lost everybody, but we had each other. We were tight, him and me, really close." She paused.

"What happened?" Brenda asked.

"He died. He died saving me."

No one spoke.

"They tore him to pieces in front of me," Trish said, a tear forming in her eye. "After that, I wandered. Then these guys-"

"You don't have to go on," Ed said.

"It's okay, Ed. These guys, they kidnapped me, raped me for days. I got away, but I was sick. Ed and his boys here found me. They saved my life."

"You're a fighter, Trish," Brenda said. "I like that."

Trish smiled. She turned to Ed. "I'm going to lie down for a while."

Ed nodded. "Sure."

"Is Trish okay?" Jeremy asked from where he and his brother were playing.

"She's fine," Ed told him. He walked over to where his

boys played and gave them both a pat on the head. "She's just tired."

Both boys nodded and went back to playing.

"That virus gave us all some nasty demons," Mitchell said. "Each and every one of us has our cross to bear."

"We'll probably head out tomorrow," Ed told Mitchell as they sat together, eating. Mitchell had made spaghetti for dinner. Ed felt that out of all the things about staying at the warehouse he might miss the hot meals more than anything else.

"Well, it's been a real pleasure having you folks here," Mitchell replied. He turned to look at Dave. "How about you folks? Care to stay a while longer, or are you planning to leave too?"

"We haven't really talked about it yet," Brenda said.

"Take your time, there's no rush," Mitchell said, smiling.

"We appreciate your hospitality," Ed said. "We're deeply indebted."

"You folks don't owe me anything. The Lord provides," Mitchell replied. "It ain't up to me to take credit for it."

Ed smiled. "We're obliged all the same."

"And you're welcome, all the same," Mitchell said. "Now eat up. We don't want to leave any of this food lying around. Those deadheads have a knack for finding dinner, even if you don't invite 'em."

They ate, mostly in silence, finishing up the entire batch of spaghetti and washing it down with bottled water. Mitchell again gave Zach and Jeremy their choice of after-dinner candy bar. Mitchell made sure to provide Ed with plenty of chocolate for the boys, knowing they would appreciate it on the road.

After dinner the adults sat together, talking. Dave was recounting a story about the greatest scavenge he had ever pulled off when they heard a loud crash echo from across the room. Everyone jumped to attention, eyes wide. Ed drew his pistol, gathering up the kids. Trish joined them, putting her arms around the boys. Brenda and Tammy drew their weapons while Dave retrieved his baseball bat.

Mitchell stood slowly, holding a hand up to ensure the others stayed quiet. Eerie silence filled the large warehouse as they strained to hear in the dim light. Mitchell took three steps forward before stopping and listening. Another loud sound ripped through the silence. Everyone jumped except for Mitchell, who stood very still, his finger to his lips.

Trish hugged the boys closer as Ed stood beside them, gun drawn, looking everywhere for movement. He pushed a flashback of what had happened to Zach at the sporting goods store out of his mind.

Mitchell stood, listening, both guns hanging from his hips, lodged into their holsters. Then he surprised everyone by whistling.

"What are you doing?" Brenda whispered.

Ed wondered the same thing.

Mitchell held up his hand in a *stop* gesture, his finger held to his lips. He cocked his head to the side, listening.

He whistled again.

Suddenly a carrier screamed from somewhere in the building, off in the shadows. The scream pierced the quiet warehouse like a thunderclap, the natural reverb of the room creating echoes that seemed to go on forever.

Mitchell looked around the room, ear still cocked. He looked directly at Ed. "Duck," he said.

"What?" Ed asked quietly.

"Duck. Right now."

Ed hit the ground.

Mitchell's right hand went to his waist so quickly it was difficult for anyone to see it move. He drew his revolver and fired off two shots so close together that they sounded like one. Behind him Ed heard the dull thud of the bullets striking flesh, followed by the sound of bodies hitting the floor.

Mitchell turned suddenly to his left, firing three more shots in quick succession, dropping three more carriers before Ed could even stand up.

The warehouse went silent. Ed stood up, and tended to

Trish and the boys. "Go climb into that shelf. Get your things ready in case we need to run," he said.

Trish nodded, rounding up the boys before walking briskly to their shelf.

"Do you think that's all of them?" Dave asked.

"Hard to say," Mitchell responded, "but gunfire draws 'em in. Last time this happened I just climbed the shelves and waited it out. The few that came to investigate got bored quick."

Mitchell pulled the cylinder from his revolver and placed it into a pouch on his belt. He produced a pre-loaded cylinder from another compartment before reloaded the gun, placing it back into the holster on his hip. "If you want my advice," Mitchell said to the group, "I'd say stay put for now. Hard to say how many of those things will be wandering around outside, looking for what made all that racket. They'll go their own way eventually and then you can be on yours."

"I think we'll stay here for tonight," Dave replied, looking at Brenda.

She nodded in agreement.

"I have to check on my kids," Ed said.

* * *

They all decided to stay one more night. As late as it was, and after all the shooting, Ed decided it would be a good idea to stay in the relative safety of the warehouse. It was better than facing carriers at night, anyway.

Mitchell seemed pleased to have his guests stay on for a while longer. The men took on the gruesome task of removing the carrier bodies from the warehouse and dumping them behind the building near a dumpster. In a rare event Ed left the boys with Trish to help dispose of the bodies. He couldn't remember the last time he'd left both boys alone.

Night fell shortly after they disposed of the bodies. Both groups alternated guard duty among themselves, but no more carriers showed up inside the warehouse. Early in the morning they heard a scream from outside, but nothing materialized.

Ed swapped guard duty with Trish right after the scream awakened her. He caught four solid hours of dreamless sleep, feeling like a new man the following morning. As much as he was going to miss the warehouse and the acquaintances they'd made, he was also anxious about getting back on track toward the city.

The next day came as expected, but no one left. They searched again for more supplies, repacked what they had, ate hot dinners, and talked afterward. They all decided it was too late to leave that day, so they rescheduled their departures for the following day.

The following day it rained, harder than ever, setting them back from their respective schedules. More food, more discussion, and another dry, safe night presented itself. They spent considerable time talking after dinner, all except for Tammy. She sat speechless for long periods; mostly looking at the floor, or off into the distance.

Two days turned into three days, three days into four. Ed could see what was happening; they were indulging in the creature comforts and the company the warehouse provided. Who could blame them? It might be temporary, but it was a respite all the same. Ed felt they deserved a few breaks after all they'd been through, so he quelled any protest.

Over the following days Ed's opinion of Dave solidified. Dave was a natural leader. As the days passed and Dave began to regain his self-confidence, Ed could see the person Dave really was.

He also saw the same characteristics in Brenda. It was as if she and Dave were co-leaders of their little group. A group that now contained a third wheel. Ed knew he'd have to watch Tammy very closely. She was the wildcard.

* * *

Ten days after their arrival at the warehouse Ed found himself lying in their usual shelf with Trish, the boys wrapped in their sleeping bags beside them. He and Trish spoke quietly in the darkness about trivial things, just passing the time and enjoying each other's company.

"We've been here a while, eh?" Ed said.

"Yeah. It's been nice," she replied.

"It has. We're going to have to leave soon, you know."

"Couldn't we stay a little longer?"

"We could, but it couldn't be for long. The longer we stay, the longer it delays us from reaching the city."

"The city is no guarantee of safety."

"I know, but neither is this warehouse," Ed replied.

"But there's so much here. Seems like it would last for a long time."

"I suppose it would for a while, but eventually it'll run out. And when it does, we'll be back on the road, possibly in the dead of winter. The last thing I want to do is spend another winter on the road."

"I guess you're right," Trish said, "but I don't like it."

"I don't either," he said.

* * *

"We're leaving tomorrow," Ed said to the group over breakfast the following day. Ed told the boys when they awoke. They were disappointed when they heard the news, but eventually they accepted it. They had enjoyed their time with Mitchell and their new friends, but finding the city was still paramount for them.

"For real?" Dave asked.

Ed nodded. "'Fraid so. It's time."

"Well," Mitchell said in his Appalachian drawl, "I do hate to see you folks leave, but I understand." He walked up to Ed, reached out his hand and shook it firmly. He hugged Trish and tousled the boys' hair. "Take the rest of the day to prepare yourselves, restock supplies and the like. And make sure those kids get those chocolate bars," he said, grinning.

Both the boys smiled back.

Mitchell knelt closer to them. "You boys mind your dad and do what he says now, you hear me?"

Both Zach and Jeremy nodded.

Ed said: "We're indebted to your hospitality and generosity. These supplies are critical for us."

Mitchell waved him off. "You folks are more than

welcome. It's nice for an old man to get some company from time to time." He paused, brow furrowed. "If you don't mind me asking, where are you folks headed? I mean, in the long run."

Ed looked at the boys. "A safe haven," he answered.

* * *

After dinner, while Ed and his group were packing, Dave sat with Brenda and Tammy. No one spoke while they watched Ed and his group inventory their supplies and prepare for their departure the following day.

Eventually Dave spoke up. "I'm going to say what everybody's probably thinking. I like that group and I hate to see them go."

Brenda sighed. "I guess I do too."

No reply from Tammy.

Both Dave and Brenda turned to look at her, eyebrows raised.

"What?" she replied.

"What do you think?" Brenda asked, her tone sharp.

"I don't know, they're all right," Tammy answered. "The kids are nice, I guess."

"Yeah," Dave said. "Ed's a stand up guy."

Dave watched the flurry of activity surrounding their new acquaintances' planned departure with uncanny interest. "We should go with them," he said.

"What?" Tammy asked, her face askew. "Why would we do that?"

"Now she speaks," Brenda said as Tammy fired her a dirty look.

Dave shrugged. "Why not? They're good people, and they're headed somewhere, at least."

"Headed where?" Tammy asked. "This 'safe haven'? What does that even mean?"

Dave closed his eyes. "You got a better plan?"

Tammy's face reddened. "Goddammit, Dave, I swear-"

"Knock it off, you two," Brenda said, holding up a hand.

Tammy stopped talking, her lips pursed. Dave looked away.

"Maybe Dave's right," Brenda continued. "Seriously, where are we headed after this?"

"Back on the road, like before," Tammy replied.

"I'm not sure I want that anymore," Brenda said. "Maybe there's something more out there, you know? Some place for us to go?"

"Fine," Tammy said, folding her ams. "Whatever you want."

"I don't want it to be like that," Brenda said. "This could be good for all of us."

Tammy didn't reply.

* * *

"So what do you think?" Dave asked Ed. Trish and the boys were nearby, packing.

Ed answered. "I don't know. I guess I hadn't really thought about it."

"I know it's out of the blue, but I'd ask you to consider it. There's strength in numbers, you know," Dave said, sporting a grin.

Ed nodded, a slight grin on his face as well. "How about you give us some time to discuss it?"

Dave nodded. "Fair enough. We'll wait for your answer."

* * *

"Maybe it is a good idea," Trish said as she and the boys packed their things. "More people could give us an advantage."

"More mouths to feed," Ed countered.

"True, but they're the types to fend for themselves."

"Maybe."

"And they can go their own way if it doesn't work out. They would have to agree to that."

Ed nodded, thinking. He could see the advantages of traveling with Dave and the girls. But there were also risks. There were always risks.

"Do you trust them?" Ed asked.

Trish nodded. "I do."

Ed thought about it. After what Trish had been through, that was enough for him.

The following day they all stood by the front doors of the Sam's Club warehouse that Mitchell Burdette called home. Everyone carried a backpack chock-full of supplies. They had gained some precious weight back, their skin turning from corpse-gray to a more natural living-pink.

"Damn, I hate to see you folks go," Mitchell said.

"We owe you one," Dave told him. "You really helped us out."

"Absolutely," Brenda added.

"Don't mention it," Mitchell replied. "I just happened upon an empty warehouse. This stuff in here is just as much yours as it is mine, but I'm glad to provide what I can."

"You took us in, maybe even saved our lives," Trish said. "Don't underestimate how important that is."

"I'm just doing the Lord's work here on Earth."

"Are you sure you don't want to come with us?" Ed asked.

"Naw. My place is here, at least for now. One old man can live for a long time on all this. Besides, who knows what new friends might be strolling down that highway right now? I'd hate to leave them an empty building. That's not much of a welcome."

"Understood," Ed said. He turned to Zach and Jeremy. "Hey boys, it's time to tell Mitchell goodbye."

Zach and Jeremy both ran to Mitchell, each hugging one of his legs. He patted them on their heads.

"Thank you!" they both yelled in near-unison.

"You're welcome, boys. It was a pleasure making your acquaintance."

The boys released his legs and ran back to their father.

Mitchell approached Tammy, who was standing off to the side of the group. He placed his hand on her shoulder, gently pulling her near.

He hugged her.

"Stay strong," he whispered in her ear. "This too, shall pass."

Mitchell watched the group, now almost doubled in size,

as they walked away from the building, through the parking lot, and back to the highway from which they'd come. They shrank to small dots in the distance before eventually disappearing altogether. He stood there for some time, even after they'd vanished from sight, watching the empty highway as the cool spring wind blew over his face.

Chapter Sixteen

In another time not so long ago the highway would have been filled with cars and trucks traveling across a country ripe with prosperity. Carloads of people would have been on their way to see friends and relatives while others might be moving to a new city for opportunity. Cars containing families would travel across the country to see the Grand Canyon, or the Rocky Mountains, or maybe to a sandy beach to bask in the glow of the hot summer sun.

Now the highway was silent and still, littered with motionless cars. Like coffins on wheels, these cars were the final resting place of thousands, victims of the worst virus humankind had ever seen. Instead of driving for a weekend getaway they had been fleeing for their lives. Unfortunately for them there had been no outrunning the virus.

Ed walked beside his two sons along the highway, a roadway with which they were already so familiar. Trish walked beside them, the portrait of a survivor. Now they traveled with some new companions; another group of hardened survivors which, through destiny, fate, or luck, had crossed paths with Ed and his sons and chosen to walk alongside them.

They walked for two days, speaking very little. There was little to say on the road. The scenery didn't change much along the same monotonous stretch of concrete, ubiquitous for miles and miles on end. After traveling for so long, for so many miles with only his sons, the sheer number of travelers accompanying him now would have been unthinkable only months ago.

Life was always throwing curve balls.

On the second night after leaving Mitchell's warehouse they camped just off the highway, in the midst of brown cornstalks. The ground was rough, but it was secluded. Trusting Dave as their sentry, Brenda and Tammy had turned in for the night. Trish had gone down quickly alongside the boys, leaving only Dave and Ed awake. The two men sat in the quiet darkness of a world nearly devoid of homosapiens, listening to crickets chirping in the wind.

Dave spoke, breaking the eerie silence. "It's killing me, so I gotta ask. Where exactly are we headed?"

Ed thought for a moment before answering. "A safe haven," he replied.

Dave chuckled in the darkness. "Yeah, I knew that. Mr. Cryptic strikes again. For real, what is this 'safe haven' exactly?"

Ed considered the question and the implications of answering truthfully. Cryptic he'd been, this much was true, but the reasons for Ed's obfuscation were becoming fuzzier as time went on. "Saint Louis," he answered.

"Hmmm. Saint Louis, huh? What's in Saint Louis?"

"Salvation, I hope."

"Based on what? A hunch?"

"A ham radio transmission I overheard."

"So that's where you've been headed all this time? Traveling on faith in a radio transmission?"

"In a word, yes, though I don't know if you'd call it faith or desperation. I'm not sure what the difference is anymore."

"Fair enough," Dave replied. A pause. He motioned toward Brenda and Tammy. "These girls, before they met me at least, they just walked. I don't think they knew or cared where they were headed. I suppose I was the same way. All of us, we just wandered, surviving from day to day."

They listened as the crickets ratcheted up their song, the distinct calls that blended into a strange and beautiful cacophony.

"I think I might like to find a place to stop now, Ed. I'm getting tired of wandering. I need a goal, a destination." He grinned. "Plus, I've never seen the Arch."

Ed laughed out loud, in spite of himself, causing Zach to stir in his sleep. "Maybe we'll take a trip to the top when we get there," he said, grinning. "I hear the line's really short now."

Two men, who two weeks ago had been ready to kill each other, sat together in the murky darkness, listening to the ornate and complicated sound of Nature's nocturnal symphony. Whether they believed in the safe haven or not, they both agreed that there was a chance it was true, and the risks to find out were worth taking.

* * *

Dave told Brenda and Tammy of their destination the following day. Tammy was nonplussed, Brenda took it in stride. After some consideration she figured that Saint Louis was as good a place as any. The group, now united in their destination, walked throughout the day and slept in shifts at night. It became routine. When it rained they hunkered down under a thin sheet of plastic.

At night Ed would sit with both the boys and talk about the city. At least some things never changed.

When the first road sign appeared, pale green and trimmed in white, bearing the words *Saint Louis* upon its face, the boys nearly toppled over with excitement. The signs made it real, no longer was the city by the river simply a bedtime story of dubious validity. It was tangible and, most of all, attainable.

They moved on, the boys containing their excitement while they trekked onward, toward the mythical city. Ed hid his concern as best he could, but he knew damn good and well that he could keep no secrets from Trish. She already knew him too well. If she was concerned, she hid it well. Sometimes Ed thought she was stronger than all of them.

Their food supplies were holding out; they'd stocked up nicely back at Mitchell's and it was paying off. They were able to avoid many of the exits, mitigating their risk. This pleased Ed immensely.

Due to the spring rains, finding fresh water was relatively easy at first. Streams and creeks ran about all over, ripe for filling canteens. As time went on and the April showers brought May flowers, the rains tapered off and the streams shrunk significantly. Larger streams dwindled while many smaller streams disappeared altogether. It became more difficult to find water easily, and their canteens ran dry more often than they were comfortable with.

Twelve days after leaving Mitchell's warehouse the group's canteens ran dry. With no water in sight, things soon became desperate. Trudging onward, they collected and boiled water from whatever shallow puddles they could find. Their thirst grew as they expended energy, and eating dried foods replenished none of the water they were losing.

The situation soon became desperate.

After spending another dry night along the roadside they got up the following morning to a very warm day. Spring was nearing its end with summer fast on its heels. With the heat came exhaustion and exhaustion ushered in more desperation.

They needed water. All other needs were now secondary.

* * *

After miles of thirsty walking, the group ran across a farmhouse sitting back in a field about a hundred yards or so from the highway. Remembering the well in the backyard of the house in which Trish had convalesced, Ed signaled for the group to stop. He pointed out the house.

They stopped, their gaze following his finger.

"There," he said, still pointing.

"After the last time I'm a little leery," Trish admitted. "It's giving me the creeps."

"But we're dying here," Brenda argued.

"I know, I know. There's just something about it..." Trish trailed off.

Brenda continued. "I say we go check it out."

"What do you think, Ed?" Dave asked.

Ed stared at the house in the distance. Trish was right; there was something...wrong about it. He wanted to pass it up, to move on to the next exit and search for bottled water or trek on to the next stream, but the pounding in his head and the scratching in this throat argued strongly against it. The boys were miserable too and they needed some relief. The next water source could be miles off. "Sure," he replied. "Why not? Let's go check it out."

The feeling remained, no matter how hard he tried to suppress it. It was only afterward, when he thought back on it, that he knew his instincts had been right all along.

By then, however, it was too late.

* * *

The group approached the front of a modest house after following a dirt and gravel road leading through an overgrown front yard. The road was well on its way to becoming covered by vegetation, but for the moment was still clear enough for them to make their way without too much effort. Ed looked around, nervous, his hand absent-mindedly resting on the butt of his pistol.

They stopped in front of the house, looking for movement or signs of danger. They saw none. A stone path cut through waist-high grass, leading to a wide covered porch, paint peeling, a gray, wooden swing hanging down from the ceiling by rusty chains.

Brenda turned to toward the group. "I'll go check around back and see if I can find-"

Suddenly the right side of Brenda's head exploded in a red mist as the crack of a shot rang out, echoing in the cool air. Her body plummeted to the ground, landing in a lifeless heap.

"Get down!" Ed yelled, grabbing both boys, pulling them down into the tall grass and vegetation. Trish ducked with them.

Another shot rang out, the explosion like a bomb.

Tammy screamed. She stood, transfixed, staring at the lifeless body of her friend.

"Tammy, get down!" Dave yelled, running away from the house and toward the high weeds. "Get the fuck down!"

Ignoring Dave's requests, Tammy stood, her eyes wide, her mouth silently moving. Her chest rose and fall as she panted for air.

"Move!" Ed yelled.

Tammy wasn't listening.

Ed drew his pistol and pointed it toward the house, firing a shot. He had no idea where the shooter was; he could only hope that he could buy her some time.

Slowly backing away from Brenda's body, Tammy shook her head. Tears leaked from her eyes as she moaned softly.

Ed fired another shot toward the house. Tammy was moving, but not fast enough. Moving quickly, Ed lifted himself above the weeds for a second or two, scanning the house for their assailant. He noticed movement in one of the windows as a man with a rifle took aim.

"In the window!" Ed screamed, firing a shot toward the figure. Ed watched the man duck back inside as the bullet caught the wooden window frame, splintering it.

"No, no, no, no," Tammy repeated, backing away slowly.

"Move your ass!" Dave yelled.

Finally Tammy dropped to her hands and knees, crawling through the tall grass. A few moments later she reached where Dave lay, belly down.

"She's dead," Tammy said, her eyes red and unfocused.

"I know," Dave replied. "We're stuck," he whispered. "That motherfucker has us pinned down."

Tammy nodded, still unfocused.

"You gotta get it together, Tammy. We're not getting out of here until that guy is dead."

Tammy nodded again.

"Do you understand me? Shoot that fucking guy, or give me the gun."

Tammy shook her head, as if clearing cobwebs. "I'll do

it," she said.

"Good. I'll get his attention; when he shows himself I want you to blow his fucking brains out. Can you do that?"

"Yeah," she replied, nodding.

"Are you sure?"

"Yeah, I'm sure."

Dave swallowed hard, gathering his courage. He took a deep breath and rose to his knees, yelling: "YOU MOTHERFUCKER! I'LL FUCKING KILL YOU!"

Dave saw movement as the sniper took his place in the window, pointing the rifle directly at him.

* * *

Tammy saw the man come into view, her rifle already aimed at the window. She'd been waiting on him. There was a scope on the shooter's rifle, a luxury she didn't have. She lined up the front sight with divot on the rear sight, exhaling half the air in her lungs as she placed her finger on the trigger. She watched as the man took his position on the window sill, lining his scope up with Dave's body.

The world grew silent; her senses cleared and sharpened. She and the target became the only things left in the world.

She gently squeezed the trigger.

The gun recoiled against her shoulder, jolting, the report from the rifle cracking the sky. The shooter's body jerked as the bullet struck him squarely in the chest. He slumped forward, lying motionless on the windowsill.

Dave hunkered back down in the weeds. "Ed, stay put! There might be more than one!"

But Tammy knew there was only one shooter. She wasn't sure how she knew this, but her gut told her she'd killed the man who killed her best friend. The only person in the world who'd ever understood her.

Seconds ticked by like hours as Tammy lay in the tall grass, her body numb with shock. Only the sound of the wind rustling some nearby wind chimes drifted through the air.

Five minutes passed. As Tammy expected, no other shooters appeared.

She'd waited long enough.

Tammy stood up, slinging the rifle over her shoulder and walking toward her friend's now lifeless body. If there were other shooters, then so be it. She was beyond the point of caring anymore.

A few more feet and she stood next to Brenda's body. She knelt, placing her hand on her friend's back. Her feet made sloshing sounds as she stepped on the blood-soaked ground. She tried to ignore that. The exit wound on the right side of Brenda's head was vicious and severe. That, Tammy couldn't ignore.

A few moments later Ed and Dave appeared behind her. She looked up at them, unable to stop the tears from welling in the corners of her eyes. She didn't want them to see her like this.

Ed and Dave said nothing. Ed placed a hand on Tammy's shoulder.

She surprised herself by leaving it there.

* * *

Ed and Dave left Tammy to her grief.

They walked out of earshot, a dozen or so feet from where Trish and the boys remained hidden in the weeds.

"Dave, I'm sorry about Brenda," Ed said. "I know she was important to you."

Dave nodded. "She saved my life."

"I don't want to sound cold, but we need to keep our heads right now. There are realities we still have to face. Are you still with me?" Ed asked.

"I'm with you, Ed," Dave replied, nodding his head. "Water, right? I mean, that's what all this was about."

Ed nodded. "Exactly. We still need to make that happen, despite all this."

"I understand. I'll go around back and look for a pump."

"You be careful back there." He paused, watching Tammy as she knelt beside her friend. "Take Brenda's gun."

Dave nodded. He made his way toward Tammy. Retrieving Brenda's gun lying a few feet away from her lifeless hand, he placed a hand on Tammy's shoulder. She brushed it off. Saying nothing, Dave left to search the backyard for a water source.

Ed watched Tammy from a distance, keeping Trish and the boys in his peripheral vision. They sat, somber and reserved, waiting. Ed hadn't had much time to get to know Brenda, apart from a few conversations along the road and some after dinner stories back at Mitchell's. In that short span of time he'd grown to like her.

Then in a second she was gone.

And for what? The only person who knew the answer to that lay dead, sprawled across the window sill.

What a fucking world.

Dave returned a few minutes later, placing Brenda's gun in his pocket. He glanced at Tammy, still kneeling beside Brenda's body. "I didn't see anything that looked like a well."

"Shit. All this for nothing," Ed said, exasperated. "What about inside?"

"You really wanna go in there, after all this?"

"Especially after all this. I don't want all this to be for nothing. There could be supplies in there, water, food, maybe guns. I think this guy might have been protecting something and-"

Suddenly Ed heard a scream from behind him. His stomach dropped as he instantly recognized the voice.

Zach.

Trish screamed. As if in slow motion, Ed turned to see a carrier on top of Zach, savagely clawing and biting at his son's throat. Zach's eyes were wide with fear, his mouth open as he tried in vain to scream again. Ed ran toward the monster, kicking it in the head with tremendous force. The deadwalker's head snapped backward upon impact as the thing rolled away. Temporarily stunned, it slowly got to its hands and knees, attempting to stand.

In a second the thing was on its feet, charging toward Ed. Ed reached for his gun as quickly as he could, but the thing was too fast. In another second it was two feet away and Ed knew he'd never draw fast enough to put a bullet in the thing.

Suddenly from out of nowhere the sharp crack of a pistol rang. The deadwalker fell to the ground in front of Ed, its body crumpled in a dead heap.

The sound of a voice echoed from the distance. "Move your asses! They're swarming!" the voice called.

Ed knew the voice immediately.

Mitchell.

Mitchell appeared, running along the road leading to the house, gun in hand.

Ed looked at his oldest son lying on the ground, attempting to sit up. His brother and Trish were beside him, kneeling, their faces a mask of shock.

Ed swooped in, picking up Zach and slinging him over his right shoulder. He took Jeremy by the hand.

Without looking back, they ran back toward the highway.

* * *

Dave watched the scene play out in front of him as if he were in slow motion. All of it happened so fast he scarcely had time to react.

Zach, his new friend's oldest son, was attacked in front of him and he wasn't able to do a damn thing about it. He watched as Ed picked up his son, dragging his younger son along as they darted toward the highway. Then he and Trish shared a look that he hoped he'd never see again.

It was all falling apart now.

Suddenly a carrier screamed from behind him. Dave turned, Brenda's gun in hand. A female carrier, still wearing the filthy and paltry remains of a Mickey Mouse T-shirt and pink sweatpants, charged at him. He froze, unable to lift the pistol. In his head he saw that little one back at the 7-Eleven, now a lifetime ago. He heard the sound of its voice as it called for its mommy.

For the first time since the outbreak, he saw a human being in front of him.

He raised the gun. His finger found the trigger, but he couldn't pull it. He stood like a statue as the Disney horror show in pink sweatpants charged, screaming, its arm hanging useless by its side. Sickening panic rose up, consuming him, overwhelming him.

A shot rang out from behind him, and the deadwalker in the sweatpants dropped to the ground with a violent crash. Dave turned, still operating in slow motion, as Mitchell strode in, gun in hand. The gunslinger's chest rose and fell as he struggled to catch his breath. "Boy, are you trying to get yourself killed?" Mitchell yelled.

Dave had no reply. He thought maybe that was exactly what he was doing.

Mitchell looked around. "Where's Brenda and Tammy?" he asked.

Dave pointed to where Brenda lay dead on the ground, Tammy still beside her, holding her dead friend's hand.

"Oh, shit," Mitchell replied.

Dave nodded.

"Tammy!" Mitchell yelled.

Tammy didn't respond. Mitchell yelled again. This time she turned her head slowly, focusing her attention on Mitchell.

"We have to leave her," Mitchell said.

Tammy shook her head. "No. I won't do it."

"There's no other choice," Mitchell replied.

Tammy turned her attention back to Brenda. Mitchell walked up to her quickly, placing a hand on her shoulder. "Come on, girl," he said.

Tammy looked at him, tears streaming down her dirty face. She opened her mouth to speak, but nothing came out.

Mitchell broke his gaze, glancing around them. A dozen carriers approached from all sides. With a pistol in each hand, Mitchell fired off five shots, taking down the closest threats with machine-like precision. He looked into Tammy's eyes. "It's time to go, honey."

"Okay," she replied, nodding.

"I'm sorry," he said.

* * *

Ed ran in a mad frenzy, his oldest son over his shoulder, his younger son's hand in his own. He heard shots ring out behind him, fired closely together, but they barely registered.

None of that mattered anymore.

Panic gripped him. Jeremy ran, keeping up as best he could, but Ed was nearly dragging him. It all happened so fast. Nobody even saw the deadwalkers coming.

They ran until they reached the highway. Ed heard more gunfire behind him. He ran, feeling the air flow in and out of his burning lungs, his head spinning from exertion and dehydration.

After what seemed like an eternity Ed could run no more. He stopped, releasing Jeremy's hand. He found a grassy area by the highway and slowly lowered Zach to the ground.

Zach's hand covered his neck. Beneath his son's small fingers Ed saw blood dripping slowly.

Shaking, Ed lifted the boy's hand from his neck.

Ed's entire mind and body went numb with white-hot, paralyzing shock.

His son had been bitten.

Chapter Seventeen

Ed carried Zach piggyback for miles, not allowing the boy to walk at all. Jeremy walked alongside them, his eyes red, rimmed with tears. Overcome with shock, Ed's world spun madly around him as he struggled unsuccessfully to comprehend the full reality of what had just happened to his son. No amount of preparation or forethought could prepare him for this nightmare. Not even Sarah.

In the face of the tragedy Dave stepped in and took control of guiding the group. He moved them along, Ed walking in a daze, until he could find a suitable place for them to set up camp and figure out what their next move was. Ed would be of no use to any of them besides his children, which was understandable enough, and Dave's intention was to allow him the opportunity to fill that role.

They walked for several more miles under Dave's direction, eventually setting up camp inside a wooded area just off the highway. Ed ventured off with the boys, walking a short distance away before setting up his own camp. With Ed tending to his sons, Dave set out to take care of their most pressing collective need: water. A fifteen minute search into the woods proved out with the discovery of a small, trickling stream. It wasn't much, but it was flowing and clean enough to boil without filtering. He siphoned off enough water to fill up the three canteens he had with him before returning to camp.

Upon his return to camp, Dave handed two of the canteens to Ed. Ed took them without a word.

"There's one for Zach and another for you and Jeremy," Dave told him.

Ed nodded in return before continuing with his work on the camp.

Dave walked away without saying anything.

Aside from the obvious, there was nothing left to say.

* * *

Ed handed Zach the canteen. The boy drank from it before lying down on his side upon the forest floor. Ed cleaned his son's neck wound before helping him into the sleeping bag Jeremy had prepared for his big brother.

The wound wasn't deep, but it was deep enough. The carrier's teeth had penetrated the skin, tearing a nasty laceration in Zach's neck.

There could be little doubt that the virus now had an unimpeded path into the boy's system.

Now it was only a matter of time.

* * *

Jeremy sat against a tree, watching his father care for his brother. He wanted to cry, but he couldn't. Not anymore. He had cried so much already he was completely spent.

Instead, he simply stared ahead, watching his father clean the wound and tousle his big brother's hair. Just trying to make Zach comfortable until the end came.

The wound was nasty, but by itself not fatal. Even Jeremy knew this. The virus, however, would be.

Jeremy knew that his father would have only one choice available to him. His father couldn't allow Zach to turn, not the way Mommy had. She hurt so bad after she got sick and the screaming… He still heard it in his dreams.

Sometimes Zach was slow, even for a big brother. He could read really good and he knew a lot of stuff about things. Sometimes though the answers were right there and Zach never saw them.

This time, however, Jeremy just knew that his big brother was fully aware of just how bad all this was. And he knew, deep inside, that Zach realized what came next.

First Mommy, now Zach.

Who would be next? Daddy? And how long would it be before the virus got to him too? Without his father and brother around, Jeremy almost hoped for it.

* * *

Trish watched Ed and the boys from a distance, sitting along with the others in their makeshift camp, sick to death with sadness and overwhelming grief. She knew how much the boys meant to Ed and how hard he'd tried to always protect them. They were his babies, his flesh and blood. His reason for living.

Zach was such a wonderful kid too. Always sweet, always helpful, with an unbreakable spirit. What happened was nothing short of devastating.

She knew Ed blamed himself. She knew this because she blamed herself too. She replayed the events in her head as she sat, trying to decide if she could have done things differently, if she could have saved the boy this death sentence. The carrier had been so quiet…no one heard it approach.

Whatever was left of her rational mind reminded her that it wasn't her fault, but that didn't change how terrible she felt. She supposed nothing ever would.

She watched Ed and the boys until she felt a tear stream down her cheek. She turned away, closing her eyes as more tears leaked out.

Mitchell walked over to her, taking a seat on the ground near her feet. Tammy sat away from the group, her back to Trish and Mitchell as she faced the forest. No one spoke while they waited for Dave to return with more water from the stream.

Mitchell then spoke softly, breaking what seemed like a holy silence. "I had a daughter once, you know? This is the worst thing he'll ever go through."

Trish broke down, sobbing. Mitchell stood, reaching out for her, placing her head on his shoulder. He held her like this, rocking and patting her back as she sobbed.

Tammy never turned around, her gaze laser focused on the trees surrounding them.

"It's not fair," Trish said to Mitchell, speaking into his shoulder.

"I know, honey," he replied. "I know. It ain't fair at all."

* * *

A few moments later, Dave reappeared from the woods with the rest of their canteens, all now full of water from the stream. He scanned the camp, taking in his fractured group. That morning Brenda had been alive and well, Zach a bright and delightful child.

But as he watched Ed cleaning his son's mortal wound, Trish sobbing into Mitchell's shoulder, and Tammy, despondent, staring into nothingness, he wondered how things could have gone wrong so goddamned quickly.

The next couple of days would carry them into some of their darkest times, he knew. He wondered if any of them could survive it.

* * *

Ed awoke, disoriented, flanked by both of his sleeping boys. He sat up, looking around, trying to remember where he was and how he'd gotten there.

A few moments passed and then it hit, hard, cold and unflinching.

The bite from the carrier.

His son was going to die.

Tears filled his eyes, the full realization of what had happened to Zach drenching him in a horrible, unjust reality. Sobs wracked his body as despair washed over him, tearing through him, leaving him vacant and broken inside. Eventually the sobbing subsided, tapering off into a free-flow of tears. He would have to figure out a way to pull himself together when the boys were awake; he couldn't allow them to see him this way, especially not Zach. Their time was so short now; they had to stay strong and get all they could from it.

Just as he had done when Sarah got sick.

It was a father's job to protect his children, to prevent harm from befalling them. It had been his job to keep his children safe and he'd failed miserably. Now the same virus that destroyed the world was incubating in his son's body, dividing and growing as he slept. Soon it would override everything that had made Zach who he was. It was the worst thing about the virus; rather than kill outright it stole one's humanity first, leaving the animated corpse to walk about and repeat the terrible cycle.

Zach would become a raving lunatic, bent on killing everyone in the group, even his own father and brother. The thing Zach would become would be nothing more than an animal masquerading as his son, devastating his body and corrupting his brain.

It would then be Ed's responsibility to end his son's suffering, just as he had for his son's mother.

Slowly and carefully, Ed sat up, being careful not to disturb the children. They rustled in their sleep, but they didn't wake. Earlier, Zach had asked him about the bite and Ed had told him a lie. It was just a scratch, he'd told the body. They couldn't be sure of anything.

Zach had accepted his father's lie, but whether or not the boy truly believed it Ed couldn't be sure. Zach was a smart boy though; if he didn't already know he would very soon. Once the virus took hold and started to change Zach the lie would collapse under its own weight.

There could be no more fibs, well-intentioned or not. Ed and his sons would bide their time together, what little they had, but the sand would eventually run out of the hourglass. And when the last grain fell through, when all was lost and his son became something else entirely, it would be Ed's responsibility to take away his son's suffering.

But not tonight.

There were too many things left to say and they still had some time remaining. Whatever time they had left, they were going to make the most of it. And then, when the time came, he'd do it while the boy slept.

Just as he had done with Sarah.

* * *

The following morning Mitchell awoke at daybreak. The others rose shortly thereafter. He watched Ed as he lay asleep with his sons, the three of them still positioned away from the group.

After Ed and the boys woke, Trish offered them some breakfast. They accepted, thanking her. She kept herself together while around them, but her tough exterior broke down by the time she returned to where Mitchell and the others sat. She cried on Mitchell's shoulder, sobbing as he held her. Eventually her tears dried up and she regained her composure as best she could.

For a while she sat beside Mitchell on the ground, her eyes puffy and swollen, her face red, holding his hand while attempting to hold back the tears.

Dave kept busy, making another trip into the woods for more water. Tammy sat, silently staring into the woods, her back toward the others.

"I brought coffee," Mitchell said to Trish, forcing a grin.

She chuckled at his attempt at mild humor.

"Want some?" he asked.

Trish nodded. "Sure."

Mitchell heated water for the coffee, preparing a rudimentary filtration system similar to the one he'd employed back at the warehouse. It was a time-consuming process, one that took his mind off their crushing problems, at least for a while. After the coffee was brewed, he poured some for Trish in a metal cup he'd brought.

"Want some, Tammy?" he asked.

Tammy shook her head.

"I'm sorry about Brenda," he said. "She seemed like a great girl."

Tammy nodded, her back toward him. "Yeah, she was."

* * *

"Daddy, will I see Mommy again soon?" Zach asked.

Ed felt his heart sink. After so much sadness he thought he could feel no more, but sorrow showed no kind regard to limitation.

"Don't talk like that," Ed told him. "We don't know anything for sure yet."

"Will I, Daddy?" Zach asked again. "Tell me the truth."

He looked at his son lying in the sleeping bag, the spitting image of his mother. Zach's face was honest; afraid but unflinching. The boy's strength was immeasurable.

Ed felt shame looking into his son's eyes. Lies would hold no water and would earn no merit with Zach. Brutal honesty was all they had left, now that everything else had been stripped away. They were all emotionally raw, completely exposed to one another as never before.

"If Heaven's real then you definitely will," Ed told him. It was as honest as he could be.

Zach smiled.

If Ed could have switched places with him he wouldn't have hesitated to do so. The universe, however, would have its way, while everyone else be damned.

* * *

Tammy sat, staring into the distance. She no longer had any appetite and no desire for water, despite her pounding headache. Her world was in upheaval. Everything had changed and there was no going back.

What will I do now? she wondered. Her best friend, the only person who ever really understood her was gone now, killed in an instant by a maniac with a gun. Pointless, all of it. She felt numb and distant, dead inside. The world, a festering shithole even before the virus, had turned even uglier and more horrible after the virus.

Now it was unlivable.

As if everything that had happened wasn't terrible enough, now the boy was infected. The virus knew nothing of compassionate discrimination. An innocent child robbed not once, but twice. First of his mother, and now of his own life.

Tammy was an outsider in this group, just as she'd been

an outsider in the world before the virus. Maybe she hadn't given Dave a chance; maybe he wasn't such a bad guy after all. But the way Brenda had sidled up to him, leaving her best friend behind to toe the line…that made it feel as if Brenda had been taken away from her twice.

It was all just so hopeless, so pointless, and so brutally painful.

In the end it was ultimately so fucking meaningless.

Suppose they did reach this so-called "safe" city? Suppose it was virus-free. Suppose she could live there for the rest of her life. What did it change? She would still be an outcast, even among the few survivors left. What could ever change that?

Nothing, really. Nothing at all.

* * *

That evening Ed remained with Zach and Jeremy. It had been almost twenty-four hours since Zach's infection and Ed knew, as they all did, that Zach had likely exhausted all the time he had left. The virus was fast, too fast. Since the virus made its first appearance three years ago no one had ever made it past forty-eight hours without showing symptoms.

Ed and the boys talked throughout the day. They didn't mention the virus anymore; it was pointless. Instead, they spoke of the good old days, the days when they'd all been a family. The days when their mother was still alive, before the world as they knew it had ended. Trips to the art museum, grocery shopping, the zoo, the first day of school, birthdays, Halloween, and Christmas. All the things that made up their lives together, the strands of experience that connected them so much more closely than genetics ever could.

Ed checked Zach's wound periodically. On the surface it seemed no worse than it had been the prior day. He could see no excessive swelling or discharge, nothing to indicate bacterial infection. The viral infection, however, was another matter altogether. It would only be a matter of time before the signs would start to show. It started with fever and it got much, much worse from there.

They napped sporadically throughout the day. Ed held

his sons close, as if their closeness would allow him to absorb their essence. He cared nothing of infection anymore; what would be, would be. Jeremy acted brave, watching his father and emulating him, but Ed knew he was devastated.

There was no guard duty for them. They didn't watch for carriers nor did they watch for the dangerous uninfected. Ed didn't care anymore. The virus had won. If its minions showed up to deliver it to the rest of his family then so be it. It was a fitting end.

* * *

Later that night Ed awoke again, surrounded by his sons. He lifted his head to look around and saw Dave on guard duty, staring into the woods. The rest of the group lay on the ground, asleep. Ed watched his sons as they slept in the dim moonlight; two beautiful, broken creatures. They'd suffered enough, hadn't they? Hadn't they all?

Where was their relief, their blessings from on high? Nowhere to be seen. They were on their own, and only Ed could bring an end to that suffering.

He would make it quick. Zach would never know it was coming. He would have to handle Jeremy's grief after it was done. How, exactly, he would do that he didn't know. It was a bridge he'd cross later. And once Ed pulled that trigger, Jeremy would never be the same again.

Ed moved slowly to avoid waking the children, reaching down for his pistol. Slowly he removed the gun from the holster, placing the barrel of the pistol near Zach's temple. The chamber was loaded; all it would take was a squeeze of the trigger. He flipped the safety off and placed his finger carefully on the trigger. One squeeze, one trivial little movement, and his son's suffering would never occur. Zach would go quickly and painlessly, without knowing the hell his mother had known before she died.

He watched his son sleep, his chest rising and falling in the dim light from the sliver of moon high above. He thought about all the things Zach should have been allowed to experience. He thought about the man his son should have become. Ed remembered holding Zach right after he was born, and in that instant he saw his son's life pass before his eyes. None of what he'd planned for his son would happen now. It was just a ghostly vision, an imagined screenplay of a life that would be cut well before its end.

With the gun to his son's head and his finger on the trigger, Ed's stomach twisted into knots. His face tingled, growing hot and flushed as adrenaline poured into his bloodstream. His heart raced. Emotions he hadn't felt in years rushed in, overwhelming him, reminding him of Sarah. Killing his infected wife was the hardest thing he had ever done.

The time had now come for Zach to die. Ed wondered: did he have the fortitude to carry it out? Could he pull the trigger and kill his own flesh and blood?

His finger squeezed the trigger, just slightly. He held it there for a moment, feeling the firing pin on the very edge of striking the cap of the shell. One click and then oblivion; a tiny scrap of lead to send his boy on his way. Ed had brought this human being into the world, now he would be the one to take him out of it.

His finger tightened slightly on the trigger. A tear fell from his eye. Tighter he squeezed. His heart beating so hard he thought it might explode. Squeezing…

He relaxed. He wondered: had they spent all the time they could together? They still very likely had another twenty-four hours. The virus hadn't shown any signs yet, so time was still available. The end would come of course, but there was still precious time left. An hour? Maybe two? What if they had another eight hours of lucidity available to them? How could he end his son's life if he still had just a bit more to squeeze out of it? Was that fair to Zach? Was it fair to Jeremy? Hadn't he killed Sarah *after* she turned?

Ed released the trigger, reapplying the safety. Do it he would, but not tonight. He placed the pistol back into its holster then lay back down between his boys. Tears leaked from his eyes, his chest convulsing as the sobbing wracked his body. Ed held his doomed son closer as Jeremy stirred in his sleep, reaching out to hug his father.

After some time Ed fell asleep, his face streaked with tears. He slept through the rest of the night, sleeping the fitful yet dreamless sleep of the damned.

* * *

Tammy awoke the following morning before the rest of the group, head pounding. She opened her eyes and saw Dave, his back to her, finishing up the tail end of his guard duty. She closed her eyes again. Her mouth was dry, her belly empty. She felt it, but so numb was she that the feelings barely registered.

Her best friend was dead. That knowledge was like a dull ache, affecting every part of her mind and body, worse than any hunger or thirst she'd ever felt.

It was all meaningless; all their effort, all their struggles, all their successes and failures. It all amounted to nothing in the end. None of it mattered now, and none of it would matter going forward. Another day of pontification and consideration hadn't changed that. It never would. She was sick and she was tired. Her future held only day after day of the same worthless grind, only to ultimately become food for the deadwalkers, or to catch a bullet from a sniper as Brenda had.

Tammy opened her eyes again, sitting up.

Dave turned at the sound of movement. "Morning," he said.

She grunted a response, too lethargic and apathetic to offer much more than that. She looked over and saw Ed sleeping with his two sons. It was only a matter of hours before the oldest one would start turning. After Zach was dead, how long could Ed expect to protect the younger one?

Tammy stood up, surveying the camp. Everyone else was asleep, blissfully and temporarily unaware of the pain that permeated each one of them. They'd remember it when they woke up, and they'd suffer through it all day until sleep could bring more peaceful relief. Then they'd do it all again the next day.

Pointless.

She glanced at Ed and his boys again. How could anyone expect Ed to carry on after the death of his son? Would he allow his son to turn into one of those…things? Surely not. That meant he'd have to do the job himself.

How could a father, any father, live with killing his own son, even if it was a mercy killing?

She knelt, picking up the rifle.

He shouldn't have to find out, she thought.

* * *

In his dream Ed was home. Sarah was there, healthy and happy, sitting on the couch of their living room. Bright light streamed in through the picture window behind her, nearly blinding in its intensity. Zach and Jeremy sat on the floor, playing with toys together. They were seven and five respectively, as they had been just before the virus struck.

Light that grew brighter and brighter obscured Sarah's face. He tried to speak to her, but found he couldn't. Her mouth moved as if to say something to him, but he could hear no sound. She was smiling, her mouth turning up into a slight sneer on the right side like it always did when she was happy. They'd often called it her "Elvis" smile as a joke.

He tried to run to the couch, to his living wife, but his legs were nearly frozen. It was as if his feet were trapped in deep, wet mud. He tried to speak again without success. Then he tried screaming. No sound came forth.

Sarah began to drift away. Ed looked down at his hand. It was filthy, stained with years of travel, and in it he held his pistol. He raised it, pointing it toward his wife, and suddenly the expression on her face changed. Her brow furrowed, her smile turned into a frown, and her eyes lost focus. She bared her teeth like an animal as she opened her mouth to scream.

* * *

The sound of a gunshot jolted Ed from his sleep.

"Tammy!" Dave yelled. He turned to the rest of the group. They were all awake now. "That was Tammy's rifle," he told them, eyes wide.

"Where is she?" Trish asked.

"She went to the woods to pee."

"With her gun?" she asked.

"Of course with her gun. We gotta go check it out. She

might have run into a carrier."

Trish looked at Dave. "Honey, I don't think she took a shot at a carrier."

"What do you mean?" he asked. A moment later a look of sick realization passed over his face. "Oh, no."

"I'm sorry," Trish replied.

Dave sat down, lost in realization. The rest of the group waited for his reaction. A few moments later Dave stood up, drawing the pistol that had once belonged to Brenda from his front pocket. "I'll take care of it," he told them. "She's my responsibility."

A few minutes later he found Tammy lying face down on the forest floor, her rifle lying beside her lifeless body. A large exit wound had destroyed the back of her head. He felt he should have been more shocked, but things were happening so quickly he barely had the time to feel anything anymore. First Sandy and Jim, then Brenda and poor Zach. Now Tammy too. Things were falling apart too quickly to patch them back together again.

Dave glanced once more at Tammy's body before recovering her rifle. True, they hadn't been the best of friends, but he hadn't wanted this. But if this was her choice, then so be it. Life went on. It was time to either get busy living, or get busy dying.

Dave walked back to camp, leaving the body where it lay.

* * *

During the second day after Zach's bite, Ed remained distant, spending all his time with Zach and Jeremy. The wound on his son's neck now showed the first signs of healing, but strangely enough the boy wasn't yet showing signs of the disease. Each extra minute was a precious gift.

Ed kept up appearances, but inside he felt he was dying. Hard and sharp in his mind throughout the day was the knowledge of what he would have to do. He felt increasingly more like a thief, stealing time for himself from his son. He was putting off the inevitable, buying time, but was it at Zach's expense? He couldn't be sure. Maybe it *was* stealing, and maybe it *was* unfair, but it was all the time any of them would have together. Wasting it seemed worse than biding it.

Throughout the day Mitchell and Dave took turns running scouting trips to see what lay in the direction they were headed. Ed overheard them as they recounted what they'd seen: buildings, streets, stoplights, and more. They were very close to the city now, the city his son had gone to sleep with every night for the past couple years. A city Zach would never get to see now.

Ed paid close attention to Zach as they spent time together throughout the second day. While there should have been signs of the virus by the second day, none appeared. They talked, they remembered, they even laughed. Ed watched his boy closely all through the day and into the evening, yet Zach showed not a single symptom of infection.

At the end of the second day, as Ed lay with his two sons in the darkness, he felt a sense of both relief and dread. Without signs of the virus he would not shoot his son. Maybe they would get a few more hours together? Maybe even another day? He only knew that whatever time they did get together he would not dare waste it.

* * *

The following morning Ed awoke before the others. Mitchell was coming off guard duty, sitting with his back against a large tree. Ed rose, being careful not to wake the boys and walked over to where Mitchell sat. It was the first interaction he had had with anyone other than Trish in the past two days.

"Good morning," Mitchell said to him as he approached. He motioned for Ed to take a seat on the ground beside him. "Good to see you up and about."

"Morning," Ed replied.

"How's he doing?" Mitchell asked.

"Well enough, given the circumstances."

"How are you doing?"

"I've been better."

Mitchell paused for a moment, gathering his thoughts. "Ed, I've been watching, and that boy hasn't showed any of the signs yet."

"I know. I can't explain it."

"I think maybe I can."

"How so?" Ed asked, his interests piqued.

"That virus," Mitchell continued, "it shows itself in a day, maybe two, tops. Am I right?"

"Yeah, that's what I've seen. Your point?"

"So nobody ever got infected by it and didn't show symptoms within two days. Nobody. Your boy, though; he's outta the first day, even the second day, and he seems fine."

"So far, yeah."

"Well, that sorta thing hasn't happened before, least not that I'm aware of, and I seen a lot folks get sick with this. A lot."

Ed's brow furrowed. "What are you trying to say?"

"What I'm sayin' is I saw this comin'."

Ed was puzzled. "How so?"

"Think about it. Why ain't *we* sick? You and me, those girls, all of us? That virus…almost everybody got it. If somebody sneezed in your direction, it was curtains. Touch a shopping cart or an escalator, and you got it. It was *everywhere*." He leaned forward and looked directly at Ed. "I'm sayin' I think it's *still* everywhere."

"But how could it be?" Ed replied. "We would have picked it up a long time ago. Unless…" His eyes widened; the revelation was like a kick to the chest. His mouth went dry as his mind raced to comprehend the impact of the next words he spoke.

"Unless we're immune."

Chapter Eighteen

Ed, Zach, Jeremy, Trish, Dave, and Mitchell left their impromptu camp around midday. They headed west, toward the city, leaving their two dead companions well behind them.

As the day wore on, Zach showed no symptoms of viral infection. The wound on his neck continued to heal as one would expect of a wound of that nature. Ed tried his best to remain cautiously optimistic. After all, there was no guarantee they were right about Mitchell's hypothesized immunity.

Despite all that, it was impossible to argue that all signs weren't pointing to Zach making a full recovery. If what Mitchell said was true, Zach was getting a second chance at life, an eleventh hour reprieve from what they'd all been certain was a death sentence.

Mitchell and Ed had told Zach the news after he awoke. He took it well, never for a moment doubting. Cautious optimism was a burden of adulthood. They told the rest of the group next and after all the horrible things they'd experienced over the past few months, the news left them completely overjoyed. A buzz permeated the camp before they left, as if a spark had ignited a fire that had been smoldering to the point of extinction just days earlier.

They walked for most of the day, stopping only for food, water and calls of nature. Ed kept both boys close by as they walked. Trish watched all of this with nothing short of absolute joy. Her happiness seemed to almost numb her of the horrible things she'd experienced up to now. Happiness was often fleeting, but Trish knew that the feeling of overwhelming joy and hope that came with Zach's second chance would stay with her for the rest of her life.

Mitchell kept up well, despite his earlier claims of geriatric inability. After watching him take the carriers down at the farmhouse with machinelike precision everyone knew his self-deprecating style was that of humility. Mitchell was one to speak softly while carrying a very big stick.

After they ate, Ed cleaned Zach's wound again before allowing the boys to walk off a short distance to play in the dirt. Ed made sure they didn't get too far away. The sight of both boys playing again filled Ed with euphoric glee. Seeing the makeshift bandage wrapped around Zach's neck only served to elevate his joy, a reminder of the bite his son had beaten.

Mitchell sat down on the ground beside Ed, groaning as he sat. They both sat for some time, silent, watching the kids play together. Brothers, reunited. In Mitchell's fingers he held a bullet, spinning it around and around, a trick he performed to keep his hands busy when they weren't doing the kind of work they did best.

A few moments later, Dave and Trish joined them where they sat. The four of them watched the boys for a while, Trish wearing a large grin.

"He's gonna be fine," Mitchell said, breaking the silence. "Ed, I know I don't need to tell you this, but your boy got the second chance most people don't."

"I know," Ed replied. "You don't know how much I know that."

"And so did you," Mitchell continued.

Ed nodded. "I know that very well too."

Mitchell said: "I had a daughter, you know."

"Do you know what happened to her?" Trish asked.

Mitchell shook his head. "She was older than Ed's boys, but you know that really don't make no difference; your babies are always your babies. Her mom and me, we divorced some years back. I was known to hit the bottle a bit back then; could be that had something to do with her leavin'. Hard to say now, so many years later. Maybe we were just too different to get along.

"Her mom moved away, took my baby girl with her. I didn't get to see her much as she grew, but I tried to make the most of it when I did. She was a good kid; good grades in school, listened to her mom and me, everything a father could ask for.

"But when the virus came along everything went crazy, and she and her mom disappeared in the mess. I tried to find her, but I couldn't. I made it to their house eventually, but by the time I got there it was long since empty. No word on where they went, or if she even survived."

"That's terrible," Trish said.

"You know, a lot of people from my generation didn't like computers and cell phones, but it's not until something is gone that you appreciate it. Before the virus my daughter had set me up with e-mail, and I could even figure out how to send her text messages on her phone. I could reach her anytime. I started to take all that for granted. After the computers and cell phones went down there was no way to talk to her. I wandered around for months, looking anywhere I could. People huddled up for a while in stores and whatnot, like refugee camps, but I never found her anywhere I looked."

"How long did you look for her?" Ed asked.

"Couple years. Eventually I just accepted what I knew was true; she was gone for good. After that I walked for a while, shacking up wherever I could find a place to sleep. Not too long ago I settled in that warehouse and then all you folks showed up. Seeing those boys again, well, it sort of brought things back."

"Why did you follow us, Mitchell?" Ed asked. "You saved our lives back there at that farmhouse."

"I don't know for sure. Maybe that feeling I got after seeing you with your boys was God's way of telling me I still had some kind of purpose left in me."

"Once again, we thank you," Trish said.

"I just wish I'd made it sooner. Maybe I could've saved Brenda. I suppose Tammy too, in a roundabout fashion."

"You did what you could," Trish reminded him. "You can't blame yourself."

Mitchell nodded.

A long pause ensued as they all watched the kids play. Eventually Dave spoke. "Immune," he said, shaking his head. "It's mind-blowing. Why'd we never think about that before?"

"I suppose maybe we all thought we were just lucky," Ed replied. Ed's response reminded Dave of his own conversation with Brenda and Tammy after killing the child carrier.

"It's also not a theory you want to test out," Trish mused.

"No, I suppose not," Mitchell said. "What happened to your boy back there, although I'd never wish it, was the test we needed."

"But there's no guarantee that we're all immune," Dave said. "I mean, some of us could still just be lucky."

"True," Mitchell said, smiling. "I think we'll all still want to be careful, just in case."

* * *

The surviving members of the group made their way west, toward the city by the river. Mitchell slowed a bit, providing some substance to his claims of geriatric restriction, but the rest of the group matched his pace without a word. Even with this mild reduction in pace they continued making good time.

After another meal and several more hours of walking they crested a hill, and upon ascension encountered a sight that made them all stop in their tracks and stare, mouths agape.

The Gateway Arch, constructed of shining, stainless steel and standing over six hundred feet above the city streets, peeked at them from just above the treetops, beckoning to them from the distance. The city Ed and his two sons had spent years walking toward was now real and tangible. After staring at the structure for some time, Ed almost worried that it might simply disappear as they neared, like a mirage in the desert. But it remained, steady and strong, clearly visible in the distance through the hazy air.

"If we keep walking until nightfall, we can probably cross that distance by tomorrow night, you think?" Dave asked the group.

Mitchell spoke: "I think so, provided my bum legs hold out."

"We'll keep our fingers crossed that you won't have any blowouts," Trish said, smiling.

Mitchell chuckled. "Honey, nothing's guaranteed by the time you get to this age, but we'll sure hope for the best."

Mitchell turned his attention to Ed, watching him as he stood in the middle of the derelict road, holding his sons' hands, staring at the stainless steel structure in the distance.

He smiled, leaving them to their thoughts.

* * *

They camped that night after walking another four hours. As they walked, the landscape began to change from farmland and residential suburbs to industrialized city. Abandoned buildings, exhibiting neglect that began long before the virus destroyed their caretakers, loomed on either side of them. Forest and fields gave way to weedy parking lots, decrepit city houses, and tattered apartment buildings.

They walked until nightfall was almost upon them, taking refuge along the base of an old wall standing sadly by itself, its three counterparts long since demolished and carried away by men no doubt long dead and gone. To avoid drawing attention to themselves they lit no fire. Luckily most of the deep chill during the nights had been replaced with milder temperatures over the past couple of weeks, and this night was no exception.

Late in the night the screams began. Ed counted eight or ten of these, each bone-chilling in its agony and fury. They were moving into carrier territory, no doubt, and Ed wondered just how safe they were camping with only a crumbling wall to conceal them. Like rats, the cities were the last refuges of the infected, and myriad city structures now surrounded the group.

Ed sat against the wall, holding Zach and Jeremy tightly, gripping them harder with each scream they heard. Everyone was awake; sleep would no doubt be hard to come by this evening. Trish sat next to Ed against the wall, peering into the inky darkness.

"I remember a time when the cities lit up the night sky," she told him. "Now they're just as dark as the countryside."

"Eerie," Ed replied. "Even after all these years I'm still not used to it."

Silence ensued as they sat.

"We're going to make it, you know," Trish told him.

"Yeah," he replied, hoping it was true.

Trish said: "Dave's taking guard duty for now. Mind if I stay here with you guys for a while?"

"I'd mind if you didn't," Ed replied.

Trish smiled at Ed and the boys, and they all returned it.

Ed put the boys down to sleep a few feet away, far enough away for he and Trish to speak in private, while close enough to get to them should trouble arise. Both Ed and Trish sat down together, their backs against the rotting wall, staring toward the city.

"Back there at the camp, after Zach was bitten," he began, "I just wanted to say thanks for your help."

Trish smiled. "No problem. It was the least I could do. You don't know how happy I am that Zach is okay."

"I am too," he told her.

More silence followed as they stared into the darkness.

A few moments later Trish said: "What do you think we'll find once we get to the city? For real, I mean. Not necessarily what you hope for."

Ed thought about the question for a while. "I don't know. I'm afraid it'll be overrun, just like all the other cities were. And if it is, I'm not sure how we'll get back out again. Of course it might all be true. There could be a safe haven on the other side of that river, just waiting for us. Either way, this may be the end of the line for all of us."

"I'm still holding out hope," Trish replied.

Ed reached around her shoulders with one arm and pulled her near. "So am I," he said. "So am I."

* * *

Two hours later Dave woke Ed for his turn on guard duty. Two hours after that it was Mitchell's turn. Then came Trish's rotation. Eventually the sun rose, basking the ruined city in bright, orange light and warming the air around them. They had made it through the night, but they were still well outside the city. What they would find there was still a mystery.

They began walking shortly after dawn, finishing five cans of beef stew and two cans of corn before taking their leave. They were making the push to the city today and stocking up on calories was the first step. Their canteens were running low, however, and the natural streams they'd used in the past to refill them were now nonexistent. Finding potable water in the city was proving difficult.

They walked along the highway, which now led them directly into a city once known as East Saint Louis. Now it was an even more crumbling and disintegrating relic of its former pathetic self. Roofs were collapsing into buildings, broken glass lay everywhere, and the bodies of the dead began to increase in number. The older corpses didn't worry them so much, it was the fresher bodies that made them all nervous.

After walking several more hours they heard another scream. The screams during the night had sounded far away, but this scream sounded close. They all stopped, looked, and listened. Ed drew his pistol, as did Dave. Trish carried Tammy's rifle now, but kept it slung over her shoulder. Zach and Jeremy remained ready, but didn't draw as they were waiting on word from their father. Mitchell's hand moved closer to the pistols he carried strapped to his hips.

"I don't think we should use the guns," Ed recommended, holstering his own pistol. He removed the baseball bat from his backpack. "If there are only a few then we can take them out without the noise. If we start firing we might as well blast a trumpet to announce our arrival."

"I agree," Dave said, holstering Brenda's pistol and removing his own baseball bat.

"I'm gonna need something here for myself," Mitchell said.

"How about a tire iron?" Dave asked.

"That'd work, if I had one."

"Well, my friend, this is your lucky day." Dave removed his backpack, rummaging through it until he retrieved the tire iron he'd procured back at the 7-Eleven with Brenda and Tammy. He felt a pang of sadness as thoughts of the two dead girls crept into his mind. Clearing his mind, he handed Mitchell the tire iron. Mitchell took it, turning it over in his hand and looking at it curiously.

"I know it's not the same as a pistol, but you'll manage," Dave said, sliding on his backpack.

Suddenly from behind them they heard a carrier scream. They watched it as it stumbled up to the highway from an embankment before bellowing out another cry. Once upon the road, it ran toward them, its right arm hanging limp. Tattered, blackened rags covered its body as it covered the distance quickly.

Ed ran forward to meet it. A few feet away, he swung the bat as hard as he could, striking the thing in the mouth. The carrier put its left hand up to block the blow, but it made no difference in the end. The deadwalker's lips and teeth disappeared into its mouth, its head snapping backward with sickening momentum from the impact of wood upon flesh and bone. The carrier fell instantly on the concrete highway, twitching as it lay there, blood oozing from the thing's destroyed mouth.

"Ed, look out!" Trish cried.

Ed looked up from the dead carrier to see two more charging him. One had a severe limp, the other was reasonably able-bodied.

Dave ran toward the carriers, first taking out the spry one with a baseball bat blow to the side of the head.

The carrier with the limp screamed before Ed smashed its head with the bat, silencing it. "We gotta get outta here!" he yelled.

They all regrouped before running away. Ed looked back to see two more carriers making their way up from the embankment and toward the road, but they were too sick or paralyzed to catch up.

They ran for several more minutes, eventually taking a break as the fatigue caught up with them. They were all still shaken from the encounter; all of them were out of breath and pumped full of adrenaline.

As they stood catching their breath Mitchell shot Dave a look of approval. "You handled yourself well, back there, son. Good work."

Dave nodded. "Thanks. That was close," he said, breathing heavily.

Trish stood, slightly bent with her hands on her knees. "We need a plan."

"Trish is right," Mitchell added. "Walking right into that city ain't gonna be easy."

Ed thought about it, struggling to come up with a plan. Had he really thought they could just walk right in? It wouldn't be easy, that was for sure now. He considered turning around, thinking maybe they could retreat and come up with a better solution. As Ed stood, thinking of a new plan, Zach tugged on his father's sleeve. Ed looked at his son and saw the fear clearly in the boy's eyes. Zach said nothing as he pointed toward the stretch of highway behind them.

As Ed turned he saw them.

All of them.

There would be no turning back now.

Chapter Nineteen

The first seven carriers encroached from behind like a pack of wolves. Paralysis gripped three of the deadwalkers so severely they were barely able to walk. The remaining four, however, were healthy and formidable.

The four able-bodied carriers charged. A shiver passed through Ed's body as the distance between his group and the oncoming ravenous animals quickly shrank. It was an absolutely terrifying sight to behold. Before he could move he watched as Dave darted toward the oncoming deadwalkers, striking the lead carrier in the head with his already bloodied baseball bat. The deadhead fell hard after the bat connected, shaking violently upon the ground as dark, syrupy blood oozed from its cracked skull. It screamed, gagging, as blood dripped from its blackened tongue. Another blow from Dave's bat swiftly and mercifully silenced the screams.

As Dave dispatched the carrier on the ground, Ed watched helplessly as the second carrier came within feet of where Dave stood. There was no way he could make the shot; the thing was moving too fast and Ed simply didn't have the skill. Ed opened his mouth to yell, to warn Dave of the approaching threat when a shot rang out, the report crackling through the air. The charging carrier dropped to the ground in heap, a small bullet hold visible in its forehead. Ed turned to see Mitchell, gun drawn and pointed.

Startled by the sound, Dave turned around and watched the carrier fall to the ground. Looking at Mitchell, he gave the thumbs up before swinging the bat at a third carrier as it approached. The bat struck the deadhead's bulky shoulder, the collarbone cracking upon impact.

Another shot rang out and the fourth carrier fell. The men looked back to see Trish on one knee, Tammy's rifle still aimed at the fallen body.

So much for keeping the guns quiet, Ed thought to himself. Although they'd had no choice but to use the guns, any hope of sneaking through to the city was now dashed.

"Boys, grab your guns!" Ed yelled to Zach and Jeremy. They drew their pistols as instructed.

Ed turned around and charged toward one of the near-paralyzed carriers, baseball bat in hand. A single blow to the head brought the thing down. It lay in a pool of its own blood; matted dreadlocks splayed out on the concrete around its head. He took the next one down, while Dave finished off the deadwalker with the broken collarbone, eliminating their most immediate threats.

"Run!" Dave yelled to the others.

They ran.

"There are more up ahead!" Trish yelled. Several more carriers had come seemingly from nowhere, limping toward them. With so many nooks and crannies in the city the deadwalkers seemed to be coming from everywhere.

"Dad, behind us!" Jeremy yelled.

Two more carriers filed in behind the group. Now they were nearly surrounded. Mitchell fired two rounds back to back, dropping both carriers behind them.

Ed heard Dave yell, turning instinctively. Behind him another deadwalker approached Dave, arms and claw-like fingernails extended, teeth bared as it gripped Dave and attempted to bite into his throat. With no time to think, Ed ran toward the attacker, swinging the bat, striking the carrier in the back. It screamed, releasing its grip and falling to the ground. Ed brought the bat down hard, splitting the carrier's head open, silencing its screams.

Two more shots rang out, both from Mitchell, and Ed watched in shock as two carriers fell to the ground just behind where Zach and Jeremy stood. He made eye contact with Mitchell, sharing a thankful look with him. Mitchell nodded in reply.

More carriers appeared from the buildings around them. With the two closest threats in front of them getting closer, Trish fired a shot to bring them down. The shot missed. Cursing, she loaded another round into the barrel and fired, landing the shot. The carrier went down, clutching its stomach and screaming. Quickly loading another shell into the chamber, Trish fired another round, taking the second carrier down in its tracks.

Jeremy and Zach fired several shots each into the crowd of rushing carriers, bringing several of them down. Despite their efforts, however, the group teetered on the edge of being overrun. More carriers were blocking the road in front of them and clear passage would be impossible if they couldn't shoot them all. With a finite supply of ammunition, they couldn't afford waste.

Ed knew they needed a plan, but with deadwalkers closing in on all sides they had no time to regroup and devise one. If only they could find a place to hide they could let things blow over while they figured out their next move. "Off the road!" Ed yelled to the group. "Stay together and follow me!"

He headed away from the road, ensuring his sons were in tow. Trish ran behind them, with Mitchell and Dave bringing up the rear. As they ran, Mitchell fired off several more shots, each one striking its target with impeccable accuracy. Ed searched desperately for a hiding place. Having successfully used a house as a hiding place while retrieving the antibiotics, he looked for a structure that might provide refuge while they figured out a plan for getting into the city.

Finally he spied an old warehouse to his right; it was in bad shape, but it was close and it was enclosed. He couldn't know if there were carriers inside, so they would just have to take their chances. As it was they didn't have much choice; they weren't any safer where they were out in the open, fully exposed.

They ran to the entrance. Ed stopped. "Take out as many as you can, any of them that might see us go in. We can hole up here for now until we come up with a new plan."

Mitchell nodded. Using both pistols he fired five shots, eliminating the closest deadwalkers before they all ran inside the building through a large metal door, rusted solid on its hinges.

Debris covered the interior of the building. Rubble from the decaying structure mixed with brown mud, orange rust, and crisp, dead leaves from outside to create a dangerous, ankle-spraining carpet. They ran deeper into the building, dodging the larger pieces of trash and rubble, in a desperate attempt to find some place suitable for hiding while things died down outside.

As they made their way deeper into the structure, running through a large, empty, debris-laden room, Ed spotted an empty door frame that he hoped led to a smaller room they could use to hide in. The group dashed through it toward the back of the building, hopping over wilted cardboard boxes, crumbling, fallen ceiling tiles and random trash littering the floor.

Suddenly Ed stopped, holding his arms out to stop the rest of the group behind him.

Before them was their worst-case scenario. Gathered around a black and white dog carcass sat a dozen or more carriers, all eating the animal's rotten remains. As Ed and the group approached from the opposite room, several of the things looked up from their putrid meal, examining the intruders with piqued interest. As Ed and the others slowly backed away, one of the carriers sitting around the dog with rotten, maggot-filled meat dangling from the corner of its mouth recognized that the intruders weren't infected. It screamed, the rotten meat dropping from its mouth, blackened teeth bared. The others quickly joined in, their arms raised and their teeth gnashing together as they tilted their heads back and unleashed mad screams.

Two deadwalkers made it to their feet before Mitchell fired twice, bringing them down quickly. The remaining carriers scrambled to their feet as quickly as they could, some more able-bodied than others. One carrier lay paralyzed on the floor, simply screaming while unable to stand. More screams resonated from behind the other carriers, deeper within the building. Ed and his group had stumbled upon what amounted to a nest of deadwalkers. They'd jumped out of the frying pan and directly into the burning, scorching fire.

Mitchell aimed at the rising carriers, but held his fire as more carriers streamed into the room from behind the group that had been eating the dog.

"Too many!" Mitchell exclaimed.

"Back!" Ed yelled. "We have to go back!"

Dave shot two more carriers as they approached too closely, their mouths stained brown from the rotten entrails of the dead dog. "Where?" he asked. "We're blocked in!"

"The carriers out front…" Trish began.

"Let's hope they didn't see us go in," Mitchell replied.

"We don't have any choice," Ed said.

Mitchell nodded. "Move!"

They all turned, now in tow behind Dave, and ran back the way they'd come, toward the building's entrance and away from the carriers behind them. They ran through the litter and muck covering the warehouse floor, listening to the screams from behind as they crossed back through the empty door frame and to the large room on the other side.

There they ran into the next worst-case scenario. More carriers from the street met them, blocking them in on both sides now. They stopped where they were, Ed frantically searching for a way out. Carriers accumulated from both sides now, gaining ground with every passing second.

This can't be the way it ends, Ed thought. *There has to be a way out.*

Suddenly Dave called out. "Here!" he cried, pointing toward a door twenty feet away. On the door was a sign:

STAIRS

They raced to the stairwell, tugging desperately at the handle while dozens of rabid carriers closed in behind them. The door resisted at first, but after a few more tugs it eventually gave way, leading to a steep set of stairs. The door now open wide enough to fit through, the group quickly filed in, climbing the concrete stairs leading to the second floor.

Mitchell brought up the rear, tugging the door closed again. Just as the latch clicked into place, a mass of deadwalkers slammed into the metal door, their faces smashed against the thin and narrow window above the door handle. The wire-reinforced glass held. With the door latched, the carriers banged madly on the metal, screaming as they struggled to understand the complexity of the door handle.

Mitchell looked around for something to brace the door, but found nothing. He could only hope that the carriers would be unable to operate the door handle, at least long enough for the group to figure a way out of their jam. Leaving the carriers to work on the closed door, Mitchell ran up the steps to meet the rest of the group.

The second floor was as decrepit as the first floor, but this level of the warehouse was completely open, save for the support columns spaced evenly throughout. Windows, mostly broken, lined the sides of the huge room, allowing in ample light from outside. A breeze flowed through the broken panes, causing bits of plastic lying about to flap back and forth in the wind like the tattered remains of long-forgotten flags. Trash, animal droppings, dead leaves and a few rotten carrier bodies littered the floor.

They ran toward the center of the room, away from the

steps and the accumulating carriers below. Upon reaching the center of the room, they they stopped to regroup. They could hear the carriers screaming from the floor below, still temporarily confounded by the door at the bottom of the steps.

"What now?" Trish asked.

Ed looked at the stairs for movement before focusing his attention back on the group. "We have to get down from here somehow, out of this building. We're sitting ducks up here."

"Fire escape?" Mitchell suggested.

"Over there, Dad!" Zach cried, pointing to an open door across the room.

"Good eye!" Ed exclaimed, ushering Zach and Jeremy along with him as they ran.

The group raced across the room toward the doorway leading to the outside fire escape. A broken exit sign affixed to the wall above it hung precariously by one screw barely embedded in the rotten concrete.

Ed peered out the door leading to the fire escape, elated at first, but ultimately disappointed. The bottom section of the fire escape's ladder had at some point been removed, leaving a dangerous twenty-foot drop down to the concrete below. While jumping from that height might not kill them directly, a broken ankle would amount to the same thing.

Dave stared at the ground below. "Shit. We're going to have to jump."

"We won't make it, not without breaking an ankle or a leg," Ed said.

"Well, if we don't, those carriers are going to tear us to pieces. I'd rather take my chances with the fall," Dave countered.

Zach's eyes lit up. "Dad! Maybe we could find some rope."

"Good idea," Ed replied. He and the others looked around for anything they could use to lower themselves down to the ground below, but they could find nothing. "Sorry, buddy. I don't see any rope anywhere."

"Wait," Trish said, walking to the door. She stepped out on the platform of the fire escape and looked out across the side of the building. She pointed toward dozens upon dozens of stacked pallets sitting beside a dumpster, just below a large second-floor window. "We could use those instead."

Ed stepped onto the platform to see for himself. The stack of pallets rose nearly halfway to the window above them. That would cut the distance they had to fall in half. That was a jump he was confident they could make.

Ed turned to Trish and kissed her quickly on the lips. "Brilliant," he said, smiling.

She smiled back.

With deadwalkers still screaming and banging on the door below, the group ran across the open room until they reached the window above the pallets. The glass was partially broken, leaving sharp and jagged shards all around the window frame, like teeth on a great white shark. Ed used his baseball bat to break out the remaining pieces of glass, just as he'd done at the Walgreens while procuring medicine for Trish, cleaning the edge well enough for the others to sit on.

Ed motioned toward Trish. Without hesitation she stepped toward the window.

"You go first," Ed said. "I'll send the boys down next."

Trish nodded, swinging one leg out, followed by the other until she sat upon the windowsill. She turned backward and reached her hand out, taking Ed's hand in hers. "I love you," she said before turning and jumping to the pallets below. A second later she landed and stumbled, nearly falling to the concrete below. She caught herself at the last second, steadying herself on top of the pallets before leaping off to the ground.

She looked up at the group and gave the thumbs up. "Send the boys down!"

Ed motioned for Zach. "It's time buddy. Be brave."

Zach nodded.

Ed lifted his oldest son up and onto the windowsill. "Don't think about it. Just jump."

The boy hesitated for a moment before jumping off the windowsill and to the pallets below. After a second of freefall, Zach landed squarely on the pallets, bending his knees as he landed. Another jump to the ground and he stood by Trish.

Next, Ed lifted Jeremy up and placed him on the window ledge.

The boy grabbed his arm. "I'm scared, Daddy."

Ed touched his son's cheek. "I know, buddy, but you have to be brave like your brother. We don't have much time."

Below them the sound of more carriers screaming traveled frightfully through the air.

"Okay," Jeremy said, hesitating only for a moment before jumping with a little too much force. He overshot the pallets and fell, landing on his shoulder before rolling off the pallets. Trish and Zach lunged forward, catching him clumsily before he struck the ground.

Ed felt his muscles tense and his heart race as he watched. Once Jeremy was upright Trish again gave the thumbs up.

"Your turn," Mitchell said to Ed. "Those boys need their daddy."

Ed nodded, climbing onto the windowsill himself. He looked down at the pallets below. It was much higher than he'd expected, but he pushed off from the ledge and fell through the air. He landed, his left foot striking the pallet hard. He heard the sound of cracking wood as his foot went through the top board, a sharp pain racing up through his leg as the jagged, broken wood gouged his calf. His leg burning with pain, Ed made the jump to the ground.

Just as Ed looked up from the ground he watched Mitchell make the leap, followed by Dave. Mitchell leapt to the ground as Dave fell from the window. Ed could see the ragged arm of a carrier reach out to capture its prey, the deadhead screaming in frustration as it swiped at nothing but thin air. Both men made it to the ground safely.

They had no time to contemplate their luck. "Back to

the highway!" Dave yelled.

They all ran. Though Ed's leg burned with pain as he took each step, he pushed onward. To stop would mean certain death.

They ran, rounding the corner of the warehouse. Suddenly dozens of carriers flanked them, some paralyzed and limping, others running with frightening strength and aggression. Before Ed could pull his gun, Mitchell had already fired off three shots. Ed watched as the three closest carriers fell to the ground, blood oozing from the bodies into pools where they lay.

Feeling like he was in slow motion compared to Mitchell, Ed finally managed to pull his pistol from his belt. He fired off two shots of his own while limping on his injured leg. One shot missed entirely, the other caught its target in the shoulder. As the carrier went down screaming, Ed fired off another shot, bringing another carrier down hard to the ground. Three more deadwalkers appeared to replace them.

They ran, sticking together, away from the oncoming carriers. They crossed an alley, Ed in the lead, followed by Zach and Jeremy. Dave crossed the alley directly behind them. As he did, a group of carriers suddenly rushed in from the alley, cutting off Mitchell and Trish, separating them from the rest of the group. Trish and Mitchell stopped in their tracks, backing quickly away from the line of infected now standing between them and the rest of their group. Mitchell shot two of the closest threats as he and Trish retreated, but more appeared in their place. Ed, Dave, and the boys ran on, unaware their friends were no longer running with them.

"Ed!" Trish yelled, catching Ed's attention. He stopped and turned to see Trish and Mitchell on the other side of a growing wall of carriers.

"Ed, look out!" Dave called.

Ed turned to see three carriers coming directly toward him. He raised the pistol and fired twice, taking two of them down. He pulled the trigger again and heard the terrible click of the firing pin striking an empty chamber. There was no time to reload as the deadwalkers closed the distance.

A gunshot sounded from behind Ed. He watched as the charging carrier dropped to the ground. Ed turned to see Dave holding Brenda's gun.

Ed turned quickly toward Mitchell and Trish, only to watch in horror as the group of deadwalkers collectively changed direction to follow their two separated companions, like a ravenous school of piranha. Mitchell and Trish ran from the mob, Mitchell firing more shots into the crowd as they ran. With each shot a body fell to the ground, the other deadwalkers stepping on them to get at their prey.

Ed stood, transfixed, unsure of what to do next. He watched as Mitchell and Trish disappeared into an alleyway, followed by dozens of carriers in hot pursuit.

"Dad!" Zach exclaimed. "What are we waiting for?"

"Ed, if we get caught in that alley we're done for," Dave said.

Ed stood, unable to answer. A few of the gimpy carriers not in pursuit of Trish and Mitchell turned their attention toward Ed, Dave and the boys, dragging their useless limbs behind them as they screamed and gnashed their teeth.

"I know," Ed said to Dave.

"Dad, what are you doing?" Zach asked.

Dave's eyes met Ed's as he shot Ed a deeply troubled look. "I'm not sure we have any other choice."

"No, Daddy," Jeremy said, his eyes tearing.

"We have to leave them," Ed heard himself say, hating himself.

Zach shook his head, speechless.

"Mitchell will protect Trish, okay guys? Then they'll meet us on the road again later, after all this has cleared." The lie tasted foul on his lips.

Zach stared at his father, the boy's face a mask of incredulity.

"We don't have any choice," Ed told him.

"We always have a choice, Dad," Zach said. He turned, running away from his father and toward the oncoming deadwalkers.

Mitchell ran as fast as he could away from the slew of oncoming carriers. Trish stayed close to his side. He turned and fired two shots before feeling the click of the firing pin as it struck an empty chamber. He reloaded as quickly as he could while running, something at which he'd always felt he was reasonably good, finishing quickly before firing three more shots into the group of deadwalkers behind them. Three bodies fell to the ground in his wake, each bullet easily finding its mark.

"Turn right!" he yelled to Trish, ducking into the alleyway. Trish fell in behind him, hot on his heels. He scanned the alley as he ran, quickly locating what he was looking for.

"In there!" he cried, pointing to a large, green dumpster. Both Mitchell and Trish ran to it, stopping short just in front of it. He gave Trish a boost as she lifted the lid, tossing Tammy's rifle inside. She then climbed in herself, falling into soft bags of old trash.

The horde of carriers in pursuit rounded the corner and and headed into the alley behind them. They quickly caught sight of Mitchell as he stood in front of the dumpster, guns drawn like an old west sheriff. He took two steps forward and then opened fire with both pistols.

* * *

"Zach, no!" Ed yelled. Zach stopped and looked at his father. Ed felt his son's gaze fall upon him, piercing right through him. They stood this way for a few seconds, silently communicating with their eyes.

Suddenly it all made sense. "Stay close to me," Ed said to Zach. "We can't get split up again." He turned to Dave. "You with us?"

Dave took a deep breath, nodding. "Until the end."

* * *

Trish's heart pounded in her chest, her lungs burned for more air. She waited for Mitchell to join her in the dumpster, but there was no sign of him. After a few seconds she heard a horrible racket as Mitchell began firing on the crowd of carriers. She'd been certain the plan had been for them to hide in the dumpster together. Apparently Mitchell had other plans.

Well, so did she.

She searched through the dimly lit dumpster, eventually finding a box solid enough to stand on. She then retrieved the rifle from within the trash bags and other petrified garbage, ensuring another shell was in the chamber. She pulled herself up on the box, the dumpster lid still closed, just above her head.

She didn't intend on allowing Mitchell to die for her.

* * *

Mitchell walked slowly toward the crowd of the infected, firing bullets into as many of them as he could. He spent the cylinders of the revolvers before placing them back into their holsters. He stooped down and retrieved two pistols with full magazines from holsters strapped to his legs, hidden beneath his pants. He raised both pistols and fired. Virtually every shot found its mark. As carriers fell, more poured in behind the fallen. Mitchell continued firing, taking them down as methodically as he could.

He spent the ammunition quickly, leaving him no choice but to reload. He placed the gun in his left hand into the leg holster before removing a magazine from his belt for the gun in his right hand. He dropped the empty magazine to the ground.

He was about to place the loaded magazine into the gun when a large carrier bolted through the pack from the rear, charging with alarming speed. Mitchell struggled to get the magazine into the pistol, but the thing was closing too fast. He backed up, picking up speed and trying to buy himself time.

Without warning a loud gunshot pierced the air from behind him. Mitchell watched as the carrier's body jerked and dropped to the ground with an unmercifully dull thud. Seizing his opportunity, Mitchell slammed the magazine into the gun just before he turned to see Trish pointing the rifle toward the crowd of carriers. He smiled at her as she stood up in the dumpster, giving him the thumbs up.

Mitchell turned back and shot three more carriers as if they were clay pidgins. He temporarily placed the freshly loaded pistol into its holster, repeating the reloading process on the second pistol. He heard another loud boom as Trish fired another bullet into an approaching carrier. The deadwalker fell face-first on the ground, blood spattering all around the body.

Pushing the magazine into place, Mitchell turned back toward the crowd of carriers, raising both pistols in the air and pulling the triggers. Mitchell watched in satisfaction as the carriers fell one by one with each pull of the trigger.

As he fired away into the oncoming crowd Mitchell heard more gunshots from the end of the alley. He quickly spied Ed, Dave, and the boys as they fired into the crowd of carriers, flanking the ravenous group of deadwalkers from the opposite end. The carriers in the rear turned toward the sound of new gunfire, dropping as bullets pierced their filthy, emaciated bodies.

"Watch your aim!" Mitchell yelled to Trish. "Ed and the others are at the end of the alley!"

Trish smiled amidst the acrid smell of gunpowder and the stench of dead carriers. They'd come back after all.

* * *

Ed caught sight of Mitchell through the crowd of deadwalkers, guns raised, placing bullets into bodies with precision accuracy. Trish was behind him, standing in the dumpster near the end of the alley, rifle in hand. They were both alive. He felt a sigh of relief leave him. "There's Mitchell!" he yelled to Dave, pointing.

Dave fired another shot, searching through crowd. Catching sight of Mitchell, Dave returned a thumbs up. The last thing Ed wanted was to see any of their group killed by friendly fire.

The carriers were now split facing two directions, flanked on either side by heavy fire. Ed, Dave and the boys shot the able-bodied carriers first, leaving the paralyzed and nearly immobile ones alone. They didn't have ammunition to waste, and they had already used up so much of it. Each shot needed to count. It seemed that Mitchell and Trish were employing the same strategy on the other side of the group of deadwalkers. One by one the crowd of carriers fell, taken down by the combined firepower of the group.

A few minutes later, the bulk of the threats were down. Ed, Dave, and the boys ran through the piles of dead carriers, dodging the cripples along the way. They quickly reached Mitchell where he stood in front of the dumpster containing Trish.

"You folks shoulda kept going," he told them.

"No, we shouldn't have," Ed said. He shot a knowing look at Zach.

"Help me out of here," Trish said from behind them. As Ed helped Trish down she kissed him before hugging him close. Ed hated himself, but there would be time for self-loathing later. Right then they needed to get moving before the place filled up with more deadwalkers.

"We gotta get outta here, pronto," Dave reminded the rest of the group. "This place is fucking crawling with these things. There'll be plenty more where these came from."

"Where to now?" Trish asked.

"Back to the highway," Ed replied. "I think we need to make a break for the city before more of them show up."

"What if the city's full of these things too?" Trish asked.

Ed didn't answer.

"Back to the highway then," Mitchell said.

The group followed.

* * *

They reached the highway quickly, stepping around the dead and wounded carriers along the way. By the time they reached the highway they were all running, out of breath and nearly exhausted. The cut on Ed's leg had stopped bleeding, the pain somewhat numbed by endorphins. It hurt, but it was manageable.

Once on the highway, they slowed to a brisk walk, attempting to keep a quick pace while not completely depleting their energy stores. Leaving the fresh carnage behind them, they passed more cars and more decayed bodies as they walked. They opted for walking the westbound lanes since there were fewer abandoned cars. After all, once the infection kicked into high gear, folks were running *from* the cities, not *to* them.

As the adrenaline stopped flowing into their systems their exhaustion became more severe, hindering their progress. Ed's limp didn't help things. They continued walking as best they could, but the pace seemed excruciatingly slow, their backpacks like dead weight.

As they neared the city, the giant stainless steel Gateway Arch beckoned them. Filling in the skyline were other buildings, only the top of the structures visible from the group's vantage point. The buildings stood like sentinels in the distance; silently looming over the city streets like the forgotten watchmen of another time.

They continued walking briskly along the highway, the carriers out of sight, but not out of mind. They fought the urge to constantly look behind them, despite the possible threats. The act slowed their forward progress and that was a risk they couldn't take. They had to be quick if they had any hopes at all of reaching the city before nightfall. If they were caught in the middle of carrier country after nightfall they were as good as dead.

They walked for some time along the road, the city growing larger in their view as they made their way further west. They remained keenly aware of their surroundings, yet saw no more carrier activity. They passed by more decrepit, crumbling buildings and disintegrating houses as they walked, but they were thankfully silent.

Eventually the highway became an elevated overpass, rising into the sky and crossing over the local roads below it. They were getting very close to the city now, but the height of the bridge worried Ed. They were even more vulnerable while crossing it, for on it there was nowhere to hide and there was very little option of retreat once committed.

They stopped at the foot of the overpass, following it upward with their eyes, watching it as it rose more than three stories above the ground. As it went on, the overpass turned into a bridge over the Mississippi River. Just on the other side of the bridge was the city, nestled squarely up against the riverbank, the tall buildings visible from their midsections to their roofs.

"I don't like this," Dave remarked, his eyes following the outline of the bridge as it rose into the air and over the water of the Mississippi river. "We get stuck on that thing and we're done for."

"We don't have much choice," Mitchell said as he observed the structure, his hand shielding his eyes from the sun. "If we want in that city then this is our route. Unless you want to swim, of course, but with the load we got on our backs and the nasty undercurrent I'd say that'd be a bad idea."

Ed's eyes followed the road. "We're too heavy with gear and the boys will never make the swim," he said. "After what we've been through, it'd be a miracle if any of us made it. No, it's a risk we're just going to have to take."

He looked toward the group for any objections.

No one countered.

With that, they began their trek up the ramp and onto the overpass.

* * *

The grade was moderate, but in their nearly exhausted state the trek took some considerable effort. They moved as quickly as they could, despite their fatigue, putting thirty yards, forty yards, fifty yards, and then a hundred yards behind them. They were committed to the overpass, now standing almost three frightening stories off the ground.

Behind them the roadway remained clear of predators, but before them they could only see to the thin, concrete line of the summit of the overpass, like a beachgoer viewing the curvature of the Earth. What lay on the other side was a mystery, and quite possibly their biggest risk yet. They could only hope the road on the other side of that crest was clear. If it wasn't, their possibility of escape was dubious, at best.

They walked, each step bringing them closer toward the

summit of the bridge, closer to knowing what lay on the other side. Safe haven or a death trap, their fate lay only steps away.

But as they neared the crest of the bridge Dave said something that made them all stop where they were. "They're behind us," he said. "Lots of them."

Ed turned. The sight was like a kick to the stomach. There were dozens upon dozens of carriers walking up the overpass ramp. They clogged the roadway, blocking the group's escape route. The carriers walked, limped, and ran up the ramp, toward the group.

Toward their prey.

"Daddy?" Jeremy said, frightened.

"Run," Ed told him. "Toward the city."

They ran. Ed ushered both boys along, ensuring they didn't fall behind. The others ran with them, toward the summit of the overpass and onto the bridge spanning the river. They were literally running for their lives now, and what lay on the other side of that roadway would either save them or kill them.

As they neared the top of the incline, the road began to level out. It was then they met their destiny head on.

Before them, littering the highway, were scores of carriers. They were wandering aimlessly, currently unaware anyone was approaching. Ed and the rest of the group stopped, standing silent and still, watching the wretched remains of humanity before them.

Ed's sprits plummeted as the horrific sight accosted his eyes. *So this is how it ends*, he thought.

From behind them a carrier screamed. Ed and the others watched in sickening horror as the wandering carriers before them finally took notice. A scream erupted, inciting the others wandering the bridge. Suddenly they all charged, the screams building in ferocity and intensity as the rest of the deadwalkers joined in the pursuit.

Ed looked frantically at the group. Trish was crying, tears streaming down her face. Mitchell only returned a somber stare, communicating what Ed already knew. There was no reaching the city. There was no safe haven. There was no future. There was no cheating death. They had only put off the inevitable, and now that time was over.

It was time to settle their debts.

Ed looked at his two boys standing in front of him, their childhood stolen from them, their innocence lost. Zach's second chance, wasted. They looked up at him for answers, for direction. *Do something!* their faces screamed silently to him. He couldn't. Nothing could save any of them now. They were beyond hope.

There was only one choice left.

As carriers raced toward them from both sides, Ed reached into his front pocket and retrieved the magazine holding the three shells he had carried with him since leaving the border town over three years ago. He ejected the magazine currently in the pistol; it struck the ground with a sharp clink.

The others turned toward him, watching. More tears streaked down Trish's face as she watched Ed, horrified, shaking her head from side to side. *No*, her face pleaded with him. *This can't be happening. This isn't how it's supposed to end.*

Ed placed the magazine into the pistol, glancing toward the carriers both behind and in front of them. They were approaching quickly from both sides now, limping, crawling, running, and walking. The screams continued, almost in unison, melding into a sickening dirge.

He loaded the first shell into the chamber of the pistol, glancing once more at Trish. She looked at him with undefinable despair as Ed placed the gun against Jeremy's head.

"No," she said, sobbing. "Ed, please…"

He looked at her, expressionless. His finger touched the trigger. There was nothing he could say.

Mitchell watched, his face tense.

Dave stood, his mouth agape, gripped by disbelief. He closed his eyes.

Jeremy looked up at his father. "No Daddy, please don't." Tears ran from his eyes.

Zach's eyes widened in shock as he shook his head, incredulous.

"I love you, buddy," Ed told his youngest son, his voice faltering as the tears began to roll from his eyes and down his cheeks. They fell from his face, striking the pavement below like a melancholy rain, mixing with the dirt and grime layering the concrete. "I only ever wanted the best for you."

A few moments passed before the terrible sound of a single shot rang out, echoing in the distance.

Chapter Twenty

Dave Porter stood with his eyes closed upon an interstate overpass, death approaching from both sides, waiting for a father to kill his own son.

His wife was dead, as were all his friends, and soon he would be as well. He suddenly recalled a memory from his high school graduation, just before accepting his diploma. His life had flashed before his eyes, a fleeting filmstrip of what might be in store for him as he lived out his life. He certainly hadn't anticipated anything that actually happened.

Then the sound of the gunshot crashed through the air like a thunderclap, causing him to jump. He kept his eyes closed; maybe he could keep them closed through it all. He couldn't watch Ed shoot his other son, nor could he watch him shoot anyone else. Maybe Ed would have mercy on them all, killing the members of their group before the carriers got them. Either way, Dave couldn't watch.

And if not? If Ed simply ended things for himself and his sons? Well, the filthy remains of humanity would make short work of Dave Porter in the end. No matter what, with his eyes closed he'd never see any of it coming.

"Dave," he heard Ed call out. He kept his eyes closed,

unable to open them.

"Dave!" Ed repeated. "Open your eyes."

Reluctantly, Dave opened his eyes, bracing himself for the worst. He was shocked; Jeremy was still alive! Dave looked at Ed, confusion painted on his face like a mask. Ed raised his pistol, still filled with two shells that had once been earmarked for himself and his two children, aimed it at the oncoming carriers and fired.

Two shots and the magazine was empty. Ed picked up the partially-spent magazine he'd ejected onto the bridge earlier, jamming it back into the pistol. He glanced at Dave again, quickly moving on to Trish and then on to Mitchell. He nodded at them. They nodded in return.

Mitchell's mouth was thin line, aside from the faintest hint of a smile near the corner of his mouth. He fired into the oncoming crowd, a symphony of small explosions, the deadwalkers dropping like flies before him.

* * *

Gunfire erupted as the group worked their way through their remaining ammunition. The eruption of sound was so loud that it was impossible to hear anything else for all the noise. As they were shot, carriers screamed in agony, falling to the ground and writhing in pain. Ed, Zach, and Jeremy all stood facing west, unloading their magazines into the crowd of oncoming carriers, changing them out with the dwindling supply as they were spent. The group stood, back to back, Ed and his sons taking down the western carriers while Ed, Trish and Mitchell worked on the carriers approaching from the East. Zach and Jeremy stood by their father, firing their guns into the swarm. Though their aim wasn't as good as the adults, the besieging crowd that was so thick the boys had trouble missing.

Breaking from the group, Mitchell backed up against the railing of the overpass, keeping all his targets in front of him and picking them off selectively. He aimed and fired. Aimed and fired. One, two, three, the carriers dropped, piling up. He repeated the process, cutting them down from all directions.

Burnt gunpowder mingled with the odor of urine, feces, blood, and spilled guts. Carriers fell as they were shot while others stepped on them, over them, or fell as they tried to do either. Copious amounts of dark, infected blood ran down the concrete, drawn into crooked streams by the relentless power of gravity. Despite massive losses the carriers continued making progress. They steadily closed the distance, awkwardly limping, walking, and running toward Ed and the rest of the group. Some of the wounded still continued to crawl toward their prey, screaming as they broke overgrown fingernails on rough concrete.

Mitchell emptied his revolvers, holstered them, then pulled the pistols strapped to his legs. He fired in rapid succession, carriers falling after each gunshot. He emptied the magazines and attempted to reload. Suddenly a massive carrier broke out from the crowd, heading toward him. Mitchell struggled to reload the pistol faster, but the carrier closed the distance too quickly. The snarling, filthy body struck him at a full run, driving Mitchell into the railing of the overpass, breaking three of his ribs and knocking the breath out of him. He dropped the empty pistol while he struggled to reach for one of his revolvers.

Grasping the revolver in his hand, Mitchell struck the carrier in the head with the gun, but the deadwalker was just too large. Bleeding from the laceration Mitchell made in its forehead, the carrier buried its rotten teeth into Mitchell's neck, tearing at the soft flesh. Mitchell screamed in agony as the carrier tore with all its might. A huge chunk of flesh and muscle ripped away, tearing an artery. Blood spurted into the air with each heartbeat. Mitchell screamed, still striking the carrier with the pistol as he bled.

Another carrier saw the opportunity and joined the attack. He tore at Mitchell's face, biting his nose almost completely off. Blood leaked from the empty cavity, dripping through Mitchell's beard, soaking his shirt. A third carrier ran toward them, now a full-blown pack, striking them all with such force that the entire group lost its footing.

Trish heard Mitchell's screams, turning instinctively to

see what had happened. She cried out as she watched Mitchell and two of the carriers topple over the overpass wall, plummeting three stories to the pavement below. "No!" Trish wailed, sadness and rage painted on her face. They screamed as they fell, the terrible sound fading for only a few seconds before it was abruptly cut short with a sickening thud.

Trish saw that one of Mitchell's attackers still remained on the bridge. She took aim, fired and dropped the thing to the ground. Fresh tears streaked down her face as she cried for the friend who had shown them so much kindness.

Ed emptied his magazine, turning just in time to see Mitchell go over the railing, falling to his death on the pavement below. The reality of their fate gripped him, and Ed steeled himself for it. Mitchell was gone, the first to go. The carriers would eventually kill them all, one by one. All he could do was buy them some time.

He took the pistol from Jeremy, firing three more shots before he heard the terrible sound of the firing pin striking an empty chamber. He tossed the gun down, removing his baseball bat from his backpack. The survivors moved closer together as the carriers closed in on each side.

Ed looked at Dave and Trish. Their expressions were all the same. Her rifle now empty, Trish took Jeremy's hand, squeezing it tightly. Ed raised the baseball bat, ready for any carrier that came within swinging range. Zach fired several more times before his magazine also ran out. He attempted to reload it, but he had very little ammunition left. Dave fired off a few more shots, saving his ammunition for the closest threats. They were tightly surrounded now with only one option left.

They would fight until they died.

As Ed raised the baseball bat in the air, preparing himself for a final attack, he heard the sound of rapid gunshots. At least five carriers instantly fell, their heads snapping backward before their bodies struck the cold pavement. More gunfire erupted, a sweet symphony of sound as the carriers around them dropped where they stood. The gunfire continued in a staccato rhythm while carriers jerked madly about before falling to the ground around them.

Ed ducked, bringing Zach and Jeremy down to the ground with him. Trish and Dave both followed as the gunfire sang. The discharge of gunpowder, the ricochet of bullets, the thud of steel striking bodies, and the screaming of deadwalkers filled the air.

Ed and the others crawled on their hands and knees toward the wall of the overpass, hunkering against it, covering their heads. Ed placed himself in front of the children, covering them as best he could while the gunfire continued. Carrier bodies jerked wildly as more bullets hit their mark, decimating the crowd. The concrete, once a grim, dark gray, was now a dark red puddle of blood.

The gunfire quickly tapered off. It was followed by the sound of a group of vehicles approaching. Ed looked up to see a military-style jeep and truck, along with men on foot heading their direction. The men wore either camouflage or black, along with flak jackets, army boots, and helmets. Some wore masks, some didn't. Hot machine guns mounted on the vehicles leaked white, stringy clouds of smoke into the air as the men on foot advanced, stopping periodically to fire on the crowds of deadwalkers. The remaining infected fell at an astonishing rate, the snipers on foot taking them down methodically.

"Hold your fire!" a man called out. He sat on top of one of the vehicles, waving his arms in the air. The gunfire stopped. The air, thick with the smoke from burnt gunpowder, wafted about, making it difficult to breathe.

An eerie silence followed the ceasefire; the only sound that could be heard was the moaning and writhing of bodies as the wounded carriers lay dying on the ground.

* * *

The line of vehicles rolled up next to the survivors, three in all, dodging the bodies of the infected where they could and simply running over them where they couldn't. The man who called the ceasefire hopped down to the pavement. He had a light brown beard and shortly cropped brown hair with a touch of gray at the temples. His shoulders were broad, despite being slightly shorter than the other men. Deep wrinkles lined his cheeks. His blue eyes caught the light of the midday sun, radiating in stark contrast with his weathered face.

"You folks okay?" he asked them.

The group remained crouched where they were. Dave watched as Ed looked at the man with a mixture of confusion and disbelief. Dave understood it well; seconds ago he was ready to die; now he didn't know what to think about anything. He wasn't sure he was even still alive. His senses were reeling from overload.

"Who are you?" he heard Ed ask. "What's going on?"

"We're here to help," the bearded man replied. Several more men joined him, all carrying rifles. The bearded man whispered something to one of the other men before the other man departed. Dave heard a gunshot to his left, followed by another as the men on foot walked through piles of downed carriers, shooting any that still moved.

"How did you know we were here?" Dave asked.

"When we hear that much gunfire, we come looking," the bearded man replied. "Look," he continued, "I'd love to explain more, but this place will be crawling with these fuckers in no time. We'd prefer to be gone by then. You're welcome to come with us, if you like." He looked around, surveying the scene and gesturing with his hands. "I very much doubt you want to stay here."

Dave looked toward Ed. When Ed didn't respond Dave answered for him. "No, we'll come."

"Good," the bearded man replied, smiling. "Is this your whole group here?"

"We had another with us…but he died on the bridge," Dave told the bearded man. It hurt to speak the words.

The bearded man nodded in response. "You're sure he's dead?"

"He fell," Trish added. "Off the bridge."

The bearded man nodded again. "I see."

"You never told us your name," Ed said, still looking confused.

"Miller," the bearded man responded.

"And the city…is it safe?" Ed asked.

"It is," Miller responded. "That's where we're going to take you."

Ed nodded. Zach and Jeremy's faces beamed.

Miller continued. "We can explain more later. For now we need to get back behind the fence."

"The fence?" Dave asked.

"Around the city. Don't worry, we'll explain."

"Sure," Dave replied. "I understand."

* * *

Ed, Trish, Zach, Jeremy, and Dave sat in the back of a green jeep. Another man, this one dressed almost completely in black, sat behind the wheel.

"Take them to triage first and then transfer them to quarantine," Miller told the man in black. "Tell Manahan to make them comfortable and then await further orders."

"Yes, sir," the man in black responded. He started the jeep and sped quickly away. As they drove, Ed watched as Miller saluted them before turning back toward the rest of the men on the bridge. As they headed west on the bridge toward the city, Ed held his sons close to him. He looked at Trish and smiled. She returned it then followed it with a kiss on the cheek. She squeezed both boys' shoulders before scooting closer to them.

Ed thought of their dead friends. Tammy, Brenda, and Mitchell, all gone. Dave's wife and friend.

And Sarah.

Always Sarah.

Dave looked out the window at the city. He turned to Ed, smiling and shaking his head. "Can you believe it? We really made it."

"I can," Trish said, smiling wide.

Dave grinned back at her.

"I wish Mommy could see this," Zach said.

Ed pulled him closer. "Me too, buddy. Me too." He

kissed Jeremy on the forehead.

As they drove over the bridge and across the Mississippi River, Ed's thoughts turned to Sarah. He had promised her he'd keep her boys safe. He wasn't sure he'd done that, but he had done what he could, the best way he could do it, and he hoped that she would be proud of that. They had, after all, made it to the city by the river.

And now after all this time, Ed could finally see her face again, something he hadn't been able to do in years.

The Jeep swerved harshly around stalled cars still stranded on the bridge. Ed gazed toward the city, catching sight of the Arch in the distance. The midday sun was beginning its descent, and bright orange sunlight reflected off the polished stainless steel surface of the massive structure. Ed recalled his last memory of the Arch, the same one he'd recounted to his children time after time, and was surprised that it looked almost exactly as he remembered.

The Jeep continued until it reached two large, chain-link gates. Two men stood behind them, both with machine guns. The gates were part of a larger chain-link fence, topped with razor-wire, running as far as he could see. As they approached the gates, he held Trish and the boys a little closer. Reality rushed in with sharp clarity as realization finally took hold of him.

They made it. They were home.

They had reached their safe haven.

About the Author

Brian J. Jarrett is a computer programmer by day, thriller writer by night. He grew up in West Virginia and now resides in St. Louis, Missouri with his family.

Also by Brian J. Jarrett

NOVELS & NOVELLAS

Into the Badlands (Badlands Trilogy #1)
Beyond the Badlands (Badlands Trilogy #2)
Out of the Badlands (Badlands Trilogy #3)
The Desolate
The Crossover Gene
It Came From the Mountain
The Saint, the Sinner and the Coward
Muster Drill
Yesterday In Black
Familiar Lies
Devil Breed

COLLECTIONS & SHORT STORIES

Walking At Night
Wishes and Desires
Dine In
Cycle

Made in the USA
Las Vegas, NV
12 April 2021

21268482R00163